SACRED KNIGHT
MANIFEST THE MAGIC

Dawn Blair

To Jaimee,
Magic happens.
Dawn Blair

MORNING SKY STUDIOS

SACRED KNIGHT: MANIFEST THE MAGIC

Copyright © 2012 Dawn Blair

All rights reserved.

This book is protected under copyright laws of the United States of America. No portion of this book may be reproduced or transmitted in any form or by any means without express written permission from the copyright holders.

The story and characters are entirely fictional. Any resemblance to actual events, persons (living or dead), or locales is purely coincidental.

Cover art by Dawn Blair

ISBN: 978-0-9830905-4-0

Morning Sky Studios
P.O. Box 5422
Twin Falls, ID 83301

Visit us online at www.morningskystudios.com

This book is dedicated to Rylan and Reid who are far too young to read this series (at the moment) and who don't yet understand about legacy, but who hold the future in their hands.

* * *

Special thanks Lexie Bradley for her wonderful and thoughtful insights into this book as well as all the enthusiasm she shared with me.

PROLOGUE

From a scroll found in the library at Dubinshire:

To the Council of Lords,

I write this in the hopes that you will allow me to continue my research before all knowledge of this important life is lost forever. Without your support, the life of St. Steigan will be wiped away in the sands of time. I seek not to raise the demons of the dead as some have suggested, but to capture what really happened.

I must begin by mentioning that the research behind this tale is intensely personal for me. 'Tis a search for the truth. Because so much of the documentation from that time has been destroyed, finding that truth might be impossible.

'Tis said that St. Steigan destroyed many lives. But how many did he help? Those that stood by him were fiercely loyal. Anyone against him felt hatred and fear. There seems to be little middle ground. How could that be?

But let's not get ahead of ourselves. Let us start from the beginning and discover his possible motivations, which of course to know for certain is impossible.

That word gets used a lot in conjunction with St. Steigan's name: impossible. Still, we must remember that he was just a man, a man with a mission.

'Tis said that St. Steigan was many things: a powerful maege, an undefeated dominus, thief, conspirator, traitor, killer. But what they don't mention is that he was also a champion.

Champions sometimes have to make hard decisions.

'Tis said that he became a saint on the same day of Queen Keteria's coronation. Some continue to speculate that St. Steigan was behind the death of...

(here the text becomes unreadable for several

paragraphs)

...the Temple.

It would be a great tragedy to let this story slip into obscurity.

Annae Bytherhourn Chitanik

Temple Historian

The Council of Lords' response to the letter written by Annae, also found wrapped with the scroll:

To Annae,

Since it is known that your father, Searn Bytherhourn, had a deep personal relationship with the target of your request, we find we must acknowledge your validity to research the life of St. Steigan. Only one who would have a familiarity to those involved could actually get the information needed to compile this important text. We do ask that you not let it cloud your judgment or your words in this regard. You must remain an objective party to safeguard your work from those who would...

(here the text becomes unreadable for several paragraphs)

...raise the dead. We must keep this history from turning to fairytales and dust like the legends of Bjarn the Fierce, Kipsa of the Lightning, and Quanst the Mouse.

We enclose the stipend requested in your letter. May the Goddess light each step in the path of this most important research. Go forth with our blessings to find out the truth and discover why this saint became a traitor.

Very Respectfully Yours,
Council of Lords

CHAPTER ONE

"Fortune favors the brave." – Terence (Roman playwright)

Steigan woke bathed in sweat. He kicked the quilts off him as though his nightmare had set them aflame in the explosive shower of hot embers chasing him to the waking world. He tried to ease his breathing, telling himself he wasn't in a room on fire with gray monsters surrounding him.

Pale morning light pressed against the edges of the cloth covering the windows giving him just enough light to see his surroundings. He could barely make out the shape of the large bureau with two long candles sitting atop like horns.

Only that he remembered blowing them out last night kept him from panicking about a demon being in his room. Still, he feared that one day he would wake face to face with the beasts that haunted him.

The same terrible dream night after night as though it were trying to tell him something. He pushed himself up against the flat headboard and sat there with his legs curled up to his chest and his arms around them. He knew what was coming next: the real terror.

He looked to the window again. The faint glow confessed he'd been very close to making it through the entire night. Close, but not quite.

As if the fighting in his dreams wasn't bad enough, he felt the tremors coming.

Realizing he had precious little time, Steigan rose and picked up his boots. He opened the wooden door and stuck his head out to look down the hall.

All was quiet.

He walked barefoot and still in his nightclothes carefully down the hall, the stone floor cold beneath his feet. Steigan turned carefully into the kitchen and found the fires unlit; he was the first one up. Once at the door, he slipped on his boots, tucked the untied laces inside, and ran into the brisk morning air.

Grass whispered against his legs as he sprinted across the sward to the stables, slid the latch, and hurried to the furthest stall in the back. With a final look toward the door to make sure he hadn't been followed, he pulled the loop hanging from the gate down around the post and collapsed into the corner. He trembled as he once again put his arms around his legs.

Not today, he thought to himself, *not now, control it.* He couldn't let this happen again. How much would he have to endure? How bad would it be this time? Every episode grew stronger.

Two nights ago, the attack had been horrible. His throat still hurt from the intense, silent screams. He hadn't even made it out of his bed then and worried his thrashings would wake Dominus Searn and his wife. But here in the stables he knew he could make as much noise as he needed and he thanked the Goddess for allowing him to make it outside tonight.

Steigan put his head on his knees and started rocking back and forth as hot pins worked across his skin. His muscles braced for attack. The tremors moving through his tightened body doubled in intensity. If only he could relax.

~~It~~ overtook him as fire and ice. He screamed without a sound even though it hurt his dry throat. His head slammed back against the wood and the hairs that caught in the rough grain of the wood pulled at his scalp like razors. Even the straw beneath him felt like flattened iron rods just pulled from a forge and his leather boots felt like stone.

Then, as if by miracle from the Goddess, Steigan could breathe. He gasped raggedly, hungry for the air around him. It smelled like heated metal. But the hot metallic taste filling his senses cocooned him with comfort. Maybe he was learning to control the night tremors.

His arms quivered anew and he felt the remission ending. "Miex'calidori," he whispered.

The sound of his own voice scared him. He'd never heard it, at least not in the two months of his memory. He tried to speak the word again and found the attempt in vain as no sound came.

Defeat rushed in with ~~the scream~~ tearing through his stomach. He choked on the next scream. The one that followed closely behind seemed to come up from the very soles of his feet. He felt the yell ripple along the tremors until it came soundlessly out of his mouth, and then another.

Steigan closed his eyes and willed the ~~pain~~ away. A pulse echoed against his protest. He fell over and his back arched. He felt like he'd snap in half, anything to end the continuous cycle of nightmares and tremors.

He woke with a start, not realizing he'd lost consciousness. He took a deep breath, choked on the inhaled dirt, and then sneezed, blowing a cloud of heavy grit into the air. Steigan tried to roll his head away from the ground, but his cheek just pushed into the fine dust covering compressed clay.

Brightness fell over him. "Steigan, what are you doing in here? Are you all right?"

Steigan looked up and raised his hand to shield his eyes from the light of the lantern Dominus Searn held. Steigan tried to speak, but no words came up. He shrugged and stood up.

"Seriously," Searn said, "what are you doing out here? You can't tell me that a pile of straw is more comfortable than your bed."

Steigan shrugged again as he lifted the loop securing the gate closed.

"You don't know what you're doing out here?"

Steigan nodded.

"Sleep walking?"

Steigan nodded again as he stepped out of the paddock and closed the gate behind him. Searn blew out the candle and returned the lantern to its hook on the wall as Steigan followed.

"Don't worry," Searn said as they walked out of the stables. "I did the same at your age. You'll grow out of it."

Steigan wanted to tell him about the night tremors, yet he really hoped Searn was right and that he would outgrow these attacks. If only he knew how to explain it to Searn. If only he could.

Steigan compared himself to Searn as they walked along. While he had long black hair which he normally kept back in a queue, Searn had short, layered black hair pushed back from his face. Searn had a couple inches more height to him and his muscles more rounded and filled-out. They both had eyes as blue as the late morning sky. Approximately seven cycles separated their ages and left Steigan wondering how long it would be until he outgrew these attacks.

They walked into the house where the scent of warm bread greeted them. Centhya, Searn's wife, placed trenchers on the table. Steigan briefly wondered how long he'd been outside for breakfast to already have been cooked. She rubbed her pregnant belly, humming softly as she went about the kitchen. As ruler of the fief, Searn could've had more servants than he did, but the kitchen seemed to be one domain where Centhya ruled. Steigan took his seat at the table and watched her go about her morning. Searn stopped beside her to kiss her cheek. She smiled softly as she put a bowl of porridge before Steigan.

Searn and Centhya sat down at the table and they all joined hands for blessing of the meal. "Goddess, Your light shines on our path. We serve in Your love and gather together for You. We praise You. We thank You for this meal which strengthens our bodies so we may carry on in Your service," Centhya said.

"So mote be it," Searn added.

Steigan mouthed the words as he nodded.

When they separated, Steigan grabbed his warm honey bread and pulled it apart. It nearly melted in his mouth as he bit into it. This alone had been worth getting through the night tremors.

"I want to head over to the Temple library this morning," Searn said.

Centhya took a gentle sip of porridge from her spoon. "Don't you have to attend Prince Tanold today?"

"That'll be a short meeting later." Searn turned to Steigan. "Ranil asked if you'd come by today. His men are out helping Cainis reap the wheat field. He'll want to keep the sickles sharp."

Steigan nodded his understanding. The thought of sweating out his frustration while pounding on hot metal had become very soothing to him. Even more, Ranil said he had a natural talent, but Steigan wondered if someone had once taught him blacksmithing skills. He also liked laboring with the other men, enjoyed hearing their talk and their laughter; it made him feel part of something. He knew they all had to work together, to do their tasks where needed, to get all the duties done for the fief.

They finished the meal in silence. Steigan nodded his thanks to both of them and rose to rinse his bowl in a bucket of lukewarm water.

Before he left the kitchen, Searn said, "Steigan, don't forget that we're going to the tri-lunar ceremony tonight."

Steigan nodded to Searn again, hating this form of communication. Taking his irritation with him, Steigan went to his room, pulled a fresh set of clothes from the bureau, and tossed them on the unmade bed. He stretched the sore muscles in his arms and legs. The ache didn't leave easily and only reminded of him how exhausted he felt after dealing with the night tremors. He lay down intending only to close his eyes for a moment, but fell asleep.

He woke some time later to the sound of a door closing. Rising, he looked out the window to see Searn's page turn a horse over to him. Searn mounted, waved goodbye to someone, probably Centhya, and started down the road.

Steigan rubbed his throbbing temples. The nap hadn't

helped him feel any better. Maybe getting out and working would loosen up his tight muscles. Within moments, he slipped down the hall, nodded to Centhya, and left for Ranil's. Once out on the open road, Steigan started to run as if he could escape his own thoughts.

He wasn't certain anything would take him that far away.

At Ranil's, he entered the forge house where the blacksmith already pounded away at the day's work. Still, it seemed empty and quiet without all the other men helping out.

Ranil looked up, his face red and wet, and grunted at Steigan. The motion broke sweat from the many pockmarks on his face and sent droplets down onto the hot coals and heating metal. Steam sizzled while the blacksmith didn't even stop hammering.

Putting on a thick black leather apron which smelled of smoke and hot metal, Steigan saw a pile of sickle blades by the stone sharpening wheel. He sat down, took up the handle of a sickle, and started pressing the wheel's foot pedal to get the round stone spinning.

Once through sharpening all the tools and hanging them for Cainis' runner to pick up, Steigan went to the forge where he took a strip of metal and plunged it into the fire.

Getting it red hot, Steigan carried it with tongs to the anvil and began pounding out a horseshoe. In short order, he had a complete set finished.

Wondering what to do next, he looked to Ranil, who answered him by pointing at some chainmail armor hanging on the wall. Steigan nodded and continued making more links.

Shortly, Cainis' runner came in with a basketful of sickles, which he dumped on the floor then picked up the sharpened ones. Steigan returned to wheel and started grinding the blades.

When the afternoon grew late, Ranil inspected Steigan's work on the horseshoes and chainmail. "Your craftsmanship is improving." The grunted statement held little emotion in it, but Steigan realized the underlying compliment and he felt like he'd actually accomplished something today, even before Ranil held a few coins out for him. Steigan accepted the money.

Ranil pumped up the forge to stoke the fire. "I'm going to work a little longer. You go on home. I'm sure Searn is expecting you for the tri-lunar ceremony."

Steigan nodded and headed out. Several people still worked in the fields, he noted as he walked back to Searn's. No one seemed to pay him much attention.

Maybe they felt too uncomfortable to speak to him.

He briefly wondered what his parents had done and who they were. He wished he remembered them. He wished he remembered anything. Since the accident, he'd had no memory. No voice either. He'd come to live with his cousin, Searn, afterwards. He wished he could ask what kind of tragedy had killed his parents and left him mute. Even more, he'd like to know what it had to do with flying monsters and fire. Had the winged demons killed his parents by burning their house? How had he escaped? Had they tried to carry him off? Had he screamed until his voice fled?

For a moment he caught a chill in the late afternoon air.

As he got to the hill before Searn's house, he heard the sounds of a swordfight. Steigan ran, afraid of what he might find, afraid of what the chill had been trying to warn him, but he found Searn in the front yard with his page working on drills.

"You can't let me get on the inside," Searn said, stepping in on Paedorin.

The page jumped back and ducked under Searn's following swing. Off balance, Searn flicked the sword from Paedorin's grip.

Searn seemed to notice that his page's gaze had drifted off and turned to see what Paedorin had been looking at.

Searn smiled when he saw Steigan. "Let's see if you can do better, if you're not too tired," he called out.

Steigan hopped the fence and picked up Paedorin's sword, the weight feeling comfortable in his hand. He barely had time to prepare before Searn rushed him. Steigan reacted, parrying Searn's thrust quickly and efficiently.

After a moment of trading blows, Searn said, "Good. Do you remember the left handed techniques we've been working on?" Searn deftly switched to his left hand with a fancy twirl.

Steigan tossed the sword to his other hand and engaged Searn in battle. Paedorin scrambled out the way as their fight expanded to the area where the page had been sitting.

Centhya opened the door and called out to Searn to come for dinner.

Searn waved to Centhya. "Very good," he said to Steigan. "Tomorrow morning we'll work on a new drill."

Steigan nodded and smiled. That meant Searn would be home tomorrow and he wouldn't feel like he needed to get out and do something. Searn would keep him busy enough.

Searn took Steigan's sword and handed both of the weapons to Paedorin. As they head into the house, Searn asked, "How did it go today at Ranil's?"

Steigan pulled the coins from a pouch on his belt as he sat down at the table. He showed the four coins to Searn ignoring Searn's scowling protest as he slid three of those coins across the wood. Steigan replaced one coin into his pouch. The three others remained on the table.

Centhya eased herself down onto her seat with a heavy breath. She smiled and rubbed her belly. She looked wobbly and exhausted from the added weight. Searn reached out and took her hand. Her eyes shined so brightly as she looked back at her husband that even Steigan felt the warmth of her love. He hoped his parents had cherished each other like this and that he'd had the sense to appreciate it.

Centhya reached over for Steigan's hand. "Bright Goddess, bless this food we are about to eat," she said. "Keep Your domini safe. Gift King Cirello with long life and a strong heart. Keep Lilinar in the palm of Your hand. Thank You for this wondrous prosperity. So mote it be."

"So mote it be," Searn responded.

Steigan mouthed the words as he did every night at evening meal. He hoped the Goddess understood his reasons for only being able to do that much. But of course She had to. She knew all. She knew why he had to be mute at this time. He wished he understood Her reasons. And just once, he'd appreciate it if Centhya prayed for his voice to return.

As he accepted a small pot of carrots which had been boiled with strickleberry blossoms, Steigan thought of the strangled word he'd actually cried out this morning. Had he imagined it all together? Had it been a sign that his voice was returning? *Please, Goddess,* he thought in his own silent prayer. There was so much he didn't understand right now and only by asking the questions he needed to would he find the answers he was seeking.

Centhya leaned toward Searn. "How was your meeting with Tanold?"

"He's in a foul mood of late." Searn signed. "His sister…" He shook his head and rubbed his fingers over his forehead.

"Did I make a bad decision?"

"You didn't. But you should know what's going on." Searn took Centhya's hand. "She's ignoring affairs of state, she locks herself away in her 'work room' most days, and she walks around the castle muttering to herself. Half the servants think she's crazy. And a work room? What could she possibly need a work room for?"

"What about her plans to educate the masses about magic?"

"She's still running headlong with that plan. Every time she mentions it in court, Tanold gets so stiff with anger. I don't think she realizes how enraged he is and how close to the dungeons she comes. Were she anyone else...."

"'Tis only a matter of time before she becomes queen, then she'll have her way. Why does she not wait?"

Searn released her hand. "Cen, why not ask me how many stars are in the sky?"

"Do you think the magic is starting to addle her?"

"With her theory that everyone has magic and can use it? That's pretty addled. All she has to do is look at her own twin brother to see that not everyone has magic. Her theory is so flawed and yet she is the only one in the kingdom who can't see it."

Centhya expelled a quick breath and she put a hand to her enlarged stomach. Searn was on his feet and by her side in an instant.

"The baby," he asked.

Centhya laughed. "Not yet. Just a swift kick. I think she's reminding me that 'tis time to get to the tri-lunar ceremony."

"Going to be a punctual child, isn't she?"

Centhya smiled and Searn leaned in to kiss her. Steigan looked away, knowing they'd forgotten he was there. As their kiss deepened, Steigan slid from his chair and went to the counter, dropping his utensils into the water bucket.

The sound broke Searn and Centhya apart.

"Ah, aye," Searn said with an edge of embarrassment in his voice. "We had better be getting ready, shouldn't we?"

CHAPTER TWO

Steigan buttoned the fastenings on the doublet he chose to wear for the tri-lunar ceremony. It had been folded in his bureau for as long as he could remember, which meant for the last two months. Running his hands over the black, white, blue, and gold material, he examined it in the mirror and briefly wondered who had made it for him. Had it been the last thing his mother had sewn before the accident?

Shaking the thought from his head, he wondered how the doublet would look in comparison to Dominus Searn's armor. In some ways, the doublet made him feel like a dominus.

He tried on a hat which usually sat in the drawer next to the doublet. It was black, which half the brim upturned, and a long black feather plume. He adjusted it on his head, tipping the hat forward over his face. Hating the way it looked on him, he returned the hat to the drawer.

He picked up the hairbrush and started to pull it through his long black hair. Tonight, he decided to leave it loose instead in the queue he usually wore. Deep black smudges remained beneath his blue eyes even though he'd washed up, taking off the day's sweat. Until he managed to get a decent night's sleep, he had a feeling they wouldn't go away soon. Stepping back, he looked himself over. Something felt different. He couldn't quite put his finger on it, but sensed it stirring in the air.

A knock made him jump.

"Are you ready?" Searn called.

Steigan opened the door, surprised at the twinge of jealousy in his stomach at the sight of Searn in his blue and gold dominus armor.

"You look very nice, Steigan. 'Tis good to get fancied up and go out, isn't it?"

Steigan nodded even while hating Searn's condescending tone. He followed Searn downstairs where Centhya waited with a pink shawl wrapped around her shoulders. Her light brown hair had been done in little curls which were pulled back into a clip and left to cascade down her back. "Why, Steigan," she said, "you look very handsome in your doublet."

Steigan tried to smile and nod while not blushing at her compliment. He didn't feel real successful at it.

Outside, Paedorin stood beside two horses hitched to an open coach. Searn helped Centhya inside and then climbed up on the seat opposite her. Steigan sat beside Searn while Paedorin climbed up beside the driver. Then they were off down the road.

The sun had nearly reached the horizon by the time they got to Lilinar. Village houses surrounded the outer wall of Lilinar. Men coming in from their field work waved to them as they rolled by. Steigan couldn't help but to wave back even though Searn merely nodded in passing.

Cooking fires burned in pits outside several of the houses. Children raced around in their games while their mothers prepared the evening meal. Steigan realized how lucky Centhya must feel being able to cook inside for it wasn't a luxury everyone had.

The coach bounced as it hit a bump at the base of the outer wall's main gate. Then they were on cobblestone where the horses' hooves echoed off the buildings. People walked or rode toward the Temple like a massive flow. Searn saluted other domini on the road. As they reached the bridge to cross to the Temple, several jumping and squealing teens ran by them. Centhya smiled and reached over to touch Steigan's knee as though knowing he wanted to run with them.

"Go," she said with a bob in their direction.

Steigan settled back in his seat and shook his head. She gave him a look which echoed the sadness he felt, but then at a call of her name she turned to wave.

Everyone seemed to know everyone else. Steigan wondered how far away he had come from that Searn needed to introduce him all the time, recalling being presented to Ranil and Cainis for the first time.

As soon as they'd rolled into the Temple courtyard, Steigan jumped from his seat to the ground. Searn climbed out behind him and helped Centhya down. "Please keep it close by," Searn said to the driver.

"Aye, Dominus," the driver responded.

Searn took Centhya's arm and guided her toward the Temple. Steigan followed behind, watching the mass of people who were currently waiting behind a roped area while men and women in red and gold armor patrolled the area.

A girl carrying a basket of flowers approached them, took out a flower, and handed it to Steigan. "Bright blessings this eve, good sir," she said.

Steigan took the flower and gave her a nod.

Searn stepped up and touched Steigan's shoulder. "Thank you," he said for Steigan.

The girl, even though she seemed a little puzzled, blushed and turned away to quickly disappear back into the crowd. Steigan noticed her look back once before totally vanishing. He raised the flower to her then tucked the stem in between the shirt and the doublet so that the flower head stuck out.

Searn shook his head, looking after her. "Classic. You're already winning hearts. I'm going to have fun keeping the girls away from you."

Steigan shrugged, once again feeling embarrassed by the compliment.

All at once he realized that he stood at the base of the Temple. He looked up at the square building surrounded by a crenulated barbican at the top. He could see more knights in red and gold armor standing up there keeping watch.

They entered through the main door into a room quickly filling with people. A blond woman slightly older than Centhya came over to them.

"Searn, Centhya, well met. How nice to see you again," the woman spoke quickly. "This must be your cousin I've heard so much about. Poor dear." She glanced at Steigan with sad green eyes.

Steigan looked to Searn, wondering why he'd been made the subject of conversation. Searn appeared just as uncomfortable.

"Aye, Helana. This is my cousin, Steigan."

Helana grabbed Steigan's hand and wrapped it firmly in her thick fingers. "'Tis so nice to meet you. What a terrible accident, tragic to lose your parents like that."

Steigan tried to smile and nod, to let her know that he accepted her condolences while pulling his hand away, but she held onto it. He felt weird knowing that a stranger knew more about his parents' death than he did.

"If you ever need anything, you just let me know. All right, dearie?"

Steigan nodded again. Searn stepped between Helana and Steigan, forcing Helana to release his hand.

"Come, Centhya, let's get you seated," Searn said, pretending not to notice Helana and her irritation, but Steigan knew from practicing swords with Searn that there was little the man missed and his motions always made with optimum strategy.

Searn walked Centhya over to a row of benches where other women were already seated. Several looked up and greeted Centhya, asking how she was doing. Centhya glided onto the bench beside them and started chatting excitedly.

Searn turned to Steigan. "Stay here with her. I'll be back after the ceremony."

Steigan sat down beside Centhya right as Helana pushed her way onto the aisle seat beside him.

"Aye," one woman with shiny red lips said excitedly, "the rumors are true. Merkor told me about this dominus they found on the side of the road." She wore dangling pearl earrings which swung as she spoke. Her deep brown hair had been pulled up into a bun and secured with pins which also had pearls on them.

Helana gasped, though Steigan thought she might be faking shock. "Really, Palinade? 'Tis true then?"

The brown-haired Palinade turned to Helana as though excited to share her news all over again. "Aye, a few months ago."

Centhya sighed. "Why would they keep it secret? Where is he now?"

Palinade seemed to have an answer to that as well. Her brown eyes sparkled as she spoke. "Why he's got to be a spy, of course. So, he's in the dungeons. All the domini and their pages are accounted for. No one knows who he can be."

Helana jumped in, proving she knew more than she

had first pretended. "I heard that the princess herself tried to attend him."

"But since no one else wears blue and gold armor except for the domini of Lilinar," Palinade continued, "I'm betting he'll be executed for impersonating a dominus and treason any day now."

A woman beside Palinade leaned into the conversation. "He's probably just a commoner who stole the armor anyway."

Palinade nodded her head, leaning back and crossing her arms as if agreeing with the woman. "You know it."

"But if he was a commoner, why not have it done and over with already? Why is he being held in secret?" Centhya asked.

"Maybe he's a knight," Helana said. "Maybe it would be scandalous if his identity was found out."

Helana looped her arm through Steigan's, catching him off guard as she cuddled close. She looked up at him with big moss-colored eyes. "I love a good mystery, don't you, dearie?"

Steigan smiled and nodded. He was beginning to hate it every time he forced a smile.

"What a nice doublet," she rattled on.

Centhya cast a piercing look at Helana. "Aye, isn't it a nice doublet. Someone put a lot of care into stitching it for him. Why don't you come down here, Helana, where there's more room. You can't be very comfortable nearly falling off the bench over there."

Helana sat up stiffly, her blond curls bouncing, and uncoiled her arms from around Steigan's. "Mother hen."

Centhya blinked and smiled. "I'm sorry. What was that?"

Helana rose and stepped around both Steigan and Centhya to sit beside Centhya and Palinade. "I was just wondering when they were going to begin."

Centhya smiled at Steigan and gave him a wink while still addressing Helana, "Very shortly now, dearie, I'm sure."

Steigan said a quick prayer of thanks to the Goddess for his muteness also leaving him unable to laugh out loud or even make an audible scoff. He looked toward the other pews across the aisle from him, noticing that the first two rows near the dais were empty. Behind those, the people filling the seats looked like they were farmers or merchants from the city.

Palinade leaned around Helana to touch Centhya's enlarged stomach. "Centhya, do tell us. Is Searn hoping for a boy or a girl?"

"I'm sure he'd love a boy to teach the sword to, but I think he's really hoping for a girl. He always refers to the baby as a girl."

The woman at the end spoke up, "I bet you're excited to be able to use your magic again."

Palinade laughed. "Oh, hush with that old wives' tale. You can use your magic during pregnancy and I'm sure Centhya hasn't stopped."

Now Centhya looked uncomfortable. "Actually, Searn and I have decided not to test the legend, just in case. 'Tis why I've been letting someone else fill in for me."

"But you are still going to the Cauldron?" Helana asked as if hoping to grab another piece of juicy gossip.

"Aye, Searn and I have made several trips. We'll do another in the next few days."

"So, how does it feel to not be leading the ceremonies?" Palinade asked.

"'Tis strange. I've forgotten what 'tis like to be part of the audience. 'Tis been so long."

Steigan looked around at the other domini in the room as the women's talk spun off to idle subjects. The domini looked so strong and tall in their armor of blue and gold with their swords hanging at their sides. He wondered about the dominus found on the side of the road and how it had been for the dominus to awaken. Had he been as confused as Steigan had felt after the accident? Steigan remembered several mad images of people standing around him talking but they were all blurred and their words incoherent. He'd faded in and out of consciousness for what felt like weeks on end. But at least he'd had family to take him in. It didn't sound like anyone had come forward for the lost dominus.

Knights in red and gold armor filed in and took various posts around the room. The last knight to enter had a red and gold cape secured to his armor. He walked to the dais centered at the front of the room and went to stand at the table at the very back. He turned so quickly on his heel that his cape gave a sharp snap. He removed his helm and set it on the table. Then he went to the statue of the Goddess and gave a salute. Without hesitation, the man turned and motioned back to the door as all the other knights came to attention. The sound and feel of synchronized movements pulsed through Steigan.

A line of paired boys and girls dressed in long wheat colored tunics entered. Steigan noticed several people across from him wave to their children. They were aligned by age and size. As the older children came in, Steigan noticed they were allowed to wear swords.

Behind them came another procession of children from smallest to largest. Here, the boys were in long green tunics and the girls wore pale yellow dresses which almost touched the floor.

Palinade stretched up in her seat. "Blessings, Urlane," she said, blowing a kiss and waving toward the children.

"Palinade, he's getting so big," Helana whispered.

The cavaliers in the wheat colored tunics took the second row while the pages and maeges stood beside the seats in the first row.

A dominus stepped forward from the doorway. "Domini, seperous macton."

The domini stood in unison. A chime rang out from somewhere above and the audience rose. Steigan helped Centhya to her feet. Several domini took positions on the balcony that surrounded the room. Two more domini, one of them being Searn, walked in and advanced toward the dais.

Once they were halfway into the room, the flower girl who had approached Steigan in the courtyard entered and began scattering blossoms along the aisle. Shortly behind her was a woman in flowing white cloth. Her slippers whispered over the floor even while her gaze remained focused and steady, unwavering, as she moved forward.

Steigan felt his breath leave him. This woman had dark brown hair the color of Palinade's and styled in a similar fashion but adorned with tiny white flowers which glittered like jewels. Little unruly tendrils found their way out to curl around her face and neck. Her dress seemed to float around her like a cloud brought in by the storm of her gray eyes.

Suddenly the air around her began to sparkle. The woman blinked in surprise, nearly coming to a stop.

"Did you feel that?" Palinade asked Centhya.

"Aye, but who did it," Helana responded.

The woman in the aisle smiled as she slowly closed her eyes. She tilted her head back, lifting her face toward the shimmering air where the glistening drops fell on her skin like mist.

Steigan felt like he'd watched a sacred moment with the Goddess basking in Her magic. He swallowed hard.

As quickly as it happened, the woman opened her eyes and resumed walking toward the dais. Only when she'd moved out of his direct line of sight did Steigan notice the knights around the room glancing nervously about, each with their hands on their hilts. They seemed to relax a little when the woman reached the dais unharmed.

The woman held out her skirt while bowing to the statue of the Goddess. "Coom ra wialca do. Sha belika ne. Ha nee. Porta quienest acay doomasha."

The sound of her voice made Steigan break out in to a sweat. Oh Goddess, not only was this woman beautiful but her voice was like magic itself.

She stepped up on the dais and turned toward the

audience. Holding her arms out, she said, "Coom ra wialca to?"

The people responded, "Coom ra wialca do. Sha belika ne. Ha nee. Porta quienest acay doomasha."

The woman turned to the caped knight standing behind her. "Sacred Knight Danis, coom ra wialca to?"

Danis nodded and saluted with a fisted hand over his heart. "High Maege, coom ra wialca do."

The woman turned to Searn. "Dominus Searn, coom ra wialca to?"

Searn saluted. "High Maege, coom ra wialca do."

"Dominus Merkor, coom ra wialca to?" the woman asked the other dominus.

Merkor put his fist over his heart. "High Maege, coom ra wialca do."

Steigan held in a sigh as well as the jealousy flowing through him. Oh, to be a dominus and have her put forth the question to him. He'd draw his sword, salute her, and then speak the words like none other have ever replied to her before.

The woman turned back toward the entry door at the back of the room and called out, "Holy Sapere Mierk, coom ra wialca to?"

The Holy Sapere entered and walked swiftly toward

the dais. He wore white robes with three gold braids hanging from shoulder to shoulder and bounced against his chest as he walked. A torch made of gold silk decorated the back of his robes. "High Maege, coom ra wialca do." His words were short. He stopped but for a moment to bow to the statue of the Goddess, then took his place on the dais. The domini closed the doors.

"I pronounce this ceremony sealed," the Holy Sapere announced, again quick and abrupt.

The Holy Sapere and the High Maege went to a table covered with a white cloth trimmed in gold. The Holy Sapere began mixing items from various bowls into a larger one.

"Cordiuth kilginta ralishad," he spoke.

"Rino'dakatle afashutin ba milecky," the woman said, her voice singing with confidence.

"Ralishadi nocturpin moalinettic pashta ghutheinen."

Steigan looked around the room, curious if he was the only one who didn't understand the words being spoken. He started with the women he sat with. They were all entranced. But when his gaze crossed the aisle to the people who seemed to be peasants he found several vacant stares and watched a few rubbing their tired eyes. It had been a long workday and Steigan discovered himself having trouble stifling his own yawn.

He felt like such an outsider. What a waste of his time.

Mierk poured his concoction into three separate bowls then stepped back so the High Maege could come forward. She placed her hands level above the table.

"Cazidor," she said.

As the liquid in the bowls ignited, Mierk threw herbs onto each fire, starting with the outer two, then lastly the one in the middle. A sweet aroma filled the air as sparks jumped from the flames leaving cinders drifting and fading away.

As the fires burned off, the High Maege poured the ashes from the side bowls into the center one, which she then handed to Mierk. She stood with her arms out to her sides as the Holy Sapere finger-painted ashes into dark circles on her forehead and palms.

"Flama'tada lutarien," he said.

The High Maege gave a reverent nod and replied, "Flama'tada lutarien." She received the bowl from him and turned to several people now lining up in the aisles.

Centhya nudged Steigan, motioning for him to get up. "Go get in line and get marked."

Steigan looked at her with curiosity. Marked for what?

With a sigh and a shake of her head, Centhya explained, "Let her smudge ashes on you and be blessed." She pointed to the dais where Searn was currently standing before the High Maege who placed a mark down his face from forehead to the tip of his nose.

"Flama'tada lutarien," she said to Searn.

With a nod, Searn moved aside for Merkor to be next then headed up the aisle.

Steigan felt someone shoving behind him. He turned just to be pushed aside by Palinade. "Oh, move out," she snapped, "I'm going for my blessing."

Centhya urged Steigan to follow Palinade, but he stood up in the aisle and motioned for Centhya and Helana to go ahead of him. He started to follow behind them. As he got closer to the High Maege, he began to tremble. He let the next few people in line go in front of him. Slowly, he moved his way back, letting the entire line go by. He walked to the back of the room and the domini opened the doors for him. He glanced back over his shoulder toward the High Maege still marking and blessing people. He wanted to return to the line. Maybe her touch against his head would bring back all the memories he wished he could recall.

One of the domini cleared his throat. Steigan nodded then exited the room. He felt his shoulders sag as he left the Temple, the heavy steps of his feet on the stone vibrating up through his legs. He crossed the courtyard pausing only to wave at Searn's driver then traversed the bridge. Three moons were rising on the horizon, casting the outskirts of Lilinar as a silhouette in their pale light.

His feet found the road back to Searn's and he started to walk.

CHAPTER THREE

Steigan opened his eyes to find morning light pressing through the triangular gap between the window curtains. He raised his hands to look at them and flexed his fingers. The night tremors hadn't come for him. He sat up. Maybe he'd been worn out by his long walk home before Searn had caught up to him or maybe by the tedious lecture about not wandering off which had followed. Either way, he was glad it was morning.

He dressed and headed for breakfast. Raised voices made him stop in the hallway just before the door to Searn and Centhya's room.

Searn gave a sigh, "I'm sorry. It means a lot to me that I help him."

"Aye, you think he's a cousin," Centhya snapped. "I understand."

"How can you of all people look at him and not see the resemblance. He's a spitting image of me seven cycles ago. Plus the birthmark on his hand... Somehow we're related."

There were scuffling noises as one of them walked across the stone floor. "I see the resemblance. Seeing him has made me wonder what our child will look like."

"So you realize why I have to do this?"

"I understand. Doesn't mean I have to like it, but I understand."

"Thank you, Centhya. I love you."

At the sound of her murmured words and kissing, Steigan stepped backwards carefully a couple of paces, then started coming noisily down the hall, continuing toward the kitchen. Searn entered a moment later.

"Guess where we're going today?" Searn said.

Steigan shrugged.

"Centhya and I are going to the Cauldron. We'd like you to go with us."

The Cauldron of Life where pregnant women went to bless their unborn children. Somehow Steigan figured that banging his thumb between a hammer and anvil would be more fun than what Searn suggested. Steigan shook his head.

"You don't want to go?" Searn asked. When Steigan shook his head again, Searn prodded, "Ah, come on. Centhya wants to make this a family event."

Steigan knew it was a lie. Centhya didn't really want him to come.

Searn continued, "We'll have a picnic, enjoy the woods, and maybe if we're really lucky we'll see some centaurs."

At the mention of centaurs, chills swept over Steigan. He felt like he should remember something. Maybe it was a sign he should go. With a bobble of his head and another shrug, Steigan agreed.

"So you'll go?"

Steigan nodded more firmly.

"Good. Let's see what we can get together for Centhya."

Shortly, they were packed and in the coach heading back toward Lilinar. Men and women worked away in the fields beyond Lilinar's concentric walls. The outer city seemed quiet now, sleepy almost, compared to the bustle of activity from last night. Instead of going left toward the Temple, the driver continued on then took an easy bend in the road to the right and approached the stone curtain which protected the castle. They rolled through the open, massive, arched gates of the inside fortification wall.

Steigan realized how much older the inner ward was compared to the outer city. It felt almost like stepping into another world all together, vibrant and alive. In the outer city, merchants occupied buildings. Here, vendors hocked their merchandise right from carts and stands. Animals were penned in little corrals and straw spilled out onto the road. Half naked children ran around in the streets. Many of the buildings looked like they might house people. In the alleyways lines of clothes hung between the buildings.

They turned left toward a tall, round, windowless tower that rose high above the city walls. Two knights stood guard outside the door, but they came forward and greeted Searn as he got out of the coach. Searn helped Centhya before he went to the door, drew his sword, and saluted the tower.

"Holicathida," he spoke boldly. He reached for the handle and pulled it open.

"Wait!"

At the sound of a voice behind them, they turned to see a man running down the road toward them. Behind him a woman tried to keep up. She ran with a hand under her belly to support it though she wasn't nearly as advanced in pregnancy as Centhya.

"Wait," said the man again as he stumbled up to them panting. "Please, Dominus…" He gasped for air.

Searn gave him a moment.

The man straightened. "May we accompany you to the Cauldron?"

The woman caught up to the man and took his arm. Steigan noticed her muddy clothes were threadbare in spots and didn't quite fit her expanding body. Bits of straw mussed up her hair and dirt covered her face like they'd been sleeping outside. Her husband didn't seem much better in appearance, yet he looked toward his wife with caring in his eyes, then back to Searn. "If you won't take both of us, at least take Chareese, please. We have money. Please?"

Chareese dropped to her knees in front of Centhya with a gasp. She tried to pull her husband down beside her. "I'm sorry, High Maege. I didn't know it was you. Walrik should've never asked."

Walrik gaped at Centhya after his wife's mention of High Maege. Still staring, he got to his knees too. "I am sorry, High Maege. Please, accept our humble apology and be on your way."

Centhya urged the woman to rise. "Nonsense. Today I am not High Maege. I am Centhya Bytherhourn. We'd love to take you as guests."

"Really?" Walrik stumbled to his feet.

"Aye." Centhya smiled as she nodded.

Walrik dug into his shirt for a slender pouch and coins clicked together softly as he pulled it out. Searn put his hand on Walrik's shoulder.

"You should keep that," Searn said. "You'll need it when the babe arrives."

Walrik looked at him completely awestruck. "Really?"

"How can we repay you then for taking us through?" Chareese asked, fear in her eyes as if wondering what would be required in exchange.

"Nothing. I said you were our guests."

Chareese took a step back. "We asked another dominus and he said he'd only take us through if we gave him a hundred gold."

Walrik grabbed her hand and they both looked to the ground as if confessing something ugly and not wanting to see the reactions of the nobles before them.

Searn's voice lowered and slowed. "A dominus asked you for payment?" His tone indicated his distaste for the ugly idea.

"Aye," Walrik said, "and 'tis not just us. Other families have been asked to pay. Some have…"

When he didn't finish, Searn prompted, "Some have

what?"

Walrik looked to Chareese. "Some have sold their other children into service to make the required payment."

Steigan looked to Searn who looked peacefully calm except for his tightening lips. He turned toward the knights at the door. "Is this true?"

"I am unaware of any transactions like that taking place," the knight replied, "but I have seen commoners bringing goods for the domini that take them through."

The second knight nodded to confirm the other's statement.

"No dominus should collect a fee for taking someone through to the Cauldron. Go to the castle and inform Prince Tanold of what we've learned here today. This will be dealt with swiftly." Searn opened the tower door the rest of the way and stepped inside. He briefly turned back with disgust clearly on his face. His lip curled as he spoke to Centhya. "How any dominus can cross this threshold and fulfill this duty after taking gold or slave is beyond me." He shook his head.

Centhya nodded as if understanding all the rage he wasn't speaking.

"I'll be right back." With one final shake of his head, he closed the door behind him and the knights retook their posts on each side of the door.

Chareese started weeping, her hands rubbing her stomach. "'Tis going to be all right. We're actually going. 'Tis going to be all right."

Walrik put his arm around his wife and looked at Centhya as though pleading with her not to change her mind now.

"Is this your first trip?" Centhya asked.

"Aye. She's so far along. We hope 'tis not too late."

Centhya put her hands on Chareese's belly. "He's moving just fine, kicking my hand and responding. I think you're going to have a strong one here."

Walrik and Chareese smiled at each other.

Behind them, the door clicked open again. One of the knights held the door open while everyone stepped inside.

It took a moment for Steigan's eyes to adjust to the blue light flowing through the tower. It moved and curled over the stone like a life form, flowing in glowing rivers that seemed to descend then climb again. Along the walls were the steps of a circular staircase lit in blue and gold. Centhya gestured for Walrik and Chareese to go first. With one arm behind Chareese's back and the other holding her hand, Walrik helped his wife up the stairs. Centhya hung back with Steigan.

"This all must seem strange to you," she said.

Steigan nodded.

"Couples make their way to the Cauldron to bless their baby with the springs' water. 'Tis said that if the baby isn't blessed, 'twill be born without magic."

At the top of the tower was a column of bright blue light. Chareese and Walrik stepped through after some urging from Searn and they disappeared in a flash of white.

"Steigan, you're next," Searn said.

Steigan stepped hesitantly up to the blue column.

"'Tis all right. Just step through."

Steigan took a deep breath, closed his eyes while holding his breath, and stepped into the column. It felt almost anti-climactic, like a door closing right in front of his face with a soft puff of air blowing against his cheeks.

He first noticed the smell of warm water and minerals and sensed the humidity on his skin. Opening his eyes, he saw a huge cave lit by glowing crystals hanging from the roof. Springs poured out of multiple holes in the wall and in the center of the cave was a large pool where several women were either bathing or getting in or out. Many had on long white gowns. One woman who emerged from the pool on two legs suddenly transformed into a centaur, her dress changing into a robe lying on her long back.

Steigan tried to step back, hoping he could just leave

the way he had come in. Instead, his back hit the rock wall.

Beside him, Searn and Centhya appeared. Searn's sword floated in a shaft of blue light similar to the column in the tower. Three other swords hung in their own pillars along the cave wall.

Steigan searched the room for someone else in dominus armor, knowing there had to be three others here, but he saw no one else.

"Oh look, a centaur is here today," Centhya said cheerfully.

"It looks like Rajed's wife. I'm going to go see if I can find him," Searn announced.

He started walking, then paused and turned back to her. "If that's all right with you?"

"I'll go prepare."

Searn leaned in and kissed her cheek. "Have I mentioned you're the best?"

"I figure I have until the baby is born, then she'll be the best girl in your life."

Searn touched her cheek. "But you were always first."

Steigan turned his attention while Searn leaned in and kissed Centhya to look at the glowing crystals hanging in long solid chains from the roof. It seemed as if they were taking daylight from the surface and dripping it down into the cave, growing like stalactites with each melted ray it brought in. He jumped as a hand touched his shoulder and Steigan found Searn finally ready to go.

Searn said, "Let's go see if we can find the centaurs." Searn left his sword behind in the column of blue light. But before he got too far, Steigan pointed at the other swords, then to the people in the room.

"Good observation," Searn said. "You're right, there are other domini here. I recognize them because I know who they are."

Steigan hoped Searn would point them out, but Searn kept walking. Steigan looked, hoping he would see a familiar face, someone he recognized from his past.

The cave narrowed into a tunnel which led in a long winding path.

A new question struck Steigan. He touched Searn's arm to get his attention and mouthed the word, "Why?" He pointed at Searn's armor.

"I'm in my armor because I want the centaurs to know I'm on official business too. They trust I'm unarmed because my sword is holding the portal open for our return and I have no other weapons visible."

Steigan shook his head, not quite understanding. "Why?" he said soundlessly again.

"Why am I meeting them unarmed or why am I meeting with the centaurs?"

Steigan held up two fingers to indicate the second question.

"I'm hoping that Rajed will know something his shamans can prepare to help you, a potion maybe."

The prospect of seeing centaurs now seemed like a good thing. He wasn't sure if he dared hope that the centaurs could help him. If he believed they could, then it didn't work…

Nay, he had to stay positive. The centaurs would have the answer.

They neared the end of the tunnel where sunlight filtered through trees and brush to fall in a scattered pattern over the rock face. As they stepped outside, Steigan took in the scent of old forest with dew on mossy undergrowth.

A man crashed into Steigan and knocked him to the ground. Searn jumped aside. Steigan tried to turn but a heavy weight on him restricted his movement, leaving him only able to see a shadow. He shouted, but no sound came.

Then the shadow began to rant, "Root rot! By all that is old and holy! Who went and said you could do that?"

A laugh came from a nearby bush making the branches tremble.

Steigan shoved at the person still sitting heavily on him. He twisted just enough to see the attacking shadow had long blond hair tied back in a similar fashion to his own.

The man climbed off Steigan. "Sorry, mate. Brambrush got a little carried away."

Steigan glared as the person offered a hand to aid Steigan up, but when Steigan refused help, he turned back to the shaking brush.

"Didn't you, Brambrush?" the man yelled at the bush. "Now tell the nice lad you're sorry."

The bush stopped shaking and seemed to lower toward the ground a bit as if sagging in sorrow. The man stretched his hand toward the bush, about to speak when a rush of air blew by them and Steigan was blown backwards off his feet. Once again, the man slammed into Steigan and knocked both of them into the dirt.

The man sat up and looked down at Steigan lying flat on his back. "I think he's challenging you too, mate," he said. "What say you we take him down together?"

"Laurient," Searn said with calm amusement in his voice.

The man jerked around as if noticing Searn for the first time. The laughter eased from his face as he looked over Searn's armor. "My apologies, Dominus."

Laurient reached down to help Steigan up for the second time, but his gaze never left Searn. Since Steigan didn't take his hand the second time either, Laurient grabbed Steigan's tunic and hoisted him to his feet as though Steigan were a child.

Laurient turned to the bush. "Later, Brambrush. I have some business to attend."

The bush shook as a fairy came out of the branches. It hovered in the air for a moment, then waved to them and flew off.

Laurient meanwhile brushed Steigan off while speaking to Searn, "I'm so sorry if I injured your page in any way." He seemed to be having a hard time not laughing as he spoke. Then, looking at Steigan, he said, "Are you all right? Not hurt are you, mate?"

Steigan glared at him.

Laurient seemed not to notice, instead picking at little bits of the forest floor still clinging to Steigan's shirt. Irritated and wanting to move away from this man, Steigan shook his head in answer to Laurient's question. He looked to Searn, wondering if they could move on.

Laurient grabbed Steigan's shoulders and started shaking him. "What's that, mate? Please, say the words! Please tell your dominus you're fine before he hurts me bad."

"Laurient," Searn said, trying to edge an inch of seriousness into the situation.

The blond man seemed to take it as a threat instead. Steigan found himself spun around as Laurient cowered behind Steigan, hands still on Steigan's shoulders. "Tell him," Laurient whispered rather quickly in Steigan's ear.

Searn tried not to laugh. "You'll get no words from him."

Laurient whipped Steigan around again with surprising strength. He opened Steigan's mouth, his thick fingers prying Steigan's jaws apart as he looked inside. "He's got a tongue," Laurient said, "but no words? A mute page?" Laurient released Steigan with a tap to his shoulders which shoved Steigan back slightly. "Why Dominus Searn, I do believe you've solved the problems of domini everywhere. Mute pages! No more of their senseless mewling. A splendid idea, mate, if I do say so myself."

"He's not my page. He's my cousin."

Laurient seized Steigan again and held him at arm's length while he looked him over. "Mute relatives! Even better!"

Steigan looked to Searn really wishing he'd do something and get him away from this crazy man.

"I saw Rajed's wife inside," Searn said. "I was hoping

to speak to him. Do you know where I can find him?"

Laurient released Steigan and faced Searn. "Probably twenty leagues from here. He had other matters to attend. I escorted Beyanda."

While Searn seemed to consider this new information, Laurient stepped around Searn and picked up a bow and quiver of arrows from the far side of a nearby tree and slung them over his back.

"My cousin was in a terrible accident. He lost his memories as well as his speech. We've been unable to help him. I was hoping the centaurs could," Searn said.

Now Laurient looked Steigan over like he was a lost case and gave a sigh. "Let's have a look."

As Laurient walked back to Steigan, he seemed to grow in size. Like a ripple of water running over a flat surface, Laurient shifted from man to centaur. Steigan couldn't help but to step away from the large creature.

"Sorry mate," Laurient said with a shrug. "I should've walked around a tree. The Shift probably isn't something you're used to seeing."

But it was more than that. The air around the centaur seemed singed and sharp. Steigan trembled involuntarily.

Laurient reached out for him. "Woah, mate, 'tis all right. I'm not going to hurt you."

Steigan held up his hands defensively then turned them inward to cover his face. His body twitched and he couldn't stop. What if the night tremors came for him now? Searn would see. Searn would know. He had to control it.

The air. Goddess! It smelled so good and so foul at the same time. He felt his body growing warm. He shook. Breath came in short spurts.

Steigan felt Laurient's hand touch his shoulder then pull instantly away. He peeked between his fingers.

Laurient looked at his hand as though he'd been shocked. "Woah, howdie! That's some fire power you've got there."

"'Tis been growing."

"'Tis super-charged."

Steigan tried to focus on their words, but he shuddered with the chills now coming over him. Had Searn known all along? Did Searn know how bad the night tremors were? He sensed Laurient walking around him.

"You know," Laurient said, "'tis almost like he's never been magic spun before."

"Impossible. How could that happen?"

Laurient gave a little shrug with a sideways tilt of his head. "Just calling it like I see it, mate."

Steigan felt like he could lower his hands now, at least

enough to wrap around him to keep warm.

Laurient took several more sidling steps around Steigan, who noticed the centaur's hands moving close to him but not touching. It was like he was pulling leaves off a shirt. Every so often he'd hold up pinched fingers as if examining one of those leaves then he'd toss it aside with a grimace.

"What do you see?" Searn asked.

"Absolutely nothing that makes sense. 'Tis like someone's taken him, jumbled him up then put together mixed pieces." Laurient gave Searn a serious look. "Sometimes accidents that happen are for a better purpose than we know."

The way Laurient's gaze slid from Searn back to Steigan made Steigan shiver. A pause let the seriousness of the look dim, then a moment of playfulness entered as Laurient gave a smile and slapped Steigan's shoulder.

"No memories can be a great thing," Laurient said. "I'd like to forget that barmaid I knew last night." He gave a laugh then turned back to Searn. "As for the voice, I'll see if I can get the shaman to make up a potion and send it by. If my friend here screamed during the accident, he may have just stressed his vocal cords and they need healing."

"And the magic?"

Laurient gave Steigan a glance that spoke more than

Steigan could decipher. "We'll hope that settles out on its own as time goes by."

There was movement behind them and Laurient snapped to attention. Steigan turned to see the centaur female, Beyanda, coming from the cave.

"Are you ready, my queen?" Laurient asked.

"I am. Let us leave."

Laurient pulled his bow from over his shoulder and started walking into the forest without another word just slightly ahead of Beyanda.

Searn turned and headed back toward the cave. Steigan watched the centaurs go deeper into the trees, then turned and followed Searn.

CHAPTER FOUR

Steigan rolled out of bed, landing on the floor in a crouched position. With steady breaths, he looked around the room. The monsters weren't real.

Relaxing, he started to stand. Then he saw the heatless fire on his skin.

'Tis coming.

The thought whispered through his head, bringing fear in its crashing wake. He stared at his glowing hands. Little gold swirls ran through him like flames beneath his skin. He turned his hands over, willing them to stop, yet knowing his time grew short.

Could he even make it outside? How bad would it be this time? Did Searn already feel it?

He took a heavy step. Goddess, he wasn't going to make it. He stumbled for the door, but staggered into a wall. He couldn't get his body to move correctly. The mirror opposite him revealed his eyes glowing with an intense blue and looked more like a cat's eyes when caught reflecting firelight. He stared at his visage, wondering what he was becoming. Was he changing into one of the monsters?

"Miex'calidori," he whispered. "Badimazulien."

The word came easier than it had the night before and the magic bubble surrounded him. He put his hand against the invisible shell and leaned into it as the ~~pain~~ flowed over him. He arched his back, his head tilting as a soundless scream tore from his throat.

Another wave of torment swept over him. His legs threatened to give way, but he locked his knees to keep them from buckling beneath him. He folded his arms on the boundaries of the bubble and laid his head on his forearms while slow cries shook his shoulders. He was only a boy. How much more of this could he take?

Chills answered him, pricking like pins bringing nothing but torture to him. He opened his mouth and exhaled short, ragged breaths. It felt like he had claws in his spine. A small weep escaped. Tears fell from his eyes.

He needed help. Someone had to be able to help him.

"Lukion trapeze vi'na radin." Words he didn't understand escaped his lips. He felt himself choking, that strange gagging sensation right before vomiting. His body convulsed.

Then it happened. He threw his head back and flung his arms wide. With a whoosh, like warm water cascading over his body, he felt power leave him.

In the cold sweat that followed, Steigan collapsed against the wall. The glow faded from his skin though he still trembled hard.

With all his energy now gone and his breathing returning to normal, Steigan crawled back toward his bed. What had happened? What were those words that chased away the night tremors? He knew he couldn't take much more. What if next time he couldn't do anything? He really did need help.

"The High Maege," he whispered his throat so sore. As he wiped sweat from his head with the blanket, he knew he had to go see her. Had it been his imagination or had she looked directly at him when the air surrounding her had started sparkling that night of the tri-lunar ceremony? She had been looking all around the room. What made him think her gaze had intentionally fallen on him?

With the barest strength remaining in his arms, he lifted his hands so he could look at them and rubbed the silver torch-like birthmark on his right palm. What did it mean? The only thing he seemed to know for certain was if he let these nightly magical assaults continue, he'd never find the answers he sought. He needed to do something.

But how could he get into the Temple to see the High Maege?

A woman screamed in the night.

Searn's shout cut across the woman's. "Steigan!"

Adrenaline rushed in and renewed Steigan's strength. He jumped out of bed and ran into the hall. Searn stood in the doorway to his bedroom.

"Centhya's in labor," Searn said. "Wake my page and have him get the midwife."

From inside the room, Centhya called out, "Searn!"

Searn flashed him one last pleading look as if willing Steigan to understand, then he disappeared back into the room.

Steigan grabbed and lit his lantern, then hurried out to the servant quarters by the stables. He knocked on the door thrice, but received no answer. Finally Steigan tried the door and found it unlocked and the room empty. Feeling panic,

Steigan ran into the stables and found a horse missing. Where had the boy gone? And tonight of all nights!

Steigan opened the stall for another horse and, grabbing a fistful of mane, mounted the horse bareback. He led the horse with his knees, briefly wondering at how he knew how to handle the animal so deftly, but now was not the time for such pondering.

Riding into the small village of the fief, Steigan made his way to the midwife's home. A chime of bones clinked softly in the wind. The rocks leading up the S-shaped pathway to the house had white symbols drawn on them which reflected in the light of the three moons.

Steigan dismounted and tied his horse to the hitching post by the path.

The air tingled as he approached the cottage. He knocked on the door and shuffled impatiently as he heard muffled noises from inside. How long did it take for a baby to be born? Would he return with the midwife too late?

The door opened and the midwife stood before him with sleepy eyes. Her loose blond hair sparkled in the candlelight of the lantern she carried. She blinked as she looked up at him. "Is it time, Searn?"

Could he really be mistaken for Searn? A delightful curiosity went through him as he wondered how far he could carry the charade. "Aye," he replied, "Centhya is in labor."

The midwife moved aside. "Come in. Let me get my things."

The midwife lit a couple more candles. Steigan stepped inside, rubbing his throat as he followed her. It hurt to speak, but he had words. He wasn't certain if the remnant aroma of incense burned here earlier in the evening made him feel buoyant or if it was his own heady joy at hearing the sound of his voice.

She wrapped her loose braid into a bun and fastened it deftly without the use of a mirror, showing she'd prepared herself in the night several times before. A moment later she had on her cloak and turned back to him. She came to a sharp stop and stared at him, fear creeping into her eyes. "You're not Searn."

Steigan briefly wondered what gave him away then realized his hair wasn't pulled back. Searn had short hair and his own had fallen over his shoulder showing the long strands. Steigan shook his head.

The midwife seemed confused now. "You are Searn's..." She struggled for the word. "Family member. Mute, Centhya said. But you spoke to me at the door, did you not?"

Steigan shrugged and shook his head.

The midwife pursed her lips as she picked up a bag from a nearby table. She paused before a shelf that looked like an altar to the Goddess with flowers, divination cards, a crystal ball, and a dagger. She picked up the blade, pulled it momentarily from its sheath then jammed it in the belt of her cloak. "Goddess help you if I find out you are lying to Centhya and Searn."

Steigan started to nod, then shook his head. He turned and headed out the door, no longer feeling comfortable with the sacred magic contained in the house. Still, he couldn't help but to smile to himself. He had his voice back and if he looked and sounded similar enough to Searn to fool someone then maybe he had a solution to his night tremors.

Without looking back, Steigan mounted the horse and reached for the midwife, who sneered at him.

"I figured Searn would send his coach or a properly equipped horse." She raised her gaze and he saw her question in her eyes. She challenged him, seeing if he would answer her.

Steigan shrugged and kept his hand out for her.

"Aye," she said disappointedly. "Getting there is what matters."

Instead of taking his hand, she turned back to the house and motioned as though drawing a symbol in the air.

"Goddess, protect this ground until I return. So mote it be." She took his hand now and let him pull her up on the horse. "You may go now."

Steigan felt her magic dance uncomfortably along his arms. First, he'd perceived Laurient with his magic and now the midwife's. He started the trek back to Searn's waiting for that moment when he could get away from the midwife and find a dark, quiet corner to sit in. Alone he could recover from the discomfort. If he started sensing everyone's power like this, he wondered if he'd be better off as a hermit.

Coming to a crossroads, Steigan caught sight of a couple riding down the street. He wondered who they could be at this late hour, and yet, he already knew.

As if sensing Steigan as well, Paedorin spoke quickly to the girl and dropped her off the horse. He pushed his mount to a gallop when Steigan pointed at him.

"Is that Searn's page?" the midwife asked.

Steigan nodded and continued back to Searn's. He took the midwife right to the door, which opened before she knocked. Searn ushered her in with barely an inquiring glance at Steigan.

Steigan rode to the stables and went inside. Paedorin waited with a brush in hand and the stall door open for Steigan's horse.

"I am sorry I wasn't here to make the run for the midwife," Paedorin said. "'Twas irresponsible. A dominus never fails in his duties."

Something in the boy's voice made Steigan question the truth in his words. It sounded more like verbatim then sincerity.

Paedorin shifted uncomfortably under Steigan's gaze. "Very irresponsible. I know you'll have to report this to Searn." Then a new light came into the page's eyes as he began to smile slowly. "Oh, but wait, you can't tell him, can you? The most you could muster is a poor sign language that no one understands."

Steigan folded his arms over his chest and kept a leveled look at Paedorin.

"You think you're so tough, don't you? But you don't even know who you are. Some refuse Searn picked up on the side of the road. But I... I am son of Haborian Setherbern and I will be the youngest dominus ever. You will not report this matter to Dominus Searn. Do you understand?"

Steigan kept staring at him.

"Dumb mute. Probably don't even know your ass from your face."

Steigan just stood there.

"What do I have to do to get rid of you? You are

dismissed. Go. Shoo!"

Steigan took one step forward and sent the page scampering into the stall. After locking the gate, Steigan turned and left the stables.

"Searn will hear about this!" Paedorin shouted.

Steigan looked back to see Paedorin looking through the slats in the door. He shrugged then left the stables.

Outside, faint bands of daylight spread across the sky. He knew he had until tonight before the night tremors would be back and he had to get to the High Maege before then.

Inside the house, the midwife settled a pot of water over the fire to boil. "She's bearing a large baby," she said to Steigan. "Fetch some spare blankets and bring them in here by the fire to warm them. We'll need them later."

Steigan nodded and started for the cupboard where Centhya stored all the linens. He passed Searn's armory and a sudden idea came to him. He picked up his pace and gathered all the blankets he could find. Then, before heading into the kitchen he went into the small room where Searn kept his armor and personal weapons and tossed a blanket over Searn's breastplate. Into another blanket he tucked Searn's sword.

His heart racing, he stole down the hall with his ill-gotten possessions and entered his room. He hid the armor and weapon away, then refolded the blankets and headed into the kitchen to place them by the fire as the midwife had requested.

He tucked his hands behind him, facing a moment of sickness. Had he just become a lying thief? Why couldn't he just go to Searn for help?

Because Searn was holding something back from him. The realization washed over Steigan. He didn't fully trust Searn. It made him feel even guiltier. After all, why should Searn trust him either? Yet, Searn had taken him into his home and taken care of him. He wasn't sure anyone else would've done the same.

This felt wrong. He would go and put the items back. There had to be another way.

But as he headed toward his room for the armor and sword, he found Searn standing in the hallway looking at the floor. Searn glanced up, pale, like a wretched combat took place in his mind.

"Women die in childbirth, you know, Steigan," Searn said, appearing shocked that these words were actually coming out. "Uncle Cirello's wife died that way. This was an ill-conceived plan on my part. I don't know how to live without Centhya. Yet this is one battle I cannot fight."

Steigan wanted to speak reassurances to Searn, but he

couldn't promise such a fate, so he kept his words to himself, glad for his silence.

Searn pushed away from the wall, shaking his hanging head. "There is naught more I can do other than wait and pray. Come ride with me, Steigan."

Steigan nodded then followed Searn out of the house. They spent the morning riding through the fief, greeting people. Afternoon found them practicing swords in the yard. Occasionally someone would come out of the house to report Centhya's progress.

Steigan started to worry. Did it really take this long for a baby to be born?

Evening approached. Steigan and Searn were leaning up against the fence and Searn had been explaining some sort of maneuver that Steigan didn't think Searn was even paying attention to, since it was the fourth time they'd discussed the move when the midwife came to call out the door for Searn. But he'd seen her when she opened the door and was already hurrying across the yard. As Steigan followed behind, Searn handed his sword back to Steigan.

Searn stepped up on the porch while the midwife spoke quickly to him. Searn's eyes widened and he rushed into the house. After a second, he poked his head back out the door with a big smile on his face. "A girl. 'Tis a girl!" he shouted.

Searn disappeared back into the house and Steigan went to the stables to put the swords away with the other duller practice weapons. Alone, he said a thankful prayer to the Goddess for not letting Searn go to the armory today where he would've discovered his own sword missing.

Steigan lingered with his hand on the hilt of his practice sword for a moment, wishing he didn't have to give up its comfortable weight.

He left the stables and walked out to the road. He'd made it through the day without anyone noticing the missing armor and sword, and yet he'd also been unable to go and return it. He hoped it was a sign that he had the Goddess' blessing to follow through with his plan of going to see the High Maege for help.

On one horizon, the sun was setting while on the other a moon was rising. Soon it would be dark. He knew the night tremors would return with the dark. His decision needed to be made now, quickly. Already he could feel the magic creeping up on him, tingling over his skin like a mass of insects. He wanted this feeling to stop.

Yet things felt so wrong and he didn't fully know why. Was it because he had stolen from Searn? Was it because he wanted to ask Searn for the truth? Was it because he knew he had to go for outside help with the night tremors? Searn was supposed to be family. Yet Searn had his own family to consider right now. If Steigan could just get these feelings to stop for a moment, he might be able to find a way to end them for good.

There was just too much and Steigan knew he couldn't do it alone.

CHAPTER FIVE

Steigan pulled back his long black hair and knotted it at the nape of his neck as he'd seen the midwife do the night before. Turning his head side to side, he checked to make sure there were no loose strands. Then he looked the armor over and adjusted the sword at his side. He ran his hand over the breastplate, thinking about how right, how familiar this felt. For the first time since he'd awoken from the "accident" he felt a sense of peace. Lastly, he donned a dark riding cloak and pulled the hood over his head.

He tussled the blankets on the bed to make it look like someone sleeping.

With the house finally quiet for the night, Steigan made his way barefoot save for socks through the house. Outside he slipped into his boots and headed to the stables where he saddled a horse.

He stopped for a moment. How was he going to get to see the High Maege? The fewer people he ran into, the better. He picked up a saddle bag and loaded a grappling hook and rope into it. Tying it to the horse's saddle, Steigan mounted and started down the road to Lilinar.

The three moons were now up and provide him with enough light for traveling even as the forest grew in thick around him. He spurred the horse, not liking the things watching him from the woods.

The branches thinned as he got closer to Lilinar and the forest seemed to draw back from the road. Moonlight lit the castle in a pale light, making it rise like a white specter behind its protective walls. Steigan rounded a turn and the dark silhouette of the Temple came into sight. An orange light lit a single window on the black wall facing him. His heart quickened. Soon, he told himself.

He rode around the outskirts of the village surrounding Lilinar, breathing deeply as he plotted what he was going to do. As he got closer to the Temple sitting in the middle of the lake island, he stared at the lit window. If only he knew which room it was.

He watched the barbican, waiting for several moments but never saw any guards moving around. A plan ignited in his head, but first he had to get into the courtyard.

Steigan rode to the bridge, then circled back into the village, and dismounted. He tied his horse to a post at a local tavern, took the rope and grappling hook, and returned to the bridge. The gates to the Temple were closed, much as he expected them to be. He moved stealthily across the bridge.

A single candle on the sill lit the slender guardhouse window, but how many knights were awake within?

Tying the rope to the hook, he tossed it up to the barbican and tested it to see if it would hold his weight. When it held against his steady pull, he started up the rope.

At the top, he retrieved the rope and loosened the hook from its catch in the stone. Keeping low, he ran along the barbican to the Temple. Atop the main building, he fastened the hook into the wall and tossed the rope over the edge. It fell through silvery moonlight toward the black water below and settled against the building. This time he couldn't give it a test except for the simplest of preliminary pulls to see if the hook might hold. He would have to trust the Goddess. Rope wrapped around his arm, Steigan lowered himself over the edge. Before fully releasing the ledge, he gave it a final tug.

The hook rocked and came loose. Steigan lost his handhold on the edge. He felt the building slid against the armor. The hook found another catch and stopped Steigan with a jerk. He closed his eyes, regained his breathing, and started down the rope.

What had he done before the "accident" to give him the strength and skill he had to do this now? What instincts were guiding him?

Shaking the thoughts from his head, Steigan refocused on what he had to do here. Only the present moment mattered. He continued down and found a locked window, but he broke the glass with his balled fist.

Shards fell against his arm and sliced into him. With a hiss, he flinched back and grabbed the rope. He circled it around his bleeding arm to keep from sliding down and to give him more leverage as he raised his feet to the window. He used his boot to knock out more glass. Then, with a kick-off from the wall, he gave himself a little swing, maneuvered into the room, and landed in a crouch.

A quick look around revealed he'd landed in a store room. So far he hadn't raised any alarms.

Opening the door, he found the hallway empty, yet lit with lanterns. Steigan moved out, careful to watch both directions until he came to a hall where a knight in red and gold armor roamed back and forth. Steigan ducked before the guard saw him. He tried another way. Unfortunately, he rounded the corner right into another knight, a woman this time. Only as they stood there face to face did Steigan realize his hood had fallen back when he had swung into the storage room.

"Dominus Searn," the female knight said with surprise. "What brings you here?"

Glad that she mistook him for Searn, Steigan replied, "I've come to see the High Maege."

The knight gave him a questioning look. "Centhya's here? I thought she wasn't due back until after the birth of your baby?"

Steigan tried to smile, but feared his nervous laugh might give him away. "My apologies. I actually meant to say the woman filling in as High Maege while my wife is out."

"You're in luck. She hasn't returned to the castle yet. But why didn't the gate guards let us know you were here?"

Steigan shook his head. "No sense in waking anyone who doesn't need to be awake. Do you care to escort me to the High Maege now?"

"Aye, I will do that." She started to lead the way, but then turned back. "Is there a problem on your fief?"

"Nothing major," he said, hoping to cut off further

questions. "I'm sure she will be able to help in no time."

"That's good. To find that stranger on the road.... Is he still living in your house?"

Steigan realized that he was the stranger that the knight referred to. Found on the road? He didn't remember any of that. Searn had said that there had been an accident. Had a carriage overturned? And *stranger*? Searn had said he was a cousin? Why would Searn say something like that about someone he didn't even know?

"You are a braver man than me," the knight continued. "I'd be afraid he'd slit my throat while I slept and with a new baby on the way.... I'd rather dispatch him –"

Quick anger overtook Steigan as he interrupted, "He's a cousin and shown nothing but kindness. I'd – he'd never hurt any of us."

The knight gave him a long look, but Steigan kept his head carefully turned away. Goddess, he hoped his slip hadn't given him away.

"How much longer?" Steigan snapped.

"Third door to the right," the knight said pointing down the hallway.

"Thank you. You are dismissed."

The knight gave a snappy nod. "Very good, Dominus Searn." She took a couple steps backward, then turned and rounded the corner.

Steigan waited for her to leave and made sure she wouldn't come back immediately or raise an alarm. With all silent, he headed for the indicated door.

His thoughts took him back in time for a moment. What had Palinade said on the night of the tri-lunar ceremony? That a person had been found in the armor of a dominus? He looked down at the blue and gold breastplate. Is that why it felt so familiar to him? "Dominus Searn. Dominus Steigan," he whispered to himself.

His chest felt like he'd had a great weight lifted and he breathed deeply. "Dominus Steigan," he said again. It felt so right. Oh Goddess, was it true? Was he the unknown dominus? What had they said about him? That the princess of Lilinar had already tried to attend him once? Aye, that was it. Tried and obviously failed.

He knocked on the door the knight had indicated. It creaked open slightly and he saw a shadow moving within so he nudged the door open further.

A woman with shoulder-length brown hair glanced up from her book. She'd been moving her fingers over a bowl on the round table, but she lowered her hand as she saw him enter. Her lips pursed as she began to shake her head, sending her tight curls bouncing, and she rolled her eyes.

"Don't take this personally, Dominus, but I hate you." She leaned over the table, hanging her head as she looked down into the bowl with defeat. "Ruined."

Steigan stepped further into the room and pushed the door closed without looking away from her.

"I told you I would attend you just as soon as I'm done. I am not yet ready to leave," she said. She moved her hand over the bowl again and a ball of light rose up out of the wooden container.

"I'm sorry to offend," Steigan replied, "but as we've just met, I don't understand what inconsiderate action I've made against you. I will leave if you wish." He didn't want her to send him away, but he did hope his words would soothe the road between them.

She drew back slightly, lifting her head to look up at him as thought assessing him for the first time. Her face softened as she tilted back her head. "'Tis I who should apologize, cousin. Come in." She went back to writing in her book. "I thought you were one of the domini currently on babysitting duty. With Father sick, Tanold has been a little overbearing in making sure I'm protected. Apparently the knights aren't trained well enough for his liking either."

Steigan stepped closer to her and pulled his hair free of the knot so that it fell around his shoulders. "Maybe he is right to not be so trusting at a time like this. But I do not wish to deceive you either. We have not been introduced, not formally at least."

With a flick of her hand, the little ball of light disappeared. Panic rose to her eyes as she started to get up from her chair and she looked as if she were about to scream. Steigan raised his hand, wishing he could will her to remain calm, but she settled back as she took a second closer look at him.

"The boy with no memory," she whispered. "The one Searn was certain had to be a cousin, maybe a child of Saleaha."

Steigan grabbed a chair and pulled it to sit across the round table from the High Maege. He leaned forward over the table on his forearms. "Thank you for confirming what I was starting to suspect. I… I still have no memory of any of it. But I need your help."

"I cannot help you. The salve to heal the gargax wounds was all I could do for you." Her breath sounded shaky as she spoke. "You were lucky I could do that much."

"I was attacked by a *gargax*?" He shook his head as the word felt strange and foreign, yet so familiar. "I've had dreams of them, me fighting them in a room of fire, but nothing more."

Again, she rolled her eyes and sighed. "Let me see your arms."

Steigan pulled up his sleeves. Only a couple faint scars remained from the gargax attack.

She leaned forward. "Incredible. But now you are having dreams?"

"Aye, nearly every night."

"Maybe now that you're fully conscious, I can help." She seemed to debate within herself. "I suppose 'tis worth a try. Sit back and let me take a look."

The High Maege moved behind him in the chair and put her hands on each side of his head without actually touching him. He forced his attention on the gray brick wall in front of him, but the power emanating from her hands made him want to pull away. Every bit of him needed to be on the defensive, not helpless within her magic.

"Nalorium breticham," she spoke. He felt her breath against the top of his head.

After a moment of silence, she started to wiggle her fingers. She made a fist then shook her hands out at the sides of his head. Leaning over so she could watch what she was doing, she placed her middle finger onto his temples. She took a deep breath and said with more conviction, "Nalorium breticham."

Steigan felt an electrical bolt go through her fingers. The High Maege jumped back. Steigan turned in time to see her looking at her hands. Noticing him, she rubbed her hands together and sidled away from him.

She held up her index finger, her hand trembling. "One moment."

She continued to wring her fingers together as she walked across the room and opened a cupboard to rummage through the contents. She pulled out a flat oval crystal and looked at him through it. With an inquisitive look, she lowered the crystal, gave it a question glance, and then raised it again. She turned back to the cupboard and took out a round stone of marble.

"Let me see your hand," she said as she put the marble ball on a nearby table and approached with just the flat crystal.

Steigan held out his hand. She took it and turned it palm up. Gasping as she saw the birthmark, her gaze came to his, and then she began to examine the mark through the crystal.

"Interesting," she said, her lips tightening.

"What?" he asked.

Keteria ignored him as she picked up the ball and put it in his hand. "Hold this in one hand." She reached down to take his other wrist. "Nalorium breticham."

The marble stone changed colors to a bright blue and grew heavy in his palm. He tried to release it, but his fingers seemed glued to it.

Keteria tightened her grip around his wrist while she studied him through the flat crystal. "What are you hiding?" she asked, her voice sharp.

"Nothing." He practically gasped out the word.

"Why do you have no memories?"

"I don't know."

Keteria's gray eyes darkened. "Why is your magic so strong?"

"I don't know."

The marble ball grew heavier in his hand as it swirled with colors, now being mostly purple.

Keteria released his wrist and walked over to the table where she leaned against it to watch him struggle with the ball as it began to grow orange. He grasped it in both hands and quickly realized his mistake as it started to drag him to the floor and neither hand could release it.

Panic rose in his chest. "What is it?"

The wooden chair cracked under his weight and pitched Steigan forward. The back of his fingers slammed into the floor under the weight of the now yellow orb. He spared a glance at her, wishing she'd do something, and then looked back to the ball.

Keteria started to move forward as it changed to green, but stopped suddenly, her mouth agape as she stared between him and the marble stone.

"Make it stop," Steigan pleaded, his fingers feeling smashed into the wooden planked floor. His vision blurred with tears so he wasn't sure if he was seeing white or if the ball actually turned to a white-gold color.

Keteria rushed forward and pulled the stone from him as though it didn't weigh an ounce.

Panting, Steigan sat on the floor and looked up at her. "What is that?"

Keteria held the ball in her palm as it started to grow pink and showed some weight in her hand. After a moment, it changed to blue, then purple, then reddish-purple, and finally settled into orange. It didn't seem to pull her down as it had him, but the stone definitely seemed heavier.

"It measures magic," she explained. "Color is the intensity of the power and the weight is the direct tap into the bloodwave. On my best day, I can get it to yellow, but I've never seen it go beyond. The weight tells me I have a typical flow from the bloodwave, nothing special." On these last two words, she turned and placed the stone on the table.

Steigan picked himself up off the floor. "So what does that mean?"

"It means that the power behind your magic and its weight is beyond anything we've ever seen before."

"You don't sound happy about that."

"Aye, I'm not." She returned the marble stone to the cupboard. "It means that no one will be able to break the magic suppressing your memories."

He watched her walk back to her table piled high with opened books. "Somehow I get the feeling you don't care about my lost memories, that it alone isn't what has you worried."

"You're right." She scowled. "With that kind of power, the fact you can control it already tells me you're a stronger maege than I am. I can't help you. I suspected that before when I told it to Searn and Tanold. My decision remains unchanged." She turned her attention back to the books.

Sudden realization came over Steigan as he put the pieces together. "You're the princess of Lilinar. You tried to help me when I was found." The shock of it brought him out of his chair to a bended knee bow before her.

"Very good. Now, if you'll excuse me, I need to get back to helping those I can help. Blessed evening to you."

Steigan rose and stood there for several more stunned

seconds. "There's more," he stammered. "I... every night I..." He couldn't bring himself to say any more and she never once looked up from her books to him.

You're a stronger maege than me. I need to get back to helping those I can help.

With a nod, he crossed the room, opened the door, and exited the room.

CHAPTER SIX

Disappointment ran through him like a fire. Steigan raced all the way back to the store room and slammed the door behind him. With his hands to his head, he screamed. He climbed out on the window sill, grabbed the rope, and started climbing up toward the barbican.

What was he going to do now?

He knew the moment he went to sleep, the dreams would return along with the night tremors. If the princess was unable and unwilling to help him…

On the barbican, he closed his eyes. A soft breeze blew against his face. "What do I do?" he whispered. He wished he could reach out and will the princess to understand. He knew he couldn't defeat this power within him alone.

As though the wind spoke to him, he felt a sudden urge to move and to do so quickly.

He gathered the rope and pulled the hook loose from its grip in the stone then ran along the barbican to the guardhouse. He saw a carriage about to leave, waiting for the drawbridge to be lowered. As it started to roll forward, Steigan jumped on to the top of the coach. With it swaying beneath his feet, he dropped to all fours, and lay flat on the wood.

The dark of night kept him hidden as he rode on the top of the coach all the way into the walls of the inner city toward the castle. As the carriage slowed, Steigan lowered himself over the side to the footman's stand. He stepped off and into the shadows as a guard moved to let Keteria out of the stopped coach. He fought the urge to chase her straight away.

Progressing deeper into the shadows, Steigan looked up at the castle walls, pale under the light of only one moon high in the sky. He flung the grappling hook and began to scale the walls. Acting on instinct, he traveled around the outside, swinging between sections and ledges, not sure where he was going, but always moving along. Guards patrolled the barbicans and never noticed him advancing. He felt as silent as the wind.

Steigan found and climbed into an open window. Through the darkness, he could make out the door from the rectangle outline of orange light coming from the hallway beyond. He crossed toward the door.

"Who goes there?" a deep voice called out.

Steigan turned and realize he's entered someone's sleeping chambers. He held his breath while he watched a man struggling to sit up in bed.

"I can hear you there. Show yourself." The man groped beside his bed in such a fashion that Steigan wondered if he was looking for a sword.

"Knight, identify yourself!"

It sounded like the command of a king. Steigan found himself snapping to attention.

The man snatched up a candle from the nightstand and lit it. "Foul guardsman! How many times have we discussed that I don't like being watched while I sleep? Step forward!"

Judging quickly by the clothes he wore and the crown he placed askew on his head, Steigan knew he'd entered King Cirello's bed chambers.

Steigan entered the candle's ring of light keeping his head bowed.

"You're not a knight."

"Nay, Majesty," Steigan said. "I am sorry, sire. I hadn't meant to disturb you. I only meant to check on your safety."

"Safety?" The king snorted, spittle flying. "With my sleep so light these days, there is no way I will be taken unaware."

"Aye, milord. But there was a minor disturbance at the Temple tonight. I wanted to make sure it wasn't a diversion tactic."

"Very wise of you, Dominus. Come closer."

Steigan kept his gaze averted as he stepped closer to Cirello. The king slid out of bed to inspect him.

Cirello gasped as he lowered himself to look at Steigan's downward tilted face. "'Tis you." Cirello stepped back, his mouth agape. He stumbled into the chair at his desk.

"Do you know me?" Steigan asked, taken back by this man's reaction.

"I could never forget. And while I've grown old, you haven't changed a bit. Have you brought him back to me?"

"Who?" Steigan swallowed hard. He felt like he'd been tossed a lifeline and he couldn't let go or he'd drown.

"My son," Cirello answered. "My true son."

It took Steigan a moment to pull himself out of this shock and recall the prince's name. "Prince Tanold sleeps in his chambers."

"Not Tanold. You brought Keteria and Tanold to me and took my son. Do you not remember?"

"I do not, but I truly wish I did."

Cirello raised his hand as though holding a sword and slid the invisible blade into the scabbard hanging empty at his side. "A disturbance at the Temple. Keteria isn't harmed, is she? She's back in her chambers, right?"

The change in Cirello's attitude stunned Steigan. "Aye, milord. She is fine and safe."

"We fought them back then? No more demons?"

"No more demons." But even as he spoke these words, Steigan swore he saw something move right by the window. As he dared a second glance, he saw nothing there.

Cirello's face tightened with rage. He reached once more for his invisible sword and took a threatening step forward. "Where is my son?"

"I don't know."

"I want him back." Cirello stood upright, his fists tight and tears in his eyes. "I want him back."

Cirello blinked, but the anger remained on his face. "Who are you anyway? Why have you come back to haunt me? I am an old man now and full of ▬▬ enough without your attack. Be but a ghost and disappear from my sight again." Cirello turned away. "Disappear!"

The door behind Steigan crashed open and two knights rushed in with their swords drawn.

"Get him," Cirello ordered. "He has kidnapped my son."

Steigan rushed past the knights and ran down the hallway, taking turn after turn with no plan in mind. He slammed into an empty chamber room and leaned panting against the door. Listening as running footfalls went by, Steigan slid to the floor and pulled his knees up to his chest and wrapped his arms around his legs. If only the ranting of an old king could be believed…

Had he really found someone who knew him?

Nay, it had to be the tricks of an elderly mind!

Steigan closed his eyes and pressed away raw emotions. Just a little sleep and he'd feel so much better.

But did he dare sleep now? If he did, the night tremors would come. If he didn't, his mind would replay the words thrown at him: *You brought Keteria and Tanold to me and took my son. Do you not remember? Be but a ghost and disappear from my sight again.* What did it mean?

Steigan woke with his arms and legs trembling. His hands seemed to involuntarily shake before his face as he held them up. The night tremors had seized him, attacked while he slept and given him no warning.

"Miex'calidori," he said.

struck him, knocking him sideways to the floor. He screamed as his body arched.

"Badimazulien," he gasped between racking agonies. His skin began to glow and he stared at the aura emerging around him. His skin seemed to crackle, feeling suddenly dry as the hairs on his arms stood on end.

Blackness rode in on the next wave of pain. "Keteria," he whispered as the darkness fell upon him.

Yet somewhere in the pitch, a soft voice called to him.

He felt light fall over him as a door creaked open. He blinked opened his eyes, only to shield his face with his arms as sharp brightness filled his vision. He tried to withdraw to the shadows once more, but there was nowhere to go.

A face came through the light toward him. Princess Keteria came into focus, but she was upside-down. With a quick look, he realized he hung by the knees from a bar in a wardrobe closet. He hissed and bared his teeth as he shielded his face with his hands.

"Go away. I'll come out as soon as the tremors go away." As he said the words, another wave overtook him. He screamed, rocking back and forth. He flicked his hand casting out a spurt of magic and Keteria gave a yelp in surprise, jumping sideways as the door slammed shut between them.

"Steigan, you've got to release the door."

He heard her trying the handle and tugging on the door. "Go away."

"Holicathida." The door opened, revealing Keteria standing there with her hands on her hips.

"You've got to get away from me. Go away," he warned.

Keteria gave a huff as she stepped forward. "Scream at me all you want. I can't hear you."

A new terror took him as he wondered if he'd gone mute again. He knew he could hear himself speak, but what if the sound existed only in his head?

"Calidori," she said with a simple wave of her hand. "Now I'll be able to hear you."

"Don't look at me like this," he said. "I don't want you to see me this way."

She scoffed. "It's a little late for that. Come on, Stegian, get down from there."

"You've got to go away. It's not safe. The magic –"

"I know." She raised her hands and made a quick gesture much like the tossing of a grappling hook. "Nalorium breticham."

Steigan's skin began to glow again. He held his hands up to stare at them, realizing there was something sticky surrounding him. "What?" He pulled at the tenuous threads as though they were thick spider webs. "What is this? What's going on?"

With her hands on her hips again, she gave an impatient shake of her head. "Looks like you've gotten yourself into a fine magic spun tangle."

"Magic spun tangle?" He furiously swiped at the webbing trying to get it off him, but it just seemed to thicken. "What's that? Get this off me."

"Do it yourself. I'm not touching it."

"Thanks. Some help you are," he growled.

Keteria shrugged. "My father always told me that if you get into a mess you should get yourself out."

"Ordinarily I might agree, but I don't know how."

Keteria stepped out of sight for a moment, then returned with a chair and took a seat. She adjusted her skirt as she crossed her legs. With one final glance at him, she began examining her nails. "You do, you just don't know it."

Steigan grit his teeth. He couldn't believe the risks he'd taken to get here only to have Princess Keteria watch and mock him. "A clue then?"

Keteria put her feet flat on the floor and leaned

forward. "Frustration got you into this mess."

"You're not going to tell me that frustration will get me out, are you?"

Keteria cocked her head. "You choose who you are, moment by moment. So tell me, what has you so frustrated?"

His skin tingled and more of the sticky web seemed to tighten around him. With an irritated growl, he tore at the webbing, but it stayed firm. He hated it that Keteria just sat there, watching. "Close the door and leave me alone."

"I can't do that."

"Close it!"

He struggled with the web even more until a movement across the room caught his eye and he looked up. It took a moment for him to focus on just what he saw. He could make out the edges of the dark closet, but the most striking feature was the violent blue balls seeming to float in the air. It was his own gaze staring back at him from a mirror on the opposite wall while his eyes were glowed. Every so often his body seemed to let off a little electrical charge which lit the immediate area around him and made the webbing sparkle in the odd blue light. He hadn't imagined that he looked so abnormal. No one had ever looked this strange!

Steigan's chest tightened. "Ahh! Don't look at me! I don't want you to see me like this. Ah, please Princess, go away."

Slapping her thighs, Keteria rose and came over to him. She leaned in. "Don't you understand? You are just magic-spun. A little extreme maybe, but what else do you expect all considering?"

His head began to hurt so badly that he put his hands to the sides and pressed inward to keep his head from exploding. "'Tis so painful."

"A little more help then," Keteria sighed. "You've got to have a clear head if you're going to get out of this."

She reached toward him. At first he flinched back but then submitted to her light touch against his forehead. Blue whips of light lashed out at her hand, circling her wrist and running up her arm. Keteria gasped as she stepped back.

With the sudden release from her, Steigan felt like he had no more energy and he collapsed to the floor as his legs released the bar.

"So that's what it feels like," Keteria muttered. "Whoa."

Steigan untangled himself from the pile he'd become to look up at Keteria. She held her hands out in front of her but didn't really seem to be seeing them. As his gaze went to her face, he noticed her eyes had gone all black. Something about that seemed so familiar. "Princess?" he asked.

Keteria reached for her face, but it was like her arms

and hands were floating and not really responding to her. "I'm fine," she said though she did have a touch of fear in her voice. "I can balance this. Me, magic spun? Not for some time now."

She turned and stepped into the room where he couldn't see her. He crawled out of the wardrobe closet to watch her glide over to the bed where she calmly picked up a pillow and continued to the window. She flicked her fingers and the window opened as she approached. Once there, she covered her face with the pillow and screamed into it. The pillow exploded, sending feathers flying out the window. Steigan swore he saw a couple of the fluffs turn into birds which flew off into the night sky. Dropping the remains of the cloth casing, she put her hands on the sills and panted.

Steigan got to his feet, holding onto the wall for support as his head spun from being upside-down for Goddess knew how long. "Are you all right?" he asked.

Keteria nodded, but didn't move.

Steigan went over to the mirror and stared into it. With his eyes still glowing in that unusual extreme blue color, he hardly recognized himself. "How can this be?" he asked, touching his cheek. "This isn't me."

With one final exhale of exhaustion, Keteria turned and sat down on the window and leaned against the side. She smiled weakly, her eyes filled with curiosity.

Her amusement brought a flash of anger. He demanded, "What are you thinking?"

"I'm wondering how long 'tis going to be until you decide to stop being magic spun. You are so stubborn."

"You keep mentioning this magic spun. What is that?"

Keteria laughed and shook her head. "'Tis all so curious. 'Tis like you've just come into your magic."

"Explain," he snapped.

"Being magic spun is like..." She struggled to find the right words. "Like a childhood illness. Something you get once and your body is protected against it thereafter. Children usually get it between the ages of four and six when their magic comes in. The degrees vary by ability and it lets the Temple know who needs magical training."

"My memory loss? Could it have something to do with it?"

"Just because you lose the memory of having chicken pox doesn't mean you're going to get it again."

"How do I stop it?" It seemed like the only question he really wanted the answer to, the one she refused to give him no matter how many times he asked.

She looked tired. "Let's start simple. How are you feeling?"

Did he know where to start? "Angry, confused, irritated, like I've had the stuffing knocked out of me." He involuntarily looked down at the remains of the pillow on the floor.

"That's not good." She looked a bit irritated and confused herself. "We'll work through it."

"How?"

She had a look of fear in her eyes as she folded her hands together as though protecting her fingers. "I don't know if I dare take any more magic from you."

"Why not?"

"When a child gets magic spun, 'tis a simple matter of a parent or trained maege to peel off a layer of magic. It clears the head and allows for the way out. But you have so much magic…"

He did have to admit that his thoughts did seem clearer than they had been before she'd touched him to peel off the magic, but the way she sat there, weak, tired, and scared, he knew there was something she wasn't telling him. "Why?"

"Why what?"

"Why do I have so much magic?"

She stood up and took a couple steps toward the door. For a moment he wondered if she would ignore him again or maybe leave. But she turned back toward him, looking at the floor. Her muscles tightened as if bracing herself. She exhaled deeply. Whatever she had to say, she didn't want to say it.

Keteria lifted her head as she inhaled, the princess in her seeming to rise to the surface. For but a moment, she seemed to sway between princess and High Maege as though the two titles conflicted with each other. It happened so fast he wasn't even sure he saw it. He certainly didn't know where she settled but she held her head high as she answered.

"Because obviously," she said, her voice sharp and tight, "you possess stolen magic."

Chapter Seven

Steigan stood accused of something he didn't understand and couldn't remember. Her tone alone alerted him to this situation not being good. "Stolen magic? What does that mean?"

"'Tis exactly as it sounds. You took someone's magical ability." She began to pace while tapping her index finger against her lips. "You thieve the power from someone, get attacked by gargaxes which no one has seen in centuries, lose your memory, and now you're magic spun."

"How do you even know I was attacked by gargaxes?"

"Very few creatures can actually puncture a hole into a

magic aura," she replied. "It doesn't seem to add up, and yet the facts point to a truly interesting and unique situation. You are a magical mystery."

"Why's that?"

"How did you steal magic in the first place if you've never encountered magic enough to learn to control it?"

~~Pain~~ tore through Steigan again and he felt like he was sweating out a high fever. When he recovered, he realized that he was covered in more of the web-like goo. "How do I make it stop?" Even before he finished the question, the ~~pain~~ returned and knocked him to his knees.

Keteria dropped down beside him, her hands hovering over him as though unsure if she should touch him or not. "I hope this is a lesson to you not to steal other people's magic," she scolded.

She seemed more interested in the situation and the amount of magic he had rather than helping him.

"I don't remember stealing anyone's magic and I don't think I would!"

"Time will be the judge of that." Her anger had returned. "I'll hear if someone in the land complains of having their magic stolen."

Steigan collapsed onto his side, still curled in a tight fetal position. "Have you heard anything yet?"

"Nay, and 'tis the only reason I'll help you. I ought to have you thrown in the dungeons."

More spasms moved through him. He cried out under the muscle cramps that constricted him. "And how bad is it going to have to get before you show your mercy?" he whimpered.

"I'm thinking, I'm thinking," she fretted.

Steigan rolled onto his back and pulled his knees up to his chest. "I'd rather have you doing!"

"Children never get this tangled. I don't..." Suddenly she was on her feet. "Oh, I know. I'll be right back. Don't go anywhere."

As he watched her flee, Steigan didn't know if could leave the room if he wanted to.

Agony seemed to spread into eternity. The floor grew cold and uncomfortable beneath him. He tried to move, but every action felt like he was pulling up splinters from the wood and driving them deep into his flesh. He tried to see if it was really happening, to see if his out-of-control magic pulled the floor up in shards, but the movement sent more dicing through him.

He heard footsteps in the hall, then the door creaked open, and Keteria entered. She dropped down beside him and put a chain around his neck. Instantly the began to subside though it didn't disappear.

Steigan relaxed, panting on the floor. "Oh, that's good. Much better."

"Here, hold this too," she said handing something toward him in her cupped hand so that he couldn't see what she held.

Only too late, after it was already in his hand with his fingers curled tightly around the marble did he recognize it as the stone of unbearable weight. Was she trying to kill him?

The stone went red and stayed there.

"Amazing," Keteria whispered.

Steigan shifted the ball in his fingers. It actually felt comfortable now. "What's amazing?"

"I've always wanted to test it, but the opportunity never presented itself. The absorption stone suppresses your natural magical abilities. The stolen magic which you're left with now is really normal."

"Which means?"

Keteria looked out the window into the night sky. "That your magic by itself might actually rival my own. Why would you need to take more?"

Steigan started pulling off the sticky coating covering his skin. "I'm sure I'm an interesting intellectual problem, but how do I deal with being magic spun?"

"Well, I'd say that a layer of magic is peeled away now and you sound like your head has cleared, so figure out how to use your magic."

Steigan sat up as he finished cleaning himself off, then he looked at his hands. "I don't know how. I kind of use it instinctively, but I don't know how I do it."

"So," she said, tilting her head, "you're telling me a four year old child is better adapted to using magic than you are, someone with stolen magic?"

"Stop it. I didn't steal magic."

"Everything about you says otherwise."

He stood up to look her in the eyes. "I don't care. I know in my heart I didn't steal magic from anyone."

"The heart feels, but the heart doesn't 'know.' There's a reason your heart is in a cage."

"And that reason would be?"

"To shield it from the very world the brain sees."

Something in her tone made Steigan come to complete calm. She looked embarrassed and dropped her gaze to where her feet shuffled on the wooden floor. She swayed, making her skirt twirl against her ankles.

All at once, Steigan felt warm and the remaining cobwebs that had stuck to him fell away and turned to dust. He reached a hand out and touched her shoulder. "I am sorry you've seen something that made you think your heart can't be trusted."

Her eyes sharpened as they darkened with anger. "How would you... How dare you presume?" She turned her back to him and crossed her arms.

He hadn't meant to injure her. He decided to ask the question on his mind. "How did you find me tonight?"

"Your magic called to me." She turned back slowly.

"And you followed your heart, that blind heart, because you knew that somewhere someone needed you. Your eyes couldn't see it, but your heart felt it."

"You made the air around me sparkle the night of the tri-lunar ceremony. It... felt... the same."

Steigan lifted the absorption stone from around his neck and, ignoring her protests, placed it in her hands. "I understand now. The magic comes from the same dwelling that kindness, bravery, and courage do: the heart. I feel it now. I didn't want to before." He stretched his hand out and flexed his fingers. "'Tis no longer the beast within, but a part of me I can't be without."

Keteria's gaze flickered quickly over him as though trying to understand something incomprehensible.

Steigan leaned close to her and whispered in her ear. "Thank you, Princess. You are very good with your guidance."

He straightened and saw the puzzled expression on her face. This was her issue to work out now. He started to leave the room.

Before he reached the door, she said, "Maybe someday I'll be able to take my own advice."

He spoke over his shoulder. "If I have to give you forever, I'll wait for that day."

CHAPTER EIGHT

Steigan returned to Searn's fief, but headed straight to the blacksmith's shop. He wasn't ready to face Searn yet.

Ranil was already at work at his forge. "Blessed morning, Steigan. You're out early this morning. Baby keep you awake last night?"

Steigan answered, "I've been out taking care of some things. Searn and Centhya needed their privacy."

He had just picked up a piece of iron with some tongs and was making his way to the forge when he saw Ranil's pale, shocked expression. Steigan shrugged. "My voice recently came back. I only wish my memories would now too." He hoped he'd recovered enough. To keep from judging the success of his words, he continued to the forge and put the iron rod into the hot coals.

Ranil picked up a larger hammer and resumed pounding his heated metal on the anvil. "What business were you out taking care of this early in the morning?" Ranil's voice had changed, tightened and raised in pitch.

The hairs at the nape of Steigan's neck stood up. He debated the next best course of action and decided the truth might be the best. "I went to see Princess Keteria. When speech returned to me, I thought she might now be able to help me with my magic."

Steigan dodged the hammer when Ranil pitched it at him, but in avoiding the makeshift weapon, Steigan didn't have time to duck from Ranil who plowed into him and tackled him to the floor. Ranil's weight knocked the wind out of him and for a moment Steigan's world spun.

"What are you doing?" Steigan tried to yell with no breath behind the words.

Ranil punched him.

Black and white stars swam in Steigan's vision. He barely registered that Ranil had picked him up and was tying him in thick rope. As Ranil finished with the knot, he pulled another rope which hoisted Steigan into the air. His gaze still fuzzy, Steigan looked down at his boots dangling several feet off the ground. He tried to speak, but his voice had once again left him.

"Merilynn," Ranil shouted as he stood back, arms across his chest, to look up suspiciously at Steigan. "Merilynn!"

A woman came running in wiping her hands on her wheat-colored apron. She stopped suddenly when she saw Steigan dangling in the air. "Ranil, what's going on?"

"Take the horse outside and go to Dominus Searn's house. Make sure the dominus and his wife are in good health."

"'Tis early yet."

"Go now, woman! Be quick about it. If Dominus Searn wonders where his charge may be at, let him know the whelp is here."

Merilynn nodded and went outside. She returned a moment later, her hands over her mouth as she stared up at Steigan. "Ranil, Searn's armor is here."

"What?" Ranil went outside to look for himself and returned carrying Searn's breastplate and sword. He held them up as though they were evidence. "Why are you in possession of these items?"

"I was borrowing them. Do you know what's out there

in the forest?" Steigan replied.

"So you admit that you were taking arms out to the forest, perhaps to meet someone. A Plenelian? Or maybe you wanted to pose as Searn?'

Steigan heard Merilynn spur his horse to a gallop and the hoofbeats quickly faded to silence.

"I've been attacked by gargaxes once," Steigan said. "I don't want to go through that again. I only thought to protect myself."

Ranil glared at him with disgust. "We'll see about that soon enough."

Steigan hung around as Ranil paced back and forth while smacking the head of a hammer into his palm threateningly.

Hoofbeats returned, but only one horse. Chills turned to panic. What if something had happened to Searn while he had been gone? How would Steigan prove he hadn't hurt Searn or his family? He thought of Annae, only born yesterday.

Searn appeared in the doorway of the forge house. "Steigan!" He stepped forward toward where Steigan was hanging.

Ranil dropped to his knee before Searn, and then stood back up to speak. "My dominus, I apprehended this thief and thought you should deal with him appropriately."

A moment later, a second horse came down the road and stopped. Merilynn appeared in the doorway, but she didn't come inside.

Searn looked between Steigan to Ranil, his expression growing serious. "What wrong-doing has he caused?"

"He freely admitted to being out last night, supposedly having gone to the princess, and he was in possession of your armor." Ranil held up the breastplate.

"Freely admits?" Searn glanced up at Steigan.

"My voice has returned, Searn," Steigan said, giving silent thanks to the Goddess for sending his voice back to him again after Ranil's thundering punch. "I didn't know 'twas going to be a capital offense. And aye, I did go out as he said."

"What about my armor?"

"Protection in case I got attacked by the gargaxes again."

"Is that what he told you?" Searn asked Ranil.

"Aye, but his words were suspicious," Ranil answered.

"You've never heard him speak before now. How would you know suspicious from normal?"

Under Searn's sharp insight, Ranil glanced to the floor.

"Lower him down," Searn said.

Without meeting Searn's gaze, the blacksmith untied

the rope holding Steigan and lowered him to the ground, then went to untie the knot.

"Ranil, I am proud of your vigilance. 'Tis good to know I can count on you," Searn said. "Come, Steigan. I believe you are due an explanation."

Searn put his hand on Steigan's shoulder and guided him out of the forge house. Searn took the reins of the two horses from Merilynn and started leading them down the road.

For a moment, Searn remained silent while watching the road as if trying to find the right place to start. Was he wondering how much Steigan knew?

Steigan decided to let on what he suspected. "My parents didn't die in an accident, did they?"

"There is a lot of confusion as to where you came from, Steigan, and you must understand that Prince Tanold wanted me to take every precaution."

His question turned to knowing. "Because I was the strange dominus found along the road and no one's sure where I came from."

"Aye, Steigan, you are that man. But we can't be certain you hold the title of dominus."

"Why not?"

"We know you are not a dominus of Lilinar," Searn

explained with a touch of sadness in his voice. "Only the domini of Lilinar wear blue and gold armor, which you were found wearing. Domini elsewhere wear red and gold armor."

After a small, uneasy pause, Searn went on, "Ranil tells me you are skilled at blacksmithing, probably trained well enough to make your own armor."

Searn continued looking at the road straight ahead and letting the implications hang on his words. The armor Steigan had been found in had to be a forgery. But then, what man would want to admit that the person they had invited into their home was a spy, even if that was the only working theory that made sense? Steigan respected the fact that Searn stopped short of calling him a fake.

"Is Steigan even my name?" he asked.

"Aye, 'tis," Searn replied, now looking at Steigan. "When we first found you along the road and you were barely conscious, we asked you who you were. You replied with Steigan."

"Then what happened?" If he knew more, maybe he could find his own memories.

"We were returning from a hunt and riding back to Lilinar so we took you with us. Princess Keteria treated your gargax bites with a salve and tried to help you regain your memories, but you were barely conscious."

"Why did you take me in?"

Now Searn looked over across the distant fields. "My aunt, King Cirello's sister, was banished about twenty years ago. No one's ever heard from her. When you showed up with the birthmark on your palm, I knew you had to be part of our family. I still hope you are her son and my cousin."

Such a deep part of him wanted Searn's theory to be right. But he realized there could be another. He watched the ground, now finding himself not wanting to look at Searn. "King Cirello thinks that he has another son who was kidnapped from him. Is that true?"

"Please realize that our king is suffering from the ravages of magic. It has taken his mind from us, but not his body. There is no kidnapped son, only a dream he believes real."

"You're saying the magic is making him crazy?"

"There is a reason I choose not to use magic to solve my every whim. My aunt, Saleaha, use to say that Cirello overused magic. 'Tis why she was banished. Now that I've seen what's happened over time, I don't think she was wrong."

"And Cirello's children?"

"Only Princess Keteria has magic. For some reason, Prince Tanold was born without the ability."

"Is it then not possible that he was switched with another baby at birth?" Steigan asked. "Maybe the Prince Tanold we know is not the true birthright?"

A myriad of expressions crossed Searn's face as he seemed to think through the line Steigan had been on. His emotions ranged from disbelief to fear to suspicion to amazement all at once.

Searn settled with denial. "Tanold bears the birthmark as well. He is Cirello's son." Then he changed the subject. "Why did you go to Lilinar to see Princess Keteria?"

Steigan couldn't help smiling and giving a scoff at his own foolishness. "I actually went to see the High Maege."

Searn also smiled. "But you didn't realize that Centhya is really High Maege and that Keteria is filling in for her."

"Aye, it took some quick explaining on my part since the guard thought I was you."

Searn hid the quick look of disappointment as he realized that Steigan had been impersonating him. "Why did you go?"

"I had hoped that with my voice returning so would my memories if I had the right help."

"Never lie to me." Searn gave him a sharp look to underline his words.

Steigan glanced down, trying to find the strength to

apologize among the feelings of inadequacy and embarrassment he felt. He had told the truth, at least part of it. How could he tell Searn that he had been magic spun, the victim of a *childhood* aliment?

Searn nudged Steigan's arm with the back of his hand and handed the horse's reins to Steigan. "It must have been important if you felt it couldn't wait until morning and it must have been personal if you felt like you had to sneak out without telling me. I will respect your privacy if you answer me but one question: did you actually get to see Keteria?"

"Aye, I did."

Searn mounted the horse and waited for Steigan to do the same. "Let us get back to the house for breakfast. Then we shall ride to Lilinar together. 'Tis time to visit with Tanold again."

They rode the remainder of the way in silence. Searn's page came out and took the horses when they arrived. Once inside the house, Searn turned to Steigan. "Go pack up your things. We'll have breakfast then we'll head for Lilinar."

Pack his things? Steigan wanted to ask what was going to happen to him, but feared Searn's answer. He found himself shaking, not wanting to break down and confess how seriously he'd needed Keteria's help. An icy lump grew in the pit of his stomach. Maybe the situation would get all so much worse if Searn knew he'd been magic spun. Would Keteria be able to explain it all to Searn and make everything well once more? Clinging to that minor hope, Steigan nodded and started to head down the hallway. But once out of sight of Searn, all the strength drained away and he collapsed against the wall.

"Is he all right?" Steigan heard Centhya ask Searn.

"I've told him, Centhya," Searn said as if he wasn't sure he'd done the right thing. "He knows."

"He's just a boy. What's going to happen to him?"

Steigan lifted his head, listening intently and so glad that Centhya had asked the question of Searn.

"I'm going to petition for him to train at the Temple," Searn answered.

"Do you think that's wise? You already made the choice when he was found to keep him here rather than take him to the Temple."

"Cen, I feared what Tanold might do with the boy. Steigan was so confused, lost. Imagine how terrifying 'twould have been if Tanold had put him in the dungeons then. But now I feel 'tis right for him to go to the Temple."

"Couldn't he stay here and we can train him?"

There was a pause and in that moment it felt as if Steigan could see the emotions playing out on Searn's face.

"He can't," Searn finally said. "We've got to think of Annae now. I can't keep the boy here. His wounds were the first sign of the gargaxes anyone has seen in a thousand years. If they are returning and if the legend of the enchantment is true, 'tis only a matter of time before the descendants of Rivic start hunting."

Enchantment? Hunting? There was so much more going on here. Steigan wondered how he fit into the puzzle.

Searn continued, "For all we know, he's the first to be affected by the enchantment. He might have gone out hunting the night before we found him."

"Have you felt anything?" Centhya asked with worry.

"I've got Annae to protect. If Steigan is going to wander at night, like he did last night, I can't risk him bringing something dangerous back with him."

Centhya seemed to realize that Searn hadn't answered her question. "Have you felt anything?"

The sound of Searn's hand banging against the table made Steigan jump. "I woke last night. It took all my strength to keep still and remain by you and Annae. I have to take him to the Temple until this is over."

"You really think this will be over?"

The sound of a chair scooting across the floor made Steigan hurry down the hallway. He heard a door slam somewhere in the house behind him. Once in his room, Steigan saw Searn outside working on sword drill with his page.

The aggression of Searn's swings told Steigan that not only did Searn know these times would not soon be over, but that they were just beginning.

Chapter Nine

The overhead sun glittered off Searn's armor as they rode into Lilinar. Steigan hung back just slightly, watching how the light played on the blue and gold. With a pang of envy, he felt so *without*.

Searn hadn't said much on the road and Steigan wanted to apologize for putting a fear into Searn's heart, a worry that neither one of them could ever prove would come to pass. Still, he felt like he'd betrayed Searn and let him down.

At the inner city, they left the horses with a stable boy and walked the remainder of the way to the castle. Steigan sensed that Searn had purposely done this so they could have a few more moments together. Would they spend it in quiet, or would one of them actually speak what was on his mind?

Vendors packed the cobblestone streets selling their wares. Peasants walked casually among the stalls making trades and purchases. There was chatter and laughter among the colors of business. Steigan decided he liked it here.

Following Searn into the castle, they went upstairs into the main hall. With no one around, Searn headed for the stairs.

"Wait here," Searn said. "I'll be right back after I've found Tanold."

Steigan nodded, feeling mute again. He waited on a balcony that overlooked the main hall. Below, Princess Keteria entered, looked around, and then started to leave.

"Don't go, sister," a deep male voice said from somewhere beneath the balcony. "I am here."

Keteria turned and smiled as Tanold stepped out of the shadows and approached.

"Searn is here to see us," Tanold said. "I saw him walk through. I'm sure he'll be back in but a moment."

"We really have to talk about father," Keteria said.

Tanold's warm reception instantly grew cold and he turned his back to her. "What is left to talk about? You are set to be queen."

"I have been visiting with papa this morning. He told me that the man who took his son has come back."

"His son?" Tanold turned slowly back to her. "We are his only children."

"We know that the night we were born, there was an assassination attempt on father's life. What if the assassins wanted to do more than just kill him, but to also take away his son, or murder his son?"

"We are his only children," Tanold insisted.

"You're not listening to me." Keteria put her hands on her hips. "He had the trauma of an attempt on his life, the birth of twins, and losing his wife in childbirth all in that night. Add losing a firstborn son to that and the pain would be unimaginable."

"How could father have seen the man who took his son? He never leaves the castle and he never takes visitors."

Keteria twisted her fingers around her wrist. "I'm not so sure he was being literal about seeing the man. I think a repressed memory is surfacing, something he wants us to know about before…"

When she didn't finish, he did. "Before he dies? Why are you doing this? Do you actually want someone else to claim the throne?"

"I've met someone whose power is as strong as my own and he has a lot of mystery surrounding his abilities."

Tanold's face hardened. "Who?"

"The boy found in the dominus armor."

"What? Would you have me believe that he is Cirello's firstborn son, kidnapped, then somehow brought back here? He's younger than we are."

"There are," she began, shuffling her feet, "there are spells that can change time."

"Has he regained his memories?"

"Nay, but he does bear the lineage mark."

"He is not Cirello's son. We are his only children."

"I am only saying that we really need to find out who he is."

Tanold took a step back, his mouth agape. "Have you fallen for him?"

"Nay," she replied, rolling back her shoulders to stand tall. "Absolutely not. That would be crazy."

Tanold began to laugh. "You look away while your cheeks redden. You are lying to me."

"The worst thing about having a twin is the fact that you know me too well."

"So what are your intentions? He could be a dangerous enemy."

"Rivic's blood, you are infuriating," she said, waving out her hand at him. "Why does everything have to be something to possess or kill?"

"We were raised that way. Never forget that. Cirello brought us up to rule the world."

"You've learned that lesson well. I haven't."

"Aye," Tanold responded. "I would marry to solidify our position and power. You want to marry for love. There is no such thing."

Keteria stepped away from him. "Ma-Mat said—"

"Don't bring the dead into this!"

"Very well. Just tell me you will begin a search into the boy's past. Every possibility must be explored."

Searn returned beside Steigan and the movement drew Tanold's attention to them. Steigan felt pinned by Tanold's dark eyes. Possess or kill. That's exactly the look he received and it chilled him.

"Prince Tanold," Searn said. "We must have just crossed paths."

Tanold's gaze stayed on Steigan for a moment longer then flickered to Searn. "Indeed, cousin. Crossed paths. I hear you have news for me."

Searn touched Steigan's arm indicating for him to follow as Searn went down the stone staircase to the main hall below. Steigan stayed a couple paces behind. He bowed to Keteria and Tanold, still feeling Tanold's nearly black eyes on him, but when the group settled he found himself face-to-face with Keteria. He found her gray eyes more pleasing and couldn't help smiling. Her face lit up and she glanced away. She seemed to be trying to return her attention to the conversation, but her gaze kept sliding back to Steigan.

"A baby girl! That's delightful," Keteria said, congratulating Searn who was delivering the news.

"We've named her Annae."

"Annae, what a wonderful name." Keteria sent Steigan another look and he realized in that instant that her excitement wasn't truly over the baby, but of their proximity. It was like part of her reached for him.

"I trust you haven't had any more trouble with the Plenelians," Tanold's cold voice cut in.

"None," Searn responded.

"Good. Then you probably want to be on your way back to your wife and baby." Tanold started to turn away.

"Milord, there is another matter."

Tanold's gaze flickered to Steigan, then back to Searn. "That would be?"

"Steigan has regained his voice."

"Aye, so I've heard, but not his memories. A voice does

no good if he cannot recall what happened to him and relate those stories to us."

"He knows he's the one found on the roadside and that he's possibly a dominus," Searn said.

Tanold raised his head. Steigan matched Tanold's height, yet under the prince's dark presence, he felt so small and mute. Steigan's vision seemed to tunnel until it seemed like only Tanold remained with him in the room.

"Does he now?" Tanold said, more matter-of-factly than curious.

"His magic is strong," Searn said.

"So I've heard."

"Don't you see? What if he's Saleaha's son?"

Tanold stepped back and rubbed his hand against his chin. It almost looked like he wanted to laugh. "Saleaha's son? Do you hear that, Keteria? A theory I can believe," Tanold said. "Our newcomer might be Saleaha's son."

At first, Keteria looked on the verge of tears. Then she blinked and nodded. "He does bear remarkable resemblance to cousin Searn. I say we could welcome another cousin to our family."

Steigan felt that her formal words concealed her true feelings, that deep down she was really upset. Or was he just wishful thinking?

"Excuse me," Keteria said, stepping away. "I have to get back to work."

"Of course, sister. So many duties to attend."

"Farewell, milady," Searn said.

Steigan watched Keteria go and listened as she reached the doorway, then started running until her footsteps faded.

Tanold laughed. "Are you sure he has his voice back, Searn? He's watched my sister, his own cousin, without even trying to say a word. Maybe the shock of close family relations has rendered him speechless again?"

"He needs training, milord," Searn said trying to return the course of the conversation.

"Training to speak, like a child babbling his first words?"

"Nay," Steigan returned sharply. "He is talking about my proper training as a dominus."

"Look at that. He does speak." Tanold gave a wry smile and looked toward the doorway where Keteria had gone. "But only, it seems, when the womenfolk are hidden away. Good thing too, for his voice is still a shade too high to be a real man."

Fire flashed through Steigan. He wanted to rush forward and wrap his hands around Tanold's throat, but Searn stepped in front of him.

Searn said, "I was hoping he could stay with the other domini in the Temple for a few weeks, train with them."

Tanold contemplated the request for a moment before nodding. "You need leave to be with your wife and child. I'm sure Mierk could find an open bed. I will have a request drawn up straight away and you may head there shortly." Tanold smiled as he looked Steigan over again. "But he will enter as a cavalier."

"A cavalier?" Steigan asked.

"A cavalier, milord?" Searn questioned, also shocked. "He does bear the lineage mark. The domini track is his right. He should be a page."

"His true heritage is unknown at this point," Tanold responded as though that was the end of the conversation.

"He won't get the magic training he needs," Searn protested. "His skills with the sword are excellent."

"Allowances will be made. I agree that his magic does need training and take your word that he can already fight with proficiency. But until we can prove his lineage, he will have to accept the knight track."

Searn seemed to know there would be no further changing Tanold's mind. He bowed. "Thank you, Prince Tanold."

Tanold started to walk away. "Do not thank me," he

said as he went. "Thank my sister for her wisdom. 'Tis at her request that I do this."

Searn gave Steigan a strange, questioning look.

Tanold stopped briefly in the doorway, turning back ever so slightly to glare at Steigan once more. "I personally would still rather have him thrown in the dungeons."

CHAPTER TEN

The smell of sweat and old stone woke Steigan. The barest moonlight came through the large window, illuminating the dormitory where he slept. It took him a moment to remember that he was at the Temple and not at Searn's. He shivered beneath his threadbare blanket.

Why had he awoken? He pulled his hands out to look at them, half wondering if his shivers were the night tremors returning. Feeling his fingers, he realized he was cold, not magic spun.

Looking around the room and listening to the light snores, he knew none of the other boys were awake yet. He wondered how long before the call to morning prayer. Rising, he started toward the window across the room. He'd already found that he liked standing at the window and looking down on the courtyard. He wondered if originally there had been a balcony as there was a gap past the window and a wrought iron railing. Maybe too many boys had used the opportunity to sneak out and the original double doors had been replaced with glass.

Passing in front of a wardrobe, he heard a whimper. Finding the door ajar, Steigan opened it. Clothing similar to what the peasants in Lilinar wore hung askew and looked as though it had been pushed aside. He reached inside intending on parting the clothes and heard a scuffle from deeper within. It made him jump.

He bent down to look beneath the cavaliers' ragged clothing and discovered a wide-eyed boy cowering in the back with his hands over his mouth. When he saw Steigan looking back at him, he turned his head away as though he didn't see Steigan and that Steigan couldn't see him either.

"Are you all right?" Steigan asked. "What happened?"

The boy whimpered and pressed further against the wall as though wishing it would absorb him.

"Are you afraid I'm going to hurt you?"

The boy trembled, still not looking at Steigan, but

replied, "The others do." His voice was a bare high-pitched whisper that Steigan wasn't even sure he'd heard.

"I bet that makes two of us who feel like we don't fit in here," Steigan said, wishing to be back at Searn's. That had seemed so simple, so quiet and comfortable. Here, well... here he wasn't sure if he had a place. Yet somehow he needed to fit in to his new sanctuary or Tanold might toss him in the dungeons before Searn could find out. *Possess or kill* still hung in his mind. It might not frighten Keteria, but it terrified him.

The boy's eyes flickered briefly toward him.

"Do you mind if I sit here?" Steigan asked, suddenly feeling very alone himself. It wasn't an emotion he was accustomed too. What about this small lad brought it out?

Shrugging, the boy said, "I couldn't stop you if I wanted to."

Feeling rejected, Steigan wondered if he'd misjudged the situation. "Aye, you could," Steigan replied. "If you want to be alone, simply say so."

"It never works."

"Look, you came in here to be away from the others, so you must want to be alone. I'm sorry to have disturbed you." Steigan started to stand, but the boy reached for him.

"Don't go," he said.

Steigan knelt down again. "Are you sure?"

The boy nodded.

"Then is it all right if I sit by you?"

The boy nodded again and Steigan slid inside the wardrobe and against the wall, pushing the clothes away from his head. He held his hand out to the boy. "Well met. My name is Steigan."

The boy flinched away from Steigan, but then when he realized Steigan wasn't going to strike him, he put his hand in Steigan's to shake it. "Well met. I'm Jaxsen Setherbern."

"Sounds like the name of a leader."

"Do you think?" For a moment, the boy's eyes were bright in the dark. He glanced away. "Nay, not me. I'm the fifth son of seven. My brothers, they will make great leaders. Me, I just want to survive this place."

Though he spoke softly, Steigan found the boy liking to talk. Maybe he just hadn't been given the opportunity before.

"I think 'tis a fine goal you've got there. I think I should try for the same thing," Steigan said.

"Truthfully? I wouldn't think 'twould be hard for you. I mean, I saw you practicing with the sword yesterday. If I was like that…" Jaxsen made invisible swings with an imaginary sword in the tight closet. "I'd be like, zip, zip, boom, biff to them." He fell back to his slouched position against the back wall of the wardrobe, his breathing raspy and gasping.

"Who do you mean when you say 'them'?"

"All of them." Jaxsen shook his head and waved his hand as though indicating the whole world. "All of them. My brothers, the stupid knights, the domini, everyone!"

"Who would be left?"

"No one."

Steigan wondered how badly this boy had to have been treated to be this angry. "Lonely world you'd have there after taking everyone out. Of course, all the strickleberries would be yours."

"Strickleberries!" he said, getting excited. "I'd pick buckets of them and then just stick my head into the bucket to gobble them down."

"And no one would tell you to wash your face afterward. Or to wash your hands before."

"Aye, that would be wonderful."

Steigan snickered at the thought and silence fell between them.

After a moment, Jaxsen turned to Steigan. "I wouldn't zip, zip, boom, biff everyone. Just the mean people. I'd let you stay."

Steigan couldn't help smiling. "Maybe I could be your general. After all, you'll be the leader and you'll need someone to lead your brave armies."

Jaxsen smiled too. "My armies. Aye, you'd be my general, the one I count on most. You'd be brave and carry my flag for honor and nobility. When people saw you, they'd know to be nice to each other."

"I do like that," Steigan laughed.

"So do I." Jaxsen curled up with his knees up to his chest imitating Steigan. He seemed so small, able to fit in this wardrobe as though it was his personal room. How many nights had he come in here?

"So why are you hiding?" Steigan asked, his voice nearly as soft as Jaxsen's first words had been.

"You'd probably laugh."

"A general never laughs at his commander."

Jaxsen looked up into the hanging clothes. "I have nightmares. Sleeping on the cold floor makes it worse."

"Sleeping on the floor?" Nightmares he understood.

"The mice," Jaxsen said, a faint wobble in his voice. "I'm terrified of mice. I can hear them scurry around the room at night. When I sleep on the floor, I can feel them crawling around me. If I wake up screaming, the other boys laugh at me. 'Tis better to come in here."

"Why aren't you sleeping in your bed? Do you fall out onto the floor?"

Jaxsen bit down on this lip and for a long time, Steigan

wasn't sure if the boy would answer the question or not. Steigan wondered if he'd pushed too far.

"Paedorin, one of my older brothers, told the others that I was afraid of mice when he was still here at the Temple," Jaxsen said. "Since he's been gone to serve with his dominus, it's gotten a little better around here, but every now and then..."

Paedorin, Steigan thought, *Searn's page.* That's why Jaxsen's family name had sounded so familiar.

"They decide to pick on you for old time's sake," Steigan said, understanding. Just thinking about Paedorin's arrogance was enough to make Steigan angry about the situation. He remembered and understood all too well how much Paedorin could get under his skin. Had he been smaller, Steigan realized he may have ended up just as cowed as Jaxsen.

"Aye," Jaxsen said. "I really hate the mice."

"So how do they make you sleep on the floor? Why don't you just get back up in bed?"

"Olierex pushes our beds together and sleeps across them."

Olierex was a name Steigan remembered from the previous evening. A rather round boy belonged to the name. He took to bullying the other kids at supper. He'd also been one of those watching Steigan fight against Searn when Searn showed Steigan's skills to Sacred Knight Danis and the other domini at the Temple earlier in the day. Because of that, Olierex had stayed clear of Steigan, obviously intimidated by Steigan's skill.

Steigan had an idea of how to stop all the boys from bullying Jaxsen ever again. He slid out of the wardrobe, but peered beneath the clothes to Jaxsen. "Then my first act as your general is to make sure you never sleep on the floor again."

Steigan stood. He heard Jaxsen clambering out of the closet right behind him.

"What are you going to do? You can't go onto the domini side," Jaxsen warned.

Morning light eased through the window, enough so that Steigan could effortlessly see the two beds pushed together with the large boy lying across the mattresses. Without warning, Steigan grabbed the blankets and wrapped Olierex up in them. Before Olierex woke enough to scream, Steigan had him well swathed.

"Don't," Jaxsen protested. "You'll only get in trouble. Then things will get worse."

Steigan tossed Olierex over his shoulder and started for the door. "Your general is going to make sure no one ever picks on you again."

The commotion had woken several others who all stared in disbelief, then scrambled out of bed in search of their shoes.

Steigan carried Olierex passed several saperes in the hallway on their way to prayers.

"Blessed morning, Saperes," Steigan said, holding tightly onto his wiggling bundle. Steigan bounced down the stairs, knowing he had to be quick now that he'd been seen and not really caring if he were gentle or not as he hurried.

The dawn air felt cool against his face as he headed down the steps to the courtyard. Steigan crossed to the well and dropped his bundle ungraciously in a pile at his feet. Olierex tried to get out of the blankets, but Steigan grabbed Olierex's feet and raised him up again. Hugging the boy's legs against his chest, Steigan leaned over the well, one leg up on the stone wall.

"Stop struggling or I might drop you," Steigan warned.

"You're mad!" Olierex screamed, trying to grab onto Steigan's leg. "What did I do to you?"

"You're scaring a friend of mine. I don't like it when people scare my friends. I thought a little terror in your heart would do you some good."

Taking a tight grip on the boy's legs, Steigan forced

Olierex all the way into the well.

"Don't drop me!"

"Only if you apologize to Jaxsen for the way you've treated him."

Steigan briefly looked back to see a sapere standing beside Jaxsen, who had his face covered in his hands. Boys and girls from the dormitories upstairs spilled out of the Temple, yet not daring to come too far into the courtyard. Another sapere and a knight stood in the doorway as though wondering what they should do.

"Jaxsen who?" Olierex screamed.

"Do you know how far down it is? Should we find out?" Steigan leaned forward quickly, giving the sensation of dropping Olierex.

"Nay. Pull me back up. Come on."

Holy Sapere Mierk came rushing out of the Temple, pulling on his long white night robes as he hurried. "What's going on here?" As he moved forward, the mass of people behind him also felt brave enough to come closer to the well. "Steigan, stop this."

"Not until he realizes what 'tis like to sleep with the mice," Steigan said, shaking off Mierk's hand as it fell upon his shoulder. Steigan hobbled around the well, trying to keep himself out of Mierk's reach.

Jaxsen ran forward. "Come on, Steigan. Let him go."

"Pull me up," Olierex hollered. "Pull me up."

Suddenly two domini were at Steigan's sides, each grabbing onto Olierex and trying to draw him back. Steigan attempted to shove them away while keeping Olierex in the well. Olierex screamed.

An arm came around Steigan's throat.

"I'll drop him," Steigan declared against the force pressing into his windpipe.

"There's spiders," Olierex screamed, wiggling so hard Steigan almost couldn't hold him. "Spiders!"

More screaming emanated from the well. Steigan's grip started to slip on the heavy wiggling boy. The force against his windpipe hardened. Steigan dropped down, still trying to break from of his own opponent and Olierex's weight shifted, making Steigan bang his elbow against the stone. He couldn't hold on any longer and released Olierex, trusting the two domini holding onto Olierex to catch him. Steigan allowed himself to be jerked back by the man with his arm around his throat.

Olierex yelled as he almost pulled the two domini into the well after him. Mierk plus another sapere rushed forward to haul Olierex out of the well opening.

The man gripping Steigan shoved him to the ground.

Steigan looked up at Jaxsen, who stared at him in disbelief. Steigan smiled as he wiped some spittle from the side of his mouth. Then he laughed as he turned his attention to the humor of the whole scene around the well.

Holy Sapere Mierk spun around toward Steigan, who knew there would now be Gohaldinest to pay! Laughing harder, Steigan threw back his head and collapsed to the cool, dewy grass beneath him. He spread his arms out and shouted part of the domini oath, "But I seek a richer treasure!"

"Take him to my office. Now!" Mierk shouted.

Several hands hauled Steigan to his feet. Surrounded by domini and knights, he marched to Mierk's office. Steigan stood in front of Mierk's desk staring at the large stained glass window until at last Mierk came in and shut the door.

"Do you mind telling me what that was all about?" Mierk asked.

Steigan smiled. "Just a little friendly scuffle between boys."

"Friendly?" Olierex shouted. Steigan hadn't noticed him in the room until now. "I was sleeping! He attacked me unprovoked."

Jaxsen stood cowering behind Olierex, his eyes filled with tears which were already spilling down his face.

Steigan raised his chin. "Aye. Friendly scuffle. Just

trying to gain my rightful place in the dormitory. You don't get serve with a good knight if you don't fight for top position. I want to serve with Sacred Knight Danis. I won't get there if I don't take down a few of the domini's pages first."

Jaxsen made a motion like he might step forward and protest, but Steigan's glare made him stop.

"Is that how things operated in the dormitory where you were before coming to Lilinar?" Mierk asked.

Steigan shrugged. "Couldn't say. But isn't everything about rank?"

Mierk's lips tightened. "'Tis also about discipline. I can't have you playing dangerous pranks that could get someone hurt or killed."

Steigan leveled his stare at Olierex. "So instead 'tis all right for pranks that frighten and disturb people instead?"

"What do you mean by that?" Mierk sounded appalled.

"Those parties involved know exactly what I mean. I've made my point. I'm done." Steigan turned toward Mierk. "Let's get the punishment over with."

Mierk stepped between Steigan and the other two boys to ask them, "Do either of you wish to explain to me what's going on?"

"They have nothing to say," Steigan stated firmly.

With a nod, Mierk looked around the room as though

taking a quick count. "Since no account of what happened is forthcoming, I have to take the issue as I understand it. We have one offended, one accessory, and five restorers of the peace including myself." He looked down at Steigan. "I hope you are prepared for the wrath you've brought down on your head."

"I accept what is to come."

Olierex let out a nervous laugh, but everyone seemed to ignore him.

"Very well," Mierk said. "Steigan, please remove your nightshirt and stand over there by the wall."

A twinge of fear went through Steigan. Maybe he wasn't as prepared as he thought. He pulled his shirt over his head and walked to where the Holy Sapere had indicated.

One of the domini slid a chair in front of Steigan with the upright toward him. "Hold onto this," the dominus said.

Between the sound of the dominus' voice and the look in his eye, the butterflies started crawling out of Steigan's stomach.

Jaxsen whimpered.

Steigan glanced over his shoulder to see what Mierk was doing. Out of a cupboard, Mierk had pulled a thick leather strap.

"Domini, seperous macton," Mierk said. The domini

responded by snapping to attention. "'Tis never easy," Mierk continued, "to punish one of our own, but we will do what's necessary. We must. Steigan, is it your wish to be a knight?"

"Aye," Steigan responded, "'tis. Until that day when I am proven to be a dominus."

"Then pray for your strength."

Steigan knew it was coming, but even so he wasn't prepared for the sharp sting of the wide leather band. He grasped the back of the chair to keep his knees from buckling right out from beneath him. On the second stroke, he thought he heard Jaxsen cry out.

As the third lash came, Steigan said, "Jaxsen, seperous macton. Domini always stand tall. Leaders doubly so."

A change came over Jaxsen, like someone had given him extra strength. He wiped the tears from his face and didn't look away as seven more lashings came to Steigan.

Mierk handed the strap to one of the domini, who then also doled out ten strikes to Steigan's back. As the strap was handed to the third dominus, Steigan braced himself into a wider stance.

By the end of these ten lashings, Steigan couldn't even breathe without his skin feeling like it was on fire. He felt his eyes beginning to water and with the heel of his palm he pressed against his lids to clear his vision. When he lowered his hands, he saw the look of glee on Oleirex's face. It renewed his resolve to not give way, so Steigan cast his gaze toward the stone ceiling.

"Coom ra wialca to?" Steigan prayed. "Coom ra wialca do. Sha belieka ne. Ha nee." The words brought him comfort.

He'd lost count of the lashings, consumed only with whispering his prayer, until Mierk stepped up beside him. "You've been served ten lashes from each of the five restorers. Jaxsen has been assessed as your accessory," Mierk said. "Do you wish to confess his guilt or will you refrain and accept his punishment?"

Even through his blurry haze, Steigan saw the fear in Jaxsen's eyes. ~~Painfully~~, slowly, Steigan turned to look at Mierk. "Holy Sapere, I accept his punishment."

Oleirex's mouth dropped open. Even Mierk seemed to be assessing Steigan in a new light, but he motioned for Jaxsen. "Please come forward."

The boy trembled toward the Holy Sapere.

"You must deliver the blows," Mierk said, handing the strap to Jaxsen. If they are not satisfactory or you cannot complete the task, the restorers will retake their lashes. Do you understand?"

Jaxsen sobbed as he nodded and accepted the strap. Steigan turned to look at Jaxsen and gave him an approving nod while hoping the boy could carry through with the task. He didn't know if he could take another fifty lashes.

Jaxsen's blows landed with savage heat upon his tender back. Not ten, but double the number. At the end, Steigan heard the straps wooden handle hit the floor as Jaxsen fled and put his face against the door. For whatever pain it had caused Steigan, he knew it had been twice as bad for Jaxsen.

"Now for the offended," Mierk said.

Olierex jumped as though loosening up for training. He wiggled his arms to get them to relax. "I can go all day, Holy Sapere, so if you need to be about other tasks please take your leave. We'll still be here when you get back."

Mierk let out a little entertained laugh. "I'm sure that's true."

Steigan closed his eyes as the round boy picked up the strap and came up behind him. "Coom ra wialca to?" Steigan asked just a little louder and faster. "Coom ra wialca do."

The first blow came. Lightning pounded through his back. Olierex squealed like a little chased pig. By the Goddess, the kid had punch.

Another blow. It had come from a sideways direction whereas all the others had been straight up and down on his back. The next strike came in the other direction. Steigan quickly realized that Olierex was practicing sword slashes with the leather band. At first they fell in the predictable pattern, but then it changed and Steigan didn't know how the blow would come.

"Stop it," Jaxsen cried. "Stop it, Olierex! You've done enough."

Steigan's mind had gone blank, numb ~~to the pain.~~

"You think so, huh?" Olierex said, firing off another rapid succession of strikes. It felt like the leather never quite left Steigan's back. "I told you, I can do this all day."

"But you don't have to be cruel!"

Steigan opened his eyes and looked through a red haze. "Jaxsen, enough," he whispered.

"He's right," Olierex shrieked. "He deserves it. I'm the one offended. He should feel my rage. There were spiders down there."

The next blow fueled by wrath made Steigan's knees buckle and he almost dropped to the floor. One of the domini stepped forward to stop him from falling, but Steigan had already caught himself on the chair and he struggled back to a standing position. The lashing didn't stop while he regained himself, though the rescuing dominus did glare at Olierex.

"Not even a moment for dignity," the dominus muttered.

"Dignity!" Olierex yelled. "Did he give me dignity?

Pulling me out of bed in the blankets and nightclothes, and all?"

Several more lashes. Steigan felt the fury building up inside him. He wanted to swing the chair around at Olierex's head. Closing his eyes, he worked at forcing the anger out of him. What returned to him were the words of the dominus oath. "The streets of Gohaldinest are paved with gold, but I seek a richer treasure."

"Like the skin on your back?" Olierex asked. "I'm going to make you bleed if it takes me all night."

Steigan felt the falsehood in the boy's words. Already his blows were softening. "Porta quinest acay doomasha. Porta quinest acay doomasha. Porta quinest acay doomasha."

"Ah, this is boring," Olierex said finally. He handed the strap back to Mierk and walked away.

Steigan didn't dare move, didn't even dare wish the punishment was over in case he found more coming.

Olierex shoved Jaxsen aside and he stormed from the room.

Mierk came beside Steigan. "You endured that bravely, son. Better than most. But I do hope this incident left an impression so you won't need a reminder."

Steigan barely felt able to nod his head though he did. With Jaxsen at his side, he started to leave the room.

A dominus handed him his nightshirt and leaned in close as they reached the hallway. "Go for a swim in the lake," the dominus said. "It'll make it feel better, well, after the initial sting. The mud on the east bank is also a great relief." The dominus spoke as if he had intimate knowledge of this fact.

"Thank you," Steigan whispered.

Behind them, Mierk called out to the dominus, "Call my secretary to me. We have work to do."

Chapter Eleven

Steigan sat down on a stool at a table near a wall so he could keep his back to it without another person accidentally brushing against him. Jaxsen slid onto a stood near him.

"I'm sorry," Jaxsen said. "I do wish you had listened to me when I asked you to stop." He started picking at the food before him.

"My fault," Steigan replied. "I didn't obey my commander. Think no more of it."

Jaxsen tossed a piece of bacon back down onto his trencher. "Why did you do it? Why did you take it all on? It was your first offense. If you'd asked for mercy, Mierk would've given it."

Mercy. The thought hadn't even crossed Steigan's mind.

"You know that most of what Mierk was telling you was designed to make you afraid enough to ask for forgiveness," Jaxsen said.

"Were you given forgiveness in their teasing? Or mercy?"

"Maybe you should ask Mierk to be allowed to skip training today. There's no way — "

Steigan leaned forward, putting his elbows on the table, or trying to before his raw back protested. "I will handle it. Speak no more of it."

"I'm sorry. Someday I will reward your loyalty."

"You did today by carrying through with your lashes. All is fair. There is no debt to be repaid."

Jaxsen looked up slowly at Steigan with eyes of the lightest blue. "Aye, there is. You've assured that no one will pick on me again."

"Eat your breakfast," Steigan said. "I want you to be strong this morning while you hold your own against the other pages in training."

Jaxsen smiled and began to eat with gusto. Steigan tried to eat as well, but the tasteless food seemed to stick in his mouth. Even the water in his cup didn't help force it down. He slid his bread to Jaxsen who seemed grateful to have more.

Sacred Knight Danis entered the room and he surveyed it quickly. His long red cloak snapped as he turned and marched for the table where Steigan sat. "I hear you wish to serve under me," Danis said.

Steigan stood up as fast as he could. "Aye, I do."

Danis grabbed Steigan's right palm and looked at it. The action flared through Steigan and he opened his mouth with a gasp but held back the sound. He couldn't show weakness now.

Danis released Steigan's hand as though tossing something sickening aside. "A pure blood member of Rivic's family wanting to serve under me. If that isn't irony."

"Prince Tanold's orders, sir, but that doesn't mean I can't rise in the ranks I've been issued."

Danis gave an accepting nod as if liking Steigan's answer. "I hear you took it pretty hard this morning. Feeling a little tender, are we?"

"Nay, sir. I'm ready."

"Good, because you won't make it to the lake until late tonight. Meet me in the stables after you finish breakfast. Eat well, because knights aren't as pampered as the domini."

"Very well, sir," Steigan responded as Danis turned

and stormed from the room with the same intimidating presence he had entered with. Steigan noticed how the boys in the room seemed to watch Danis with fear or reverence while the girls got dreamy eyed.

Before reaching the door though, Danis made a gesturing motion with his hand as he passed by one of the cooks. Steigan sat down only after Danis had left the room.

Jaxsen reached across the table and pulled up Steigan's hand. "Sorry." Jaxsen gave an apologetic smile as he realized he must have hurt Steigan. "'Tis true then. You are a member of Rivic's family. No wonder you're so strong. 'Tis in your blood."

Curious now, Steigan reached over and looked at Jaxsen's right palm. There was no birthmark. "How can this be? You're in the domini track."

"My great-great grandmother had a brother who bore the mark. She gave birth to three girls. My great grandmother also had only girls. My father was born from one of those women, but he didn't bear the mark. I can prove my lineage through my family tree only. It seems that the enchantment wants to keep the line truly pure. Heritage makes me a dominus." Jaxsen pointed at Steigan's hand. "The birthmark makes you a true dominus."

A cook came over and set a bowl of hot porridge down

in front of Steigan, who looked up curiously. "Danis' orders," the cook answered before walking away.

Using the spoon provided in the bowl, Steigan began to slowly stir and let it release some of the heat. "So, how many generations out can someone still bear the mark?"

Jaxsen looked around the room. "Urlane bears the mark, but he's the youngest son of Merkor, so he's a direct line. Searn, you were living with him, right? Does he bear the mark?"

"Aye."

"He is the son of Tanisha, who was Cirello's sister, so the mark will bear one generation out. Um, Henrald!" Jaxsen stood and looked around the room. He pointed to a table on the other side of the room where several little boys were eating. "Over there, the boy with the black curls, that's Henrald. He's Jalinda's son. Jalinda is Searn's sister."

Jaxsen was speaking fast now, and Steigan had a hard time keeping up but he nodded hoping Jaxsen was getting to his point.

"He doesn't bear the mark," Jaxsen continued. "But Searn does. Meaning, the mark can only pass through one woman, not two."

"How do you know all these families?" Steigan asked.

"My mother is a Temple historian. My family lives in

Hallon. I've made these genealogical charts for my ma." Jaxsen looked away, embarrassed at admitting this.

Steigan chuckled. "That's very nice of you. Sounds like you could follow in her footsteps."

"As I said last night, my brothers will be the great leaders. I'll be the one recording what they do."

Steigan felt himself suddenly envious. A family, brothers, knowing where everyone was and where they had come from. He looked down at his porridge. "That's not all bad. Someone needs to. A record of where we've been is important. A blank slate of our past is no good." He took out the spoon, licked it clean before setting it aside, then raised the bowl to his mouth and drank the porridge down. When he finished, he stood up. "I don't want to keep Danis waiting. I'll see you later?"

"Aye," Jaxsen said. "Take it easy."

"Don't really have a choice right now, but thanks anyway."

Steigan left the hall and headed for the stables across the bridge. Inside, Danis brushed down a horse.

"Armor," Danis said, pointing to a wall. "Put it on."

Seeing the chainmail hanging from a nail, Steigan cringed at the thought of its weight against his skin. He crossed over to it and started to lift it. The links were even heavier than they looked. "I don't think I can," Steigan grunted.

Danis turned slowly. "I say we find out if you can or you can't. Put it on."

Steigan knew his training tunic and a layer of padding would be between him and the chainmail, but these tunics weren't the softest material he'd ever worn. He thought of his black, blue, gold, and white doublet he still had in his pack. That was the softest material he'd ever worn. Fine clothes. When his every instinct told him he should be use to hardships and that he had to be prepared for the worst, it seemed almost a contradiction that he would possess clothes of the finest cloth. Even his own tunics he'd worn at Searn's were finer than what he currently wore.

After donning the padding, Steigan reached up and took the chainmail off the wall. He started to separate the bottom so he could slip it over his head. He turned to Danis. "I can't."

"You would refuse my order?"

Steigan felt pinned by Danis' question. He wondered if he could possibly slide into the chainmail, if it were possible at all. "I do not wish to refuse."

"I sense there is an underlying truth you wish to speak."

Steigan stood conflicted with his own emotions. He wanted to ask for mercy, to say that the weight of the chainmail on his back would hurt him so much more when he could barely stand the weight of the shirt. Yet, his own actions had brought on the punishment for which he now suffered. He had to continue to serve.

"Mierk says Olierex stopped at about forty lashes," Danis said. "You sought solace in prayer rather than asking for mercy or seeking abatement. Yet now it seems like you've reached a breaking point. What pulls you from your faith to make you disobey now? What was it that pushed you to such a point this morning where you felt the need to torture another?"

Steigan didn't like the hard questions with which Danis challenged him. He started to pull the chainmail over his arms and closed his eyes. The pain would be fleeting, but certainly less intense than Danis' words.

Danis stopped him and took the chainmail away from him. "Answer my questions."

Steigan felt his jaw flex. "I don't know."

"Aye, you do. I suspect that your answer will be the same if you only let yourself find what you seek."

Steigan looked up at Danis and realized that the Sacred Knight wasn't being harsh with him out of meanness, but rather out of wanting him to dig deeper within himself to find a diamond within.

"I hated knowing that my new friend had been hurt by that bully," Steigan answered. "He could no longer stand up for himself after being so pushed down. I had to help him. I took my punishment because hurting another was also wrong. One injustice done does not correct another. If I had gone unpunished, it would've continued the cycle, so it had to stop."

"You chose for the cycle to stop with you, so that you didn't become seen as a bully too."

"Aye."

Danis leaned over to look Steigan in the eyes. "So why did you turn to prayer, to your faith when it got tough to endure the lashings? What gave you the strength to go on and not give in?"

Steigan drew back. "What is it you want me to understand? I feel trapped, blinded here."

"I want to test your resolve. That same resolve you showed this morning. You looked before you leapt earlier, so why do you hesitate now?

"Because I don't know why I have to put this armor on. There are only the two of us and I haven't been told that we'll be riding out on a dangerous mission." The words spilled from Steigan so fast he couldn't really say that he'd planned any of them.

"Does that matter?"

Steigan hated the question being fired back at him so quickly. "I have to consider the agony that the chainmail will put me in."

"So your faith is conditional? You were willing to help the weak when you didn't know you were going to get hurt, but now you refuse to do your duty for the Goddess because it might inconvenience you?"

Steigan wondered if the Sacred Knight truly did want to be mean to him and break him. He wished Danis would just take his sword and strike him down as unworthy. "I took my punishment with honor. Am I not due a little respect for that?"

"You want respect now?" Danis gave a sarcastic laugh as he turned completely around. "You want someone to show compassion for you so you can go away and lick your wounds? You want people to feel sorry for you and take it easy on you?"

Steigan felt the tears burn into his eyes. He made a grab for the chainmail, but Danis tugged it away. The movement sent pain rippling through him and he collapsed. Involuntary tears fell from his overfilled eyes.

"Stand up, boy!" Danis commanded.

"I can't. Just, please, go away."

Danis started to pace. "Maybe I misjudged you, boy."

Steigan pressed his eyes shut tight, letting the tears hit the ground where they soaked into the hardened clay. He knew he couldn't take any more.

"I guess I did misjudge your strength. I thought your heart might be full of compassion, honor, faith, and loyalty. Now I see the truth." He paused. "This makes Prince Tanold very right in his choice to make you a knight."

Something about that statement gnawed at Steigan. He sat back on his heels. "And what truth would that be?"

"You will fight for others tooth and nail, but you have to be put to the sword's edge before you will fight for yourself. When you do finally get to that point, you want to go through it alone. That is why you pray rather than ask someone to stop. 'Tis how a knight thinks, not a dominus." Danis reached out to Steigan, who took the offered hand to stand. Then Danis rehung the chainmail.

"I do have a mission for you," Danis continued, "but 'tis not one where you will be required to wear armor or anything more than you have on right now. If riding hurts, you may walk. But as you are out, I want you to reflect on how others will still give you compassion even if you do not feel you are able to give it to yourself."

Still feeling a little numb emotionally and raw physically, Steigan said, "I am ready. What is this task?"

"Spend the next three days after breakfast going out into the forest. Take a blanket with you, but let no one else see it." As if to highlight his words, Danis showed him a pack on the floor where a blanket was rolled up inside. "Sleep. You will need it. I suspect the boys in the dormitory will give you no quarter since they know of your injuries. Your nights will not be restful."

Danis gave a pause to let Steigan comprehend what all he was saying, then continued, "Return before nightfall and soak in the lake. Join me in my quarters for supper. We will be having a 'discussion of what you've learned on your mission.' You will tell the others you are scouting. No one must suspect your deception or this privilege I'm extending will be revoked. Soak again in the lake before heading out for the day. Do you understand?"

"Aye," Steigan nodded. "As much of it as I can."

"Why do you say that?"

"Because your questions bother me. I will have much to think about. I appreciate your guidance."

"We have only begun, Cavalier Steigan. My student has much to learn, though I'm sure we both agree you have the heart of a dominus. Proving it to the world is another matter."

Steigan watched Danis' red cloak flutter behind him as he walked from the stables. Steigan admired Danis' confidence. If there was anyone who could make him a better person, if not a true dominus, it would be Danis.

Chapter Twelve

Steigan lay in the lake up to his neck in the cold water and stretching his back across as much of the mud as possible. Soft pink light brightened the horizon. Soon, the bells would ring and call everyone to morning prayer.

"Not yet," Steigan whispered to himself. He wasn't ready to get up from his spot. Today was his third and last day of refuge. Tomorrow, training would resume. But now…

He pinched his nose and slid completely underwater, letting the dark lake take him in. The mud oozed around him like silk. He wished he could lie here all day.

Surfacing, he pushed his long black hair out of his face.

He wondered what Danis would choose to talk about tonight. The first night they'd spoken about the questions Danis had asked him earlier in the day. Steigan didn't know if he had all the answers, or if he even hit upon what diamond Danis wanted to find within himself. However, Danis had made a few notes on what Steigan had said.

"Why are you writing that down?" Steigan had asked.

"There is a deep truth in that statement and I want to remember it, remind you about it later," Danis answered.

Steigan had found the Sacred Knight well worthy of his title. The man was thoughtful, determined, faithful to the Goddess, and loyal. The noblest man found among the peasants.

Last night they had talked far too late about subjects ranging from the state of the Temple, warfare strategies, and passages in the Lilton. Danis had promised to find him a copy of the Lilton, the word of the Goddess as left by Rivic, for Steigan to take out into the forest with him to read today.

Bells began ringing, calling everyone for morning prayers. He wasn't ready, but Steigan started to get up. As he pulled his leggings over still wet skin and pulled the lacings tight, he turned to the Temple.

Something was wrong. Those weren't the slow, easy bells for morning service.

A person moved through the bushes surrounding this side of the lake, ripping through the brambles. Urlane appeared, his face red. "Steigan, come quick!"

"What's going on?" Steigan asked.

"Olierex pushed Jaxsen in the well."

"*Pushed him?*"

Urlane gave him a hard look. "Pushed him."

"Is he all right?"

"We don't know. He's still in the well, no one can see him, and he's not answering.

Steigan pulled his tunic over his shoulders, ignoring the ~~kiss~~ still lingering there. Urlane turned and went back through the bushes. Steigan followed.

The journey around the lake to the bridge seemed to take forever even though Steigan ran his fastest and passed Urlane who'd had a head start on him. His footfalls thundered on the wood bridge. Even before he reached the gatehouse, he could see the crowd gathered around the well, though it once again seemed to part as Mierk came out of the Temple as it had the day Steigan had held Olierex over the well. While all had their attention on the Holy Sapere, Steigan had to fight his way through the crowd.

Steigan arrived at the well ahead of Holy Sapere Mierk and looked inside to pitch blackness. By the Goddess! Had

Jaxsen survived the fall? How far down did it go? There was only one way to find out.

Grabbing a dagger from the belt of a nearby dominus, Steigan cut the bucket from the rope and started unraveling it into the well.

"What's going on here?" Mierk demanded, now reaching the well.

Steigan already scaled down into the well. Raw skin moved over the tight straining muscles. He tried not to think about the ~~====~~, but rather getting to the little boy trembling down in the water below. Jaxsen would be all right. Steigan had to keep that thought.

"Jaxsen, hold on," Steigan called. "I'm coming."

Above him, Mierk leaned over the opening of the well. "Steigan, get back up here right now."

Steigan ignored him. Goddess, for as long as it took him to get here and for the number of people standing around above, why hadn't anyone else started down the well for Jaxsen?

His eyes adjusted to the dark as he went lower. Water dripped off the walls making the stone slick beneath his bare feet. Only now did he realize that he'd left his boots behind at the lake.

Soon, he came to the water and dropped down into it.

Everything at this level was pitch black, He felt around the slimy circular walls of the well.

"Jaxsen?" he called.

No answer. That meant Jaxsen had gone underwater. Steigan stretched out his feet, trying to touch the bottom. He didn't feel an edge, nor did his feet bump into anything floating in the water.

"Jaxsen?" he called out once more, hoping.

He pulled up some rope to give him some slack and wrapped it around his wrist before diving underwater to see how deep it was. Deeper than he wanted to know. Colder than the lake too. He'd have to let go of the rope.

With one more breath of air filling his lungs, Steigan dove down and started kicking into the abyss. He felt something knock against his shoulder and realized that it was the end of the rope. He kept going.

The sides of the walls started to curve inward, more sludge than stone. Surely he had to be close to the bottom with it closing in around him like this.

A cold limb brushed against him. Steigan grabbed it. Dead weight pulled him down. Steigan twisted, letting a bubble of air escape his lungs which went across his face and for a moment, Steigan wasn't sure which way was up or down. He pulled the body close to him and let his own buoyancy win the struggle for the correct direction. Once he was straightened out, Steigan kicked for the surface.

They broke the waterline and Steigan gasped for air. The rope smacked against his face as if announcing its whereabouts. Steigan grabbed on, knowing that a lot now depended upon that rope.

"Jaxsen?" Steigan called, worried because he had yet to hear the boy take a breath.

Jaxsen lay limp in his arms, completely nonresponsive and cold.

Steigan looked up toward the top of the well, a mere pinpoint of light above. How would he crawl out of the well with Jaxsen unable to hold onto him? His initial plan had included Jaxsen being conscious. Steigan started to shiver. Getting out of the water would make it all that much worse. His muscles were already starting to cramp.

You will fight for others tooth and nail, but you have to be put to the sword's edge before you will fight for yourself, Steigan recalled Danis' words. *When you do finally get to that point, you want to go through it alone.*

By the Goddess, he was at the sword's edge, Jaxsen with him, and he was alone. He was all he and Jaxsen had right now.

Steigan tried to position Jaxsen on his back and tied the

rope around both of them. His skin burned and brought tears to his eyes. As he tried to pull himself up, Jaxsen's weight shifted pitching them both backwards. That wasn't going to work.

He tried scaling the wall with one arm wrapped around Jaxsen but only got a few feet up before losing his grip on Jaxsen and he had to release the rope to avoid dropping the boy.

Back in the water with nothing to stand on, Steigan put the boy over his shoulder and started an overhand crawl up the rope. His arms began to tremble and he had to stop and just let himself dangle for a bit before he could resume.

Halfway up, as sunlight started to come into view, the tears stung his eyes far worse than the fire in his back. He let the angry tears fall knowing that by the time he reached the top there would be no difference between sweat and tears.

"He's coming up," someone called from above.

Steigan wished he had dropped Olierex down the well.

Hot ~~pain~~ swept out of his spine and down his arm like someone spilling scalding water on him. The pins and needles sensation quickly gave way to ~~shooting~~

As he neared the top, a dominus reached over the side to grab him. Steigan reacted quickly, kicking away from the wall and spinning on the rope. "By the Goddess, don't touch me!" he hollered.

Mierk rushed forward to usher the dominus back. He must have known that Steigan's punishment still inflicted its intended ~~pain~~.

Within moments, Steigan had climbed up high enough for Danis to take Jaxsen from him. Steigan felt relieved to know the Sacred Knight was there.

Steigan pulled on the rope and pushed himself hard enough from the well to land his stomach against the side of the well. He grabbed on and dragged himself out, slithered ungracefully onto the ground. He breathed in the dirt, puffing up little clouds of small grit. He so badly wanted to roll onto his back, but the imagined ~~pain~~ kept him still.

"Stay back," he heard Danis warning people as he carried Jaxsen toward the Temple.

The Holy Sapere spoke to someone nearby, but Steigan didn't care. He trembled as the feeling of more scalding water cascaded down his neck and over his back.

A blanket fell over Steigan, its soft warmth bringing unbearable weight to his shoulders. He cried out. Then angry at himself for his weakness, he screamed with rage. The sound shocked the person standing nearby and in the scuffle of feet, Steigan realized that Olierex was the one that had moved. Livid wrath made Steigan want to rise.

"Do you feel like you can get up now?" a dominus asked dumbly beside him.

Rage still focused on Olierex, Steigan climbed to his feet and knocked away the dominus' weak attempt at help. Olierex shrunk back as the blanket fell off Steigan. The dominus picked it up and tried to put it back around Steigan. Venomously, Steigan made a grab for it and realized that his fingers wouldn't move. They were still cramped from clinging so tightly to the rope.

Where had Danis gone? Why wasn't he here? In looking around, he saw that it was Dominus Colwyn trying to help him.

With hands that didn't feel like his own, Steigan clutched the blanket for what little warmth it offered. "Where's Jaxsen?" he asked, his voice raw.

Dominus Colwyn responded, "He's been taken to the infirmary."

"Is he all right?"

"I don't know. I've stayed with you."

Steigan started walking toward the Temple, knowing he shouldn't take his emotions out on this thick-headed dominus.

"Do you feel strong enough to go to the Holy Sapere?" Colwyn asked.

Steigan looked around, taking a quick count. The dominus had four knights behind him. He wanted to ask if Colwyn thought he'd already had enough punishment. Mierk wouldn't be happy that Steigan had disregarding his orders to get out of the well.

Goddess, had any of this been worth it? Jaxsen hadn't responded. Had he gone down to merely recover the body? It had taken him too long to get around the lake, too long to get down into the well, and far too long to get back up. How many lashes was that worth?

But better to take them now while he was already cold, sore, and numb than to wait. He nodded to Colwyn and began to follow him.

"You've proven to me that you have the heart of a dominus," Colwyn said. "'Tis only a matter of time before your lineage is proven and your rightful place restored."

Colwyn's words gave him little comfort.

They were at the foot of the stairs to the Temple when the dominus stopped again. "I realize this may not be an appropriate time, but I want you to know that when you become a page, I'd like you to serve with me," Colwyn explained. "I hope 'tis all right with you for me to put in that request."

Steigan licked his lips, tasting salt on his tongue. He

smelled like fish and this guy wanted Steigan to serve as his page? Steigan pushed tangles of his black hair out of his face and walked glumly toward the Temple, wondering if the dominus would question his obvious lack of enthusiasm.

Before he reached the Temple door, Olierex pushed in front of Steigan, tears in his eyes and his arms spread wide to keep Steigan from opening the entry before him. "I'm sorry," Olierex said. "I didn't mean to do it. It was stupid and I didn't really mean to knock him into the well. He's just so small. He didn't weight anything…" Olierex started to sob. "I tried to catch him…"

Dominus Colwyn nudged Olierex aside and let Steigan enter first. After all, Steigan already knew the way to the Holy Sapere's office. With every step, he tried to count the number of people who would be listed as offended, accessories, and restorers. Certainly he wouldn't be held accountable for so many people. Would Danis be as gracious in granting Steigan refuge a second time? How many more days would he be lying in the mud on the east side of the lake. He wondered if he could just cocoon the soft soothing mud around him and use a reed to breathe through.

The door to the Holy Sapere's office was open, waiting for him. Mierk sat behind his large desk. Steigan went to stand in front of it, hoping to get this over quickly. Olierex stood at his side with Colwyn on the other side of him.

Mierk looked up from a piece of parchment he'd been reading and it rolled closed as he released it. "I've received a primary report from the infirmary. Jaxsen is alive, but 'twas quite a fall. He's broken a few bones and is scraped up from hitting the wall during the fall. He's breathing now, but his lungs were filled with water. There's no guarantee he's going to wake up."

Steigan rubbed his hands against his face. Why hadn't he come back earlier? He saw the sun rising. He knew he'd be called for morning prayers soon. Why hadn't he just gone back?

"This leaves us in a very unusual predicament," the Holy Sapere said.

"It was an accident," Olierex cried out.

Mierk looked at the round boy with sad, knowing eyes. "That it may be, but I have heard from several that you were the aggressor. What's more, the offended may never wake up and this is a matter I'd rather have dealt with swiftly."

The cold seemed to seep deeply into Steigan and he shivered. He felt frozen.

"What's even worse," Dominus Colwyn said, "is that while we were standing around wondering what to do, only one person did what needed to be done."

Mierk nodded. "Cavalier Steigan, you showed supreme bravery today going down for your friend. You will stand in for the offended."

Steigan scoffed, wondering how many lashes that would be.

"You are, in all rights, also the restorer," Mierk said. "You did your utmost to make things right again."

The words seemed to melt through Steigan's numbness and he realized he'd been brought to Mierk's office not to be punished. "Things aren't right if Jaxsen doesn't wake up."

"That decision is in the hands of the Goddess now." Mierk turned toward Olierex. "Please remove your shirt."

Olierex bawled as he moved out of the line and undressed. The sound reminded Steigan of the first time he'd heard Jaxsen crying in the wardrobe and it galled him. He hated how the anger flashed inside him.

The dominus pushed a chair in front of Olierex as he had done for Steigan just a few days ago. Mierk retrieved the strap from the closet.

Steigan let the blanket fall to the floor and stretched his fingers, still cramped and unwilling to completely straighten. The strap's handle fit perfectly within his clawed hand. As he approached Olierex, he wondered at the weight of the strap. It felt so light. How could it inflict so much pain?

"How many lashes do I get to give?" Steigan asked.

"Ten for being restorer and..." Mierk's voice faded out.

Steigan realized the Holy Sapere couldn't bear to bring himself to say the next words, so he filled them in for Mierk, "As many as I want for the offended. I can keep going until I feel better."

Mierk's face blanched at it being put so bluntly, but he nodded.

Olierex grasped the back of the chair, his knuckles already white.

Steigan leaned close to Olierex and said, "Spread your legs apart to brace your stance. I wouldn't want you to go down after only a couple strikes. After all, I can do this all day."

Olierex sobbed.

Steigan raised the strap as he watched Olierex's shaking shoulders. "Feel free to attend other business if you need, Holy Sapere. We'll still be here when you get back."

"I'm sorry I pushed him. I didn't mean for him to fall in the well," Olierex said.

"But he did," Steigan yelled at him. "You chose wrong, as I did a few mornings ago. Now you must take the punishment like I did."

Olierex stood just a little taller as though he'd been

reminded of an honor deep within his soul.

Mierk paced, waiting for the first blow almost with a look of glee on his face. Colwyn just looked sad and weary. Much like how Steigan felt now.

Steigan lowered the strap and dropped it on the floor by Olierex's feet. He leaned close to Olierex. "I forgive you."

Olierex collapsed onto the chair sobbing.

Turning toward Mierk, Steigan said, "I'd like to change and go see my friend. May I be excused?"

Mierk raised his disappointed gaze from the strap lying on the floor to Steigan and swallowed a hard lump. "Aye, you may go."

As Steigan reached the door, the dominus stepped up beside Mierk. "I want him as my page," Colwyn said.

Mierk responded softly, "Just wait. I don't think he's done amazing us yet."

CHAPTER THIRTEEN

Steigan walked into a room which didn't look too different from the dormitory except the beds were separated by hanging white sheets. Only a few of the beds were occupied and several people gathered around one in particular.

"Bring the yarrow and the rosemary," Keteria said.

The shock of hearing her voice froze Steigan. He couldn't believe she was here, but then she turned and reached for a handful of bandages someone held out, and then went back to the patient. Or she started to. All at once, her back stiffened and she turned back toward Steigan, her eyes filled with surprise. She shook her head. "I should have known."

"Known what, milady?" a nurse asked her.

"Nothing. Just keep working."

Steigan stepped closer, wondering if they were working on Jaxsen when a voice behind him asked, "How are you doing?"

Danis stood next to the door. Steigan hadn't seen the Sacred Knight in his full armor complete with red and gold helm since the night of the tri-lunar ceremony. Steigan dropped to bended knee before Danis.

"Tired, sir," Steigan responded to Danis' question.

"Rise," Danis said. "Go see your friend."

Steigan went over to Jaxsen's bedside, or as close as he could get without interfering. Jaxsen breathed faintly through his open mouth. He looked gaunt and ghostly pale, like he'd been pulled back from the very depths of Gohaldinest. On the bed, his tiny fingers twitched as they worked away on him.

Keteria moved out from the others and headed to a nearby cupboard. Steigan followed her. "Is he going to be all right?" he asked.

"If he is strong enough," she replied.

"What are you doing here? This seems beneath you to be tending to the wounded."

"I heard the bells. I knew it had to be serious. Since I'm still filling in for Centhya as High Maege, 'twas my duty to be here." She took out a vial and shook it.

"I'm glad you are. I'm sure you'll do everything you can for him."

Keteria looked back to Jaxsen. "To be truthful, I thought it would be you." She started walking back toward the bed, her hands full of the supplies she'd gathered.

"Me? Why?" Steigan asked, still following her.

"I heard what happened the other day."

"And you thought I'd go for revenge?"

Keteria turned and spoke quietly under her breath as though the others in the room couldn't hear, "Given your condition, I'm not sure you have total control of your emotions."

Steigan bit down on his quick response. Instead, he asked, "What's that supposed to mean?"

"I've got this, milady, if you need a moment," the nurse said.

Keteria grabbed Steigan's arm and pulled him from the room. Out in the hallway, she turned to him. "Stolen magic is very unstable. Who knows what you are capable of with that power backing you?"

Steigan noticed that Danis also moved into the hallway

with them, looking in both directions as he took a position with his back against the wall.

"Do you know how you were found?" Keteria asked. "In the blue and gold armor of a Lilinar dominus. Please realize what we all thought that meant."

"Which was?"

"That you'd stolen the magic from one of our domini then killed him for his armor."

"And has that viewpoint changed?"

"Tanold sent men out in every direction to search all the fiefs of Lilinar. All the domini and their armor were accounted for."

Steigan shuffled uncomfortably knowing that Danis overheard all of this. "Why are you telling me this?"

"Because I want you to know. You are not just a cavalier. You are better, higher than that."

"Am I?" He flashed a look to Danis who glanced away down the hallway. "There are some who would say your brother's choice to make me a cavalier was right on."

"But he doesn't understand the magic inside you like I do. It makes me afraid of what you could do. I believe you were sent to us for a reason, more than just going into a well for a little boy."

"Yet you still thought the emergency bells were for

me."

"Aye, I did." Keteria looked toward Jaxsen. "Your broken, battered body is one I hope I never see. Not again at least." She didn't look at him again as she went back into the room. Danis moved to follow her, but stopped Steigan in the doorway as he tried to rush in after her.

"This isn't a good time to start fighting for yourself," Danis said. "She needs some space."

Steigan peered around Danis toward Keteria, who stood over Jaxsen continuing her work. "Was she really that worried about me?"

"Aye, she was." Danis looked over his shoulder at her. "Her heart runs very deeply for her people."

"Is that all I am to her? One of her people?"

Danis put a hand on Steigan's shoulder. "We'll talk more of this later. Go in and visit your friend. But respect my order to back off from Keteria. While she's here, 'tis my duty to make sure she's protected. Understand?"

"Aye, sir."

Steigan went inside and pulled a chair up beside the bed now that things seemed to have settled down enough that a few of the nurses had moved onto other patients. Jaxsen lay there, his skin white as ash. One of the remaining nurses stitched a gash in Jaxsen's arm. Steigan knew that if Jaxsen felt the needle piercing his skin he'd be moaning ~~in pain~~ but he made no sound. When the nurse finished, Keteria put a poultice over the area.

"You can take his hand," Keteria said. "He'd probably appreciate your strength being there for him."

Steigan started to reach out, but stopped. He watched Keteria and she gave him an urging smile and nod, so he slid his fingers beneath Jaxsen's tiny hand. "Is there anything else I can do? Is there no magic that will help him?"

"Ach!" said the nurse. "Magic doesn't heal the body. Only time and prayer does that."

Keteria looked away as she rolled her eyes, then she resumed her work.

Steigan held his friend's hand next to his forehead and closed his eyes. The fingers felt so cold and frail. "Come on, Jaxsen," he whispered.

A tap on his shoulder woke Steigan. He opened his eyes to see the room much brighter now. How long had he been asleep? Raising his head, he saw Keteria kneeling down beside him.

She glanced over her shoulder toward the nurse a short distance away. "How is your back?" she whispered.

"I'm fine," he replied.

"Not one person who has ever had to go lie in the mud

on the east side of the lake is ever fine. Especially not if you've had to do it for... what, three, four days now? I can make a salve. There is also magic that will work on minor injuries."

"I'd rather have your energy spent on Jaxsen."

She shrugged. "There's nothing more we can do for him right now."

"Fine." He shifted his aching muscles in the uncomfortable chair. "As for me, the mud is good enough for me. I endured the flogging. I'll endure the healing too."

"That man is cruel. Besides, you've gone above and beyond." She looked up toward the ceiling with a shake of her head. "It takes a special person to befriend a bullied child then risk his life to help that boy."

Dominus Colwyn entered the infirmary and came over to Jaxsen's bed. "Any change?" he asked.

Keteria touched Steigan's arm before leaving. Steigan wished Colwyn hadn't come along and made her feel like she needed to dismiss herself.

"Nay," Steigan replied.

"I was really hoping to see you back at practice today, but I guess other matters were more important."

Danis followed Keteria out of the room. Steigan wished he could go too. "I was still supposed to be scouting for Sacred Knight Danis today."

"What is he having you scout for?"

"I'm not at liberty to say."

"Oh, right." Colwyn sounded like he totally didn't believe Steigan. Maybe Colwyn saw through the story. Did it matter?

"If you have an issue, please take it up with Danis."

"Have you taken a break today?"

"Nay," Steigan said, not wanting to say that he'd napped most of the morning away.

"I don't understand your devotion to this kid, but I do admire it," Colwyn admitted. "Still, you need to take care of yourself too. Eating, sleeping."

"Things I can do when Jaxsen gets better."

"What if he doesn't?"

Steigan swallowed hard. "I can then…" The words weren't coming out easily. "I'll eat and sleep then." After being mute for months, he knew what it was like to not fit in even while knowing he was capable of so much more. Jaxsen had potential but it had been buried by bullies too jealous to see all that he could give. Steigan couldn't figure out how exactly to explain this to Colwyn, wasn't sure if the dominus was capable of understanding. But it was the thought that backed his faith for Jaxsen's recovery.

"I've come for another reason too," Colwyn said. "Holy

Sapere Mierk would like to speak to you. I'll sit here with Jaxsen if you'd like, while you go see Mierk."

"If he wakes…"

"I'll come get you straightaway if there's any change at all."

Steigan stood and stretched his aching muscles. Even if he hadn't had a strenuous few days, he wasn't use to being so stationary.

"Go out to the kitchen after you see Mierk," Colwyn pleaded. "Please. You need to at least eat."

Steigan nodded. With one last look at Jaxsen, he left the room and headed straight for Mierk's office without looking directly at anyone he passed in the hallway even if they tried to speak to him. At Mierk's office, he knocked on the door.

"Come in," Mierk called from inside.

Steigan entered and bowed his head. "Dominus Colwyn said you wished to speak to me."

Mierk motioned to a chair. "Aye, come, take a seat.

Now that he was standing, the last thing Steigan wanted to do was to sit again, but he did.

"I asked you to come here for an issue I hope will be mutually beneficial," Mierk began. "The Goddess favors those who help Her."

Steigan nodded though not quite sure he understood

what he'd have to offer.

"How far would you go to help your friend?" Mierk asked.

"I'd do anything to help him."

"I figured as much. Not many would go to the lengths you did. There is still more we can do. I have a proposal for you."

"Which would be?"

"A question first." Mierk shifted as though physically trying to figure out how to phrase the question perfectly so it wouldn't be mistaken. "Do you still have no memory of your life before the accident?"

Accident? Had Mierk not been informed that Steigan knew the truth?

"Nay," Steigan replied. "I'm sorry."

"'Tis all right. This isn't a test. Merely a question." Mierk leaned forward. "It does put you in a unique situation where you are an outside observer."

Steigan felt like he played a game, a pawn being moved into position. Hadn't Keteria just called Mierk a cruel man? Had it been a subtle warning for Steigan to watch himself?

Mierk continued, "The Temple grows mired in rites and ceremonies. We can no longer see a clear direction. But you, you know none of this."

Or was the man simply asking for help to fix a situation Steigan had seen himself. It seemed fair enough to answer Mierk's unspoken questions. "'Tis true," Steigan said. "The ceremonies aren't accessible to the masses. Several people were bored at the tri-lunar ceremony because they didn't understand it. If they understood, they'd feel like they were participating." He suddenly felt like he'd over spoken. "If you don't mind the observation."

Mierk gave a smile and nodded. "I appreciate your honesty. 'Tis exactly what we've needed and I agree with you. The people do need to know and relate."

Putting his fingertips together, Mierk leaned back in his chair. "This is where I'd like your help. We're too entrenched in our own dogma. We need someone who sees clearly. Someone who can give the people what they want. You've been out among the people, lost even, and found your way back. The Goddess guided you and tuned you in to a song we can't hear. I'd like you to help us revive what we've lost."

Steigan remembered Keteria's words: *You were sent for a reason. More than just going into a well for a little boy.* Was this what she had meant?

He wasn't sure he understood completely. "So what is it you'd like me to do?"

"We want you to review where we're at and make

suggestions. Don't you think 'tis better to serve in the all compassionate love of the Goddess then to serve in Her truth when no one is truly capable of knowing Her infinite wisdom?"

"I don't know. What if I'm wrong?" he asked. How could one know exactly how to interpret the infinite wisdom of the Goddess?

"Please, you cannot be wrong," Mierk smiled gently. "Let us just look at your friend, Jaxsen, for proof. 'Tis Her truth that he fell into the well, that he was meant to die and return to Her. Yet you served in Her love first by befriending the poor boy then risking your own life to save him where others just pondered about what to do. You have remained at his side, working your strength into a litany of a prayer which would ask the Goddess to return him to you. No one speaks better of knowing Her compassionate love than you. Do you not see that this has all been laid out for you for a reason?"

"I would be glad to help out the Goddess in any way that I am able," Steigan replied. "If you think I have a fresh viewpoint, then I am willing to give it." His words were a brave façade, covering the fear growing in his stomach. Even when he'd been facing the nightmares and the night tremors, never had he been this scared.

"Good. I, in turn, will speak directly to the Goddess in

behalf of returning your friend to you."

Steigan leaned back in his chair. If Mierk could speak directly to the Goddess, why did he need Steigan's help? Couldn't the Holy Sapere ask the Goddess for traditions to give the people of the land? He held his tongue. Maybe such questions were beyond his comprehension.

"I understand your desire to remain with Jaxsen during his hopeful recovery, so I will have a scribe bring his texts directly to you in the infirmary," Mierk said. "You may work there."

"Thank you." Steigan rose from his chair and bowed before leaving. As he made his way back to Jaxsen's bedside, he wondered why he felt a life-changing decision had been made.

Chapter Fourteen

The next three months passed with such swiftness Steigan felt like he'd spent each moment just waking from another dream. Jaxsen had regained consciousness and made a good recovery, though he'd developed a slowness along the left side of his body. Everyone seemed to agree that was a small price to pay for not having lost his life entirely.

Steigan's bargain to review the Temple's texts had been moved to the library and he put in extra hours after his normal training. If he wasn't in the Temple library working there, then he was taking supper with Danis where they continued their talks of beliefs and truths from the Goddess.

Steigan found a lot of this time finding its way into the texts as he worked on translations where sometimes the writing was so old it was either illegible or unintelligible.

He'd also taken to working with Jaxsen in the morning, helping the boy to increase his skills and defend his handicap. Now, several additional people joined them in the morning before prayers to learn from Steigan.

Centhya resumed her position as High Maege which meant he saw more of her and less of Keteria. Unfortunately, Searn wasn't coming around at all. Steigan wondered why Searn didn't want to visit him. He tried to ask Centhya about this, but sensed she didn't find anything out of the normal. Centhya occasionally brought Annae with her to the Temple and Steigan would sit with the baby in Centhya's chambers while Centhya attended her duties. It made him feel like he was still part of the family.

Then there were times when Keteria came to the Temple to search the library for an old text or scroll and Steigan could watch her from a distance.

"You really like her, don't you?" Jaxsen asked.

Steigan dragged himself out of his thoughts to realize that he'd been staring at Keteria as she walked down the hall while pretending to ignore him. But he'd seen her back stiffen as they came into proximity. She had felt him there, much like he could feel her too. Steigan glanced down at Jaxsen. "Aye, but 'tis more than that. I look at her and I see I'm no where I need to be magically. 'Tis so frustrating."

"I'd take sword skills over magic any day."

"Uh-huh," he muttered, not really listening to Jaxsen. "What's she doing?"

Down the hallway, Keteria tossed a book at a scribe. She screamed something at the man, decided she needed the book as she snatched it back, turned, and fled down the hallway. Danis followed close on her heels.

"I'll meet you back at the dormitory," Steigan said to Jaxsen.

"You're going to follow and find out what she's doing?" he asked.

Steigan shook his head. "She's the princess. Why would I interfere?"

Jaxsen sensed his pretense. "Of course."

With a wink, Steigan hurried down the hallway. He followed the echoes of Danis' determined steps and brief flashes of a red cloak. Steigan guessed where they were going before actually finding himself outside of Mierk's office. The doorway had remained ajar and Steigan pressed himself flat against the stone wall outside to listen.

Keteria's voice was the first he heard. "I ask for a book

to look up a certain reference and this is what I get! A lie?"

"Keteria, my dear," Mierk sighed, "I wouldn't think of it as a lie. Rather, I thought you'd be happy to see this."

"Why would I be happy?" It sounded like she slammed the book on Mierk's desk.

"'Tis not your dream to make magic accessible to the masses? Do you not realize that part of your dream is also making the Goddess' truth understandable by the people."

"Not like this. This isn't truth—"

"Nay," Mierk cut in quickly, "not as originally spoken. But 'tis close enough, don't you think?"

"You tempt the dungeons, Holy Sapere. This is a palimpsest. Please tell me you didn't overwrite all originals."

"Milady, you are not yet queen nor are you High Maege any longer. You hold no weight here other than that which I deign to entertain. You cannot make any threats against me."

"Then when I am queen –"

Mierk's composure broke and it sounded like he pounded his hands against his desk. "I will still have the power. I handpick your guards. Dare I say that some might be more loyal to me?"

"The originals?" Keteria pleaded. "Please tell me they are intact, that all of them haven't been overwritten. I do need them as reference." Anger vibrated through her voice though she tried to corral it within accentuated words.

"I have had a set moved to a separate library. They will still be accessible to Temple personnel."

"Will you *entertain* my rights as a former High Maege to have access to those books?"

"But of course, milady." Steigan could almost see Mierk's snake-like smile. "I wouldn't want to tempt the dungeons."

"Thank you, Holy Sapere." Her skirts rustled like she was bowing. "I will be in the library for the moment. Please send someone to escort me to this new library."

"Very well, milady."

After a pause, it sounded like Keteria might be leaving. As Steigan looked for a place to duck and hide, he heard Mierk speak again.

"Do tell me, milady... these gargaxes you assured us were returning, where are they? It seems we only have your word that the boy's bites were from a gargax. I've seen no beasts flying in the night sky other than the ones that should be there."

Keteria picked up her pace and left the room with Danis behind her. As Danis' gaze checked the hallway for threats, he stopped when he saw Steigan hiding in the shadows. Danis reached out for Keteria's arm and stopped her.

"I want you to know, milady," Danis said, "that the knights will never turn against you. You have our support."

"Thanks, Danis."

Keteria resumed walking, but Danis motioned for Steigan to go upstairs to his chambers. Steigan acknowledged the message and started down the hall in the opposite direction of Danis and Keteria.

Outside Danis' door, Steigan waited so long that he soon slumped down against the wall and fell asleep. He woke to find that the window opposite him had grown dark. He stood up and went to look out wondering what had awoken him.

The whole world seemed to vibrate. He could feel a hum going right through him. He could feel *them* out there. Who, he couldn't identify. Just *them*. Chills swept through him. A warm wave seemed to flow over him then flushed back with bitter coldness.

Footsteps came as someone ran up the stairs. Danis appeared from the stairwell. "Steigan," he said, out of breath, "did you feel that?"

Steigan nodded, glad that someone else had felt it too. "Aye. What was it?"

Danis ushered Steigan toward his chambers. "I think it was a sign that Princess Keteria's theory is right."

"Her theory?"

"Come inside." Danis waved his fingers over the handle to his chambers and the door unlocked.

Steigan followed Danis inside. The Sacred Knight flicked his fingers to light candles around the room. Once Steigan closed the door behind him, Danis turned.

"Let's deal with the more serious question first," Danis said, removing his helm and shaking out his short blond hair. "Why were you eavesdropping on Keteria's conversation with Mierk?"

"She looked upset," Steigan answered quickly. "I wanted to know why."

"She's royalty. 'Tis like her job to be upset and distasteful of everything."

Steigan hated the way Danis phrased that and he hung his head. "Aye, sir."

"You don't want to believe me? That's fine." Danis started removing his armor. Steigan went to assist. Once the armor was put away, Danis sat down in a padded chair and offered the other wooden one to Steigan. "I do like that you took initiative to find out what was going on. A knight's greatest defense is in being silent and watching what others are doing. So what did you learn?"

"That Mierk is having the Temple's books replaced with translations. 'Tis my doing. I helped him with that."

"You did what was requested. You don't bear all the burden of blame either."

"Blame?" Steigan asked.

Danis looked uncomfortable. "Mierk should know better than to challenge Princess Keteria. He won't win, but he also won't admit his wrong?"

"But if Keteria is trying to bring magic to the people, why would she be angry over what Mierk is doing?"

"She wants education of the language, not a translation. She feels that loses the original intent."

Steigan tried to see it from Keteria's point of view. "A translation also leaves room to leave out things that one might not want others to know. Or to modify it to suit one's purpose."

"Exactly."

Steigan thought for a moment. "So why was the book Keteria was looking for so important?"

"She was looking for a reference."

"For?" Steigan prodded.

"Something to prove her theory, the one I mentioned in the hallway. She believes that magic is becoming unstable,"

Danis said.

"Unstable, how?"

"'Tis her theory, not mine. I can't speak as to why she believes this. Besides, we have other issues now."

He hoped Danis was referring to the same thing he thought was an issue. "Mierk's threats made against Keteria."

"I have to know where your loyalties lie."

Steigan opened his mouth to say that they lay with Princess Keteria, but that felt like a betrayal of his oath to protect the Goddess. Mierk had proven his connection to the Goddess in the healing of Jaxsen. Without Mierk's prayers and the Goddess' mercy, would Jaxsen have survived?

"Steigan?" Danis asked.

The dominus oath came to him. "This is what they mean when they say the streets of Gohaldinest are paved with gold, isn't it?" Steigan asked. "A life of choices each made for your own profit?"

Danis leaned forward in his chair. "You are not a dominus and Tanold's mind won't change easily. Accept the fact that you will be denied your rightful title."

"But if they prove my lineage and that this is not just cleaver trickery," Steigan said holding up his right palm, "then they will have no right to deny me my title."

"You live in a world of false expectations. You believe

everyone always tells the truth and is as honorable as yourself. If someone does prove your heritage, Tanold will bury it."

Possess or kill. The truth of Danis' words rang through.

Danis leaned back and crossed one leg over the other. "The only way you will gain enough power to fight back is by one day taking over my title. So tell me, where do your loyalties lie?"

"My duty is to protect the Goddess and the royal family," he said slowly, thoughtfully. "But if members of the Temple or the castle cross each other, I have no choice but to weigh the merits of the situation and determine who betrays the Goddess. When one no longer serves in Her love, then that one is my enemy."

"Would you be capable of striking down Mierk if he proved to be false?" Danis asked. "How about *Queen Keteria?*"

"You always do ask hard questions."

"One must always know how to answer the hard questions. Easy queries never hold the life changing challenges."

Steigan felt the truth in Danis' words. "I still don't know if I would have a right to execute a death sentence. If their actions were inappropriate, wouldn't a council hearing be more in order?"

"I think you enjoy avoiding giving answers." Danis smiled.

Steigan shrugged.

"You do realize there are a lot of situations where there is no other choice?" Danis asked with a serious expression.

"But everyone does deserve the chance to speak for their actions. If they give me opportunity that is the choice I would chose. If I absolutely had no choice…"

As Steigan's voice faded out, Danis's blue eyes grew icy cold. "Your weakness betrays you. You can't afford that. Choose!"

"My loyalty is to the Temple first, the royal family second."

"So if Keteria was betraying the Temple and Mierk ordered you to, you would kill her?"

Steigan closed his eyes, trying hard not to see the scene in his mind's eye and failing. "Aye, but it better be a good reason," he said. "Not over some lousy rewritten books."

"At last, an agreement." Danis looked toward his bookshelves. "Are you ready to work on your magic?"

"Aye," Steigan returned eagerly. The only time he got to work on his magic, it seemed, was when Danis spent these evenings with him. But Danis had spent weeks on magic theory with very little practical application. Maybe now…

"Let's start by talking about gargaxes," Danis said. "'Tis written that they will return. Unstable magic might be a sign that the time grows close. We must be ready to defeat them."

Steigan tried to hide his excitement, but could barely keep from smiling. Tactical magic. He was ready to start throwing spells! But, he had to wait and not push Danis or the Sacred Knight might think he was over eager and not ready to pay attention. "How does magic being unstable mean that they'll be back?" he asked. "Where did they go and where do they come from?"

"They are magic based creatures born from power," Danis began. "They start off as Shant'olin, hungry for the most powerful magic there is: the soul. Then they enter a metamorphosis and transform into a gargax. Very hard, leathery body that's practically impossible to kill."

"But it can be done?"

"Aye, but not as you think. If you cut it to pieces, it will roll back together and reform. This creature does not bleed. It absorbs the energy of most spells. Only fire spells seem to be effective against it. That, or impaling them to the ground."

Steigan made a mental note. Was this why he was in the burning room in his nightmares? "Why are these effective?"

"Magical fire burns hot and fast, consuming all its magic rapidly. Because it does and the gargax is created from magic, the gargax becomes a new fuel source. As for impaling it to the earth, all magic returns there to be renewed. That's why, even though you can draw energy from the surroundings, your best magic will be that which you drawn on from being grounded."

Steigan saw his opportunity to go from theory to application. "How do I get grounded and pull magic up?"

Danis' expression became flat as he started to look uneasy. Steigan even noticed his gaze dart to the window.

"How am I to learn to defeat these gargaxes or anything else if you're only going to teach me theory and no practical applications?" Steigan asked with irritation.

"What I am about to tell you must not leave this room," Danis said.

Conversations that started out like that rarely had a good ending. Still, Steigan nodded hoping he'd soon find out what people were keeping from him.

Danis continued, "Prince Tanold told Mierk to keep you busy with other things so your magic training wouldn't happen."

"Why?" Steigan felt shocked by this news, though he

already should've guessed.

Danis held up a finger to mark another moment of silence from Steigan. He had more to say. "Centhya came to me and asked me to do what I could to train you."

"Centhya? Searn knew this would happen, didn't he?"

"I think Searn suspected, but Centhya knew what she risked in asking me and Searn wouldn't endanger her like that. So, realize that us sitting here discussing magic could be considered treason." Danis paused, letting that sink in. "I continually ask myself how far I want to push that fine line. You need to know how to use your magic, but in teaching you am I serving the Temple or the royal family?"

"Which is why you asked me who I was loyal to?"

"Your answer was clear." Danis looked to the window again. "With that, I think I should bid you blessed evening."

"My answer was *clear*?"

Danis stood. "Aye. In your heart, you already serve Princess Keteria. Therefore, by extension you must also serve her twin. I must respect Prince Tanold's wishes."

"I said I serve both Temple and royal family equally and fairly." Steigan blinked as he tried to recall what he'd said and what Danis had perceived deeper in his words. "I won't be led by blind justice."

"If Mierk wanted you to kill Keteria over *some lousy*

translated books, that's exactly what you should do." His voice was harsh and bitter. "His word is the Goddess' word." He pulled his door open with a quick jerk.

Steigan stood up, walking in a confused haze toward the doorway. "But you told Keteria that you won't turn against her if Mierk ordered it." He wasn't sure where this conversation had become so cloudy.

Danis' eyes grew sad, as if he wanted Steigan to understand a deeper truth. "So where do you think my loyalties lie?"

It came all at once, the pieces falling into place. "With Keteria and the royal family."

"Now you know why I can't train your magic and why I do not truly deserve the title of Sacred Knight." Danis swung the door wide and motioned for Steigan to go through. "Blessed evening to you, Cavalier Steigan."

CHAPTER FIFTEEN

Steigan felt numb from his last encounter with Danis as he walked back to the dormitory. Was there no one he could trust?

He wandered through the dark dormitory between the beds with arms and legs juxtaposed in odd sleeping positions and he felt an odd pang of envy at their innocence. All of them. Did they not know how easily their guiding teachers could betray them?

Steigan pulled his nightshirt from a trunk at the foot of his bed and tossed the clothes onto the bed as he sank down onto it. He put his head in his hands, wishing he could bury the memories and words as easily. Goddess, what was he going to do? If no one would teach him magic, how would he manage on his own?

"Steigan," Jaxsen whispered, "Are you all right?"

Steigan looked over to the domini side and saw Jaxsen sitting up. He wanted to say he was fine but couldn't. "Go to sleep."

Jaxsen slid out of bed and came over to Steigan. "Where have you been? I thought I'd see you at supper. Or evening prayer." Jaxsen took a seat beside Steigan and tucked his legs under him.

"I want to learn magic," Steigan admitted. "This cavalier tract has me bound to its training. I thought I might get help, but it's not coming."

"I'll teach you."

Steigan thought about telling Jaxsen of Tanold's orders, but stopped short. No one would notice two boys hanging out, especially when they'd already been friends for months. If Jaxsen didn't know he was committing treason and Steigan pretended he didn't know, what harm could come? Besides, he had a good case to say that it was the Goddess' will that he learn magic.

"We'll get started tomorrow then?" Steigan asked, letting excitement flow over him.

"How about now?" Jaxsen said, jumping off the bed. "I can't sleep."

It seemed odd. Jaxsen was usually the first one snoring. "Why can't you sleep?" Steigan asked.

"I don't know. I've just got this under-the-skin kind of feeling."

Steigan could relate to that. He looked around. "We can't do it here or else we'll wake the others."

"We could go down to the courtyard."

"Too much of a chance a sapere or dominus would see us. I do have a place though."

They slipped out of the dormitory and down the hall to the stairs. Steigan led Jaxsen to the store room he'd first entered when he'd come from Searn's to see Keteria. They took a lantern from the hallway to light the room. Steigan dropped a cloth at the base of the door to keep the light from seeping beneath.

"Very good," Jaxsen said, but Steigan wasn't sure if the comment referred to his trick to make the light unseen out in the hallway or the room itself.

Jaxsen started clearing off a table. "Do you know any spells?"

"I've done some," Steigan admitted, "but not with awareness of what I'm doing. Magical fire seems to be the only one I feel like I'm controlling."

"*Cazidor*? 'Tis a start. If we do anything noisy, we'll use a magic bubble, *miex'calidori*. Do you know that one?"

Steigan nodded eagerly. "That's one of the ones I did, but I didn't know what it was for." Magic bubble. That's why Searn had never heard him having the night tremors.

"So you've probably also done *badimazulien*. That gives you air within the bubble."

"Aye." Steigan felt like a weight had been lifted off his shoulders. In Jaxsen, he'd found someone who understood and could give him control of the magic he knew instinctively. Now he would learn so much.

"Can you think of any others?"

Steigan found his mind a complete, enthusiastic blank. "Nay. But I'm ready. Let's do this."

Jaxsen paced around the room rubbing a finger over his chin and he looked around. "I'll find something tomorrow that we can burn and I'll teach you a supped up fire spell, but for now we'll stick with other basic spells. Let's see…" He tapped his finger against his cheek now then went digging into a box he found on a shelf. He pulled out a small red candle. "Oh, I know. Here we go."

He placed the candle on the table and held his hands over it. "Palixa jotal."

The candle transformed into a sword.

Steigan picked up the sword and examined it. "You're kidding me?"

"'Tis a simple transformation spell."

"Simple! A small candle to a sword! Why doesn't every blacksmith use this instead of forging swords? A rock to a breastplate!"

"I'll show you," Jaxsen said, indication for Steigan to put the sword back down on the table, then he held his hand over it again. "Nalorium breticham."

The image of the sword wavered, showing that it was just a candle.

"Did you see it?" Jaxsen asked. "Direct translation of that spell is 'the truth of the magic.' Basically it reveals the magic underlying an occurrence or condition. If something is false, it will reveal itself. Would you want to be on a battlefield with your transformed sword and armor and have your enemy discover its true nature? Besides, 'tis also easy to dispel the magic. Radin lukion."

The sword turned back to a candle.

Steigan had an idea. "You said it also works on magical conditions? Could it be used to see if my birthmark was real or fake?"

"Sure."

"Check for me, please?" Steigan asked, holding out his hand. It would solve a lot of questions if the birthmark wasn't real and Keteria and Tanold already knew it.

"Nalorium breticham," Jaxsen said.

The torch-shaped mark on Steigan's right palm didn't change. "'Tis real," Jaxsen confirmed.

"Guess so," Steigan said with disappointment.

Jaxsen pointed to the candle. "Your turn."

It took several attempts before Steigan could turn the candle to a sword. Twice he even melted it onto the table, to which Jaxsen laughed and transformed it back.

"Very good," Jaxsen said after a successful attempt where the candle didn't even seem to hesitate before the transformation. "See? 'Tis not that hard –"

The window behind them shattered and wind gushed into the room, temporarily blinding Steigan as his hair blew into his face.

"What is that?" Jaxsen shouted.

Steigan raked back his hair to see a large gray demon perched on the windowsill folding up its wings. Eyes of the darkest red stared back at them as it tucked its shoulders in to move through the window.

"By the Goddess," Jaxsen gasped, "'tis a gargax."

The gargax maneuvered through the window while

Steigan stood frozen. It tilted its long triangular head and licked its muzzle with a long tongue. Those reddish eyes seemed to glow unnaturally as it watched him, moving toward him with almost serpentine flow. It hissed.

Jaxsen jumped back, colliding into Steigan.

The gargax closed its mouth then snarled, revealing rows of sharp, pointed teeth.

Steigan looked to the table, wondering if the sword was real enough. But he'd lost his concentration on the spell and the sword was only a short red candle again.

He felt torn between fascination in this creature and fear. This was the sort of monster which had bitten him. How had he ever gotten away when he felt so paralyzed by terror now?

The gargax took a rocking step forward, a kind of hop, on its spindly legs, little arms reaching for them. It opened its mouth as it spread its wings. "Hungryzzz," the gargax hissed.

Jaxsen shuddered.

"Now would be a good time for that supped up fire spell," Steigan whispered to Jaxsen.

Jaxsen held out his hands and, as Steigan noted, they didn't tremble. "Cazidor palikiem."

Steigan raised his own shaking hand out before him and tried to focus as well as Jaxsen had. "Cazidor!"

Fire erupted around the gargax driving it backward, shrieking in pain. Totally engulfed, the gargax surged forward in an earsplitting rage. The sound broke Steigan's feet from their place. He grabbed Jaxsen's nightshirt and pushed him from his frozen spot toward the door. Yanking it open, the cloth at the base squeezed under and jammed it from completely opening.

Steigan grabbed the cloth and jerked hard to free the door.

"Go, go, go!" Jaxsen yelled at him.

Steigan pushed Jaxsen out. But as he glanced back over his shoulder to see where the gargax was, he found the burning creature heading for the window. He couldn't let it get away. Steigan slammed the door, barring Jaxsen on the other side. "Hey monster," he called to the gargax, "where do you think you're going?"

Jaxsen pushed the door open. Steigan stopped it with his foot then fell back against it to shove it closed. The small boy's strength couldn't match Steigan's weight.

"What are you doing?" Jaxsen called from the other side.

Steigan put his hand on the door. "Palixa jotal." The door changed to stone as though part of the wall. He knew it wouldn't keep Jaxsen out for long, but hoped it would startle and catch him off guard enough to buy Steigan some time.

"Cazidor," Steigan said, focusing now on the gargax. More magical fire swallowed the gargax.

At the table, Steigan put his hand over the candle. "Palixa jotal."

The candle transformed to a sword. As he picked it up, he noticed that the stone wall had reformed back to a door. He recreated the wall and the sword changed back to a candle. It seemed like he had a choice: protect Jaxsen or have a sword.

The gargax charged at him, its mouth open. In a sudden rush, Steigan's dreams came back to him: fire, monster, wood, and stone. Those nightmares were now real and he'd come face to face with the demon. Fear sunk so deeply within him he wanted to flee. He turned to the door, needed to run, but he faced a stone wall.

The gargax continued to shriek. With its wings spread, it charged toward Steigan, who fell back against the wall as the giant curtain of demon descended upon him. He threw his arm over his face.

Was this how he'd been bitten before? He wasn't even sure how he had time to think such a thought. It had been right there, right upon him. Why hadn't he felt its teeth?

"Hold it!" Prince Tanold shouted.

Hearing the prince's voice, Steigan looked up. The

gargax posed above him, its head wiggling back and forth in anger. It struck out at an invisible barrier holding it, sending red sparks flying. The gargax no longer burned, but it was significantly charred.

With footsteps all around him, Steigan realized he was looking at the feet of several domini and Prince Tanold. He tried to scoot along the wall away from the gargax, who still tried to extend its toothy maw toward him.

The gargax seemed trapped inside a bubble. As Steigan slid away, it charge for him and rocked the bubble into a couple of the domini.

"I said to hold it," Tanold snapped.

Steigan wasn't sure if Tanold was yelling at him or the domini, but he held his position anyway.

One of the domini whispered incantations madly, trying to keep the bubble around the gargax from shattering.

"Bring her in," Tanold said.

Steigan looked toward the area where the door had been and found two people entering through it. One was Princess Keteria. The other was a tall, slender man just a few years older than Keteria. He wore long robes of black with gold trim. Around his head was a simple golden circlet with a blue teardrop gem hanging from it. Following him was a woman in a dress of white and gold which seemed to float as she walked. She also wore a green traveling cloak but had pushed it back off her shoulders to free her hands.

"Can you do it?" Tanold asked Keteria.

Keteria looked around. "Aye, but to hold it, I'll have to go with it."

"Too dangerous."

"'Tis either that or we'll all have to go through to track it down later," she replied looking annoyed.

Tanold spoke to the man in the black robes, "Will she be safe? Can you see?"

The man closed his eyes and exhaled deeply.

"We don't have all day," Tanold said.

"She will be safe," the man confirmed.

"Do it." Tanold turned to the woman in the white dress. "Leloran, prepare to get us out of here."

She stepped further into the room and took a look out the window. Then she began working an incantation.

The man in black pointed at the doorway. "The solid wall was a great idea. It'll give us a couple more moments."

Tanold nodded then turned to one of the domini. "Merkor, take care of the door."

"Aye, milord."

Keteria came over and handed a little wooden box to the man in black robes. They shared a glance that Steigan couldn't interpret.

The door changed back to wall as Steigan felt someone collapse beside him. He realized it was Jaxsen.

Keteria put her hand over the bubble containing the gargax. "Radin'loo malleit trapesa rhosh'a." She took a small step to the side and vanished along with the gargax.

"Dimension shift," Jaxsen whispered, his eyes wide.

Tanold bend down to Steigan. "When Mierk asks you, we weren't here. Got it?"

"I could erase the vision of us from their minds," the man in black said.

Tanold stayed in a position where he could look directly sharp into Steigan's eyes as he spoke to the other man. "This one's lost enough of his memories already. I'm hoping tonight's experience will jar those memories back."

"I'm ready," the woman, Leloran, said.

Tanold stood. "Let's go."

The domini, Prince Tanold, and the man in black stepped closer to Leloran as she said, "Talcor dun proximitious." A white light expanded from the back wall, enveloping the party.

Steigan raised his arm trying to shield his eyes from the light while still seeing what was going on. As the light faded, Steigan found himself and Jaxsen alone in the room with a light breeze coming through the destroyed window.

"What just happened?" Jaxsen asked.

"I have no idea," Steigan said, getting quickly to his feet, "but I think we best get back to bed before we're asked."

Back in the dormitory, Steigan lay awake listening to the footsteps on the stairs. He felt he needed to go, but go where he didn't know. Bunching up the blankets in tight fists, he willed himself to stay in bed and tried to keep his eyes closed.

He wanted to go hunting.

The gargaxes were here.

Flipping over, Steigan stared toward the window. He thought he saw a ghost pass by and he forced his eyes to shut, unwilling to see any more.

He covered his head with the blanket.

Sometime later, in the middle of the night, Steigan fell asleep. That night, his dreams of demons returned.

Except now he knew the gargaxes truly did exist.

Chapter Sixteen

Steigan woke in a cold sweat from his second night of nightmares about the gargaxes in a tangle of coarse blankets, drenched and breathing deeply. Outside, it was still dark. Still, he could see boys on the domini side of the room throwing back their covers and getting up.

He needed to go too.

Steigan rose, dressed, and moved through the darkness with the others. He felt like he was aware of them, yet couldn't really acknowledge their presence. He wondered if the others felt the same. They moved as a mass toward the armory and got weapons. Steigan dropped a chainmail shirt over his head, but left it at that for armor.

Dimly aware that the others were moving toward the main doors of the Temple, Steigan took the stairs for the battlements.

Danis stood at the door waiting for him. "I had a feeling you'd come this way," Danis said. "Go back down to the dormitory."

"You know I can't do that," Steigan said.

"None of you will be leaving the Temple grounds tonight."

"We need to be out there."

"The domini of Lilinar have already gone. There is no need for our young to be out there too." Danis widened his stance as if physically backing his words.

"'Tis our obligation. Will you stop us every night?"

"The domini will be done with them tonight."

"So you're telling me that magic is fixed?" Steigan asked. "We both know better."

"Well, if I can't talk you out of it, then I guess I'm going with you."

Steigan stopped completely, awestruck and wondering if he'd heard Danis correctly.

Danis opened the door. "After you."

"Why are you doing this?" Steigan asked after stepping

out on the battlements, still in shock. "Why are you letting *me* go? And why do you want to go with me?"

"It's long been speculated that when the gargaxes return, so will the reincarnation of Rivic. I have to know if you are that person."

"Why would I be?"

"What other explanation could one possibly accept for your sudden appearance, your power, and why the first gargaxes sighted seemed to be coming for you?" Danis said.

Steigan hurried along the battlements. Two moons, both nearly full, gave plenty of light to see his way as he jumped from the main building to the outer wall. He didn't wait to see if Danis safely made the same jump. He kept going.

Reincarnation of Rivic! What a preposterous notion.

Hearing a commotion in the courtyard below, Steigan looked down to see several knights rounding the young domini back into the Temple. Several more knights stood before the gatehouse. There was no way he'd be able to open the gates with it being guarded like that.

He looked for other options. He didn't want to swim across the lake. With his armor, that sounded like a sure way to drown.

He needed another idea. One that didn't involve asking

Danis to give an order to lower the bridge.

Danis seemed to sense his thoughts. "You do have an idea, don't you?"

"Working on it," Steigan replied.

The sight of several torches coming from the castle drew his attention. A party of domini were riding out into the forest after the gargaxes. But there was one person with them who shouldn't have been: Princess Keteria.

Danis swore under his breath when he saw her. "She should not be going out."

"I agree," Steigan said sourly. "We've got to get over there."

"Let me help you out with that."

Steigan wanted to tell him not to help when Danis touched his arm. "Talcor dun."

He felt a whoosh as though being pulled forward. When his eyes came back into focus, he realized he was standing next to the stables on the other side of the lake. Danis passed him and went into the stables.

"She really shouldn't be out here," Danis said from inside the stables. "We'll follow behind and make sure everything…"

Danis' voice faded as Steigan walked away, feeling a desperate need to go. He wasn't interested in following behind. As he turned the corner of the building, there stood a massive gray unicorn. Steigan barely came up to his shoulder. Dark eyes watched him. The unicorn tossed its head, shaking its black mane. Long black hair covered its hooves.

Steigan held out his hand toward it. The unicorn settled and pressed its head against Steigan's palm, then drew back and gave a bow by extending a foreleg and lowering down to the other knee.

With one last look back over his shoulder to make sure no one watched, Steigan climbed on the unicorn's back. It rose up, lifting him easily off the ground.

Danis called out, "Steigan?"

With a hold of the unicorn's mane, Steigan leaned close and the unicorn took off into the forest. The night air felt good on Steigan's face. Of course he'd been riding with Searn before, but this felt so different, so wild, so free and natural. He let the unicorn lead him deeper into the forest even though he knew he was moving away from the domini leaving the castle. They were on the trail of the gargaxes too, but the unicorn knew the fastest way. Steigan wasn't sure how he understood all of this; he just did.

Steigan slid off when the unicorn finally stopped. "Thanks, Telimas," he said, unsure of how he knew the unicorn's name. Telimas stomped its large hoof against the ground and whipped its head up and down while snorting. Steigan felt its agitation and apprehension, translating it into his own nerves.

Steigan looked around and saw a cave before him. He wished he'd had some torches now, for the night's two moons didn't give him much visibility inside. Moving slowly and staying near the sides of the cave, he let his eyes adjust to the growing darkness.

"Who enterz?" a gargax hissed.

A beguiled power reached out to him, wrapping slimy tentacles around him. Steigan felt himself slouch as he closed his eyes and lowered his head. He partially reopened his eyes to give an evil glare into the blackness before him. "'Tis I, brotherz," Steigan heard himself say though he felt like he spoke from the other side of a tunnel.

Beasts moved toward him in the blackness, their outlines becoming more visible as they got close. He raised his gaze to the ceiling where he saw more hanging upside down like bats, some stretching out their wings.

"What reportz haz you?" the lead gargax asked.

"They comez," Steigan replied, unable to stop the words, "the domini and their princess, Keteria."

Too late, Steigan felt movement behind him and a spear thrust between his ribs. Heat rather than ~~pain~~ flared through him, though he felt blood bubble in his throat and mouth. He looked down to see a horn sticking out the front of his chest through the chainmail mesh.

Steigan turned as much as he could even though it caused him great agony. He had to see. "Telimas?"

The unicorn dug in its hooves into the ground as it pulled the horn out of Steigan. He staggered and fell to the floor, helpless at the feet of the gargax. With his hand on his chest, he expected to find it warm with blood but instead he found cold ooze. He turned his head and spit, but it wasn't blood that came out either but putrid black foam.

The gargaxes were coming for him. In this position, he couldn't pull his sword to defend himself.

Telimas charged forward and the gargaxes retreated.

Spitting out more dark and bubbly mucus, Steigan noticed a white gold glow around his chest. He scrambled to his feet. Grimacing at the hole in his chainmail, he said, "They poisoned me."

Telimas snorted then moved back out of the cave. Steigan knew the unicorn had cured him and now he had a job to do. He drew his sword.

"You betrayz us," the gargax growled.

"I never willing joined your side. When did you do it? When you bit me and left me for dead on the side of the road?"

He charged the gargaxes. They swarmed around him. Steigan slashed at the nearest of the beasts, sending pieces flying.

"Cazidor!" Sword swinging in one hand, Steigan used the other to cast spells, moving right through the mass as he did. "Cazidor. Cazidor."

Fire spewed in all directions. Gargaxes dislodged from the ceiling and dropped down on him. His sword rose to meet them, casting them aside. If he wasn't there, Telimas was, spearing the gargaxes on its horn and flinging the demon against the wall. Steigan impaled gargaxes, one after another, to the ground continuing even as he felt the blade growing dull.

Once all the gargaxes in the cave were defeated, Steigan sent one last burst of fire spells into the cave. Telimas waited while Steigan gave a final inspection just to make sure.

The others would be here soon. Would they smell the charred remains? Would they know what had happened here? Would they walk right on by?

Steigan mounted Telimas and gave a look back before starting for the Temple. He hoped the domini would find the eradicated cave and head back.

He'd succeeded in keeping Keteria safe.

Chapter Seventeen

The next day, several parents of children in the domini tract came to the Temple and removed their offspring. Those remaining speculated if the former had been expelled for their actions of trying to break out the previous night, or if their parents feared the activation of Rivic's enchantment. Steigan suspected it might be a little of both.

Even as Mierk tried desperately to explain that the Temple continued to be the safest place for the boys and girls to be, Steigan knew Mierk could hold the children back from hunting no more than their parents could.

Steigan went to bed that night with an uneasy mood.

Maybe the pull of two of the three moons had an unsettling effect on him. He didn't sleep well. Whatever feeling it had been, it was gone in the morning light.

Steigan went down to breakfast, sitting as usual with Jaxsen, when Searn came in. Searn wore his domini armor as well as a blue and gold cape similar to Danis' red cape.

"Steigan, you've got to come with me now," Searn said.

"What's going on?" Steigan asked before hurriedly shoving one more bit of eggs and cheese into his mouth.

Searn glanced around at all the boys staring at him. "I'll explain outside. Get your things."

Steigan ran upstairs and packed. Nearly finished, Jaxsen came in.

"Where are you going? You're not leaving like the others, are you?" Jaxsen asked.

"I don't know. Searn needs me, but that's all I know," Steigan replied, pulling the tie on his small pack containing all his belongings.

"I looked out the window on my way up here. He's got a horse packed with an extra set of dominus armor. It looks like Danis is going too."

Steigan tossed his pack over his shoulder. What had happened? He hurried outside where he found Mierk, Searn, Danis, and Colwyn huddled together by three horses just as

Jaxsen had said.

"I think this is a mistake," Mierk said firmly. "His training isn't finished and his magic is wild. Besides, Colwyn has lay claim for him to become his page."

Danis' face tightened. "He's in the knight tract and since he's a cavalier the claim is mine."

Mierk rounded on Danis. "Things change fast."

Steigan's breath caught as he slowed down, as if sneaking up on the party. Had they found out new information about his lineage?

Mierk's lips were pressed tightly together.

Searn saw Steigan coming. "All your belongings packed?" he asked, as if indicating that Steigan wouldn't be returning.

"Aye," Steigan answered.

Mierk stepped directly in front of Steigan. "I must protest against this. You are still needed here and you still need to be here."

Steigan wanted to ask if Mierk wanted him around only to help create more palimpsests, but Searn cut him off. "You sound like he's going away forever, Holy Sapere," Searn said, making Steigan question his earlier assumption that Searn knew he wouldn't be coming back. "'Tis a short venture."

Mierk turned swiftly back toward Searn and hissed, "But this is highly irregular."

"These are highly irregular times." Searn used the hand closest to the scabbard to tilt the sword forward a bit as if drawing special attention to it as he stepped up to Mierk. "I told you from the very beginning that his sword work was more than adequate and to focus on the magic. One would almost think you were stalling. Maybe when he returns you will remember your place in his training."

"I –" Mierk began stammering.

Searn jumped in sharply. "Every moment you delay us you stand in the way of Prince Tanold's orders. I have humored you, but how long do you think Prince Tanold's anger will hold when he finds out why we've been kept?"

Mierk's eyes narrowed on Steigan. "Take him."

Mierk and Colwyn stepped back while Searn, Danis, and Steigan mounted their horses. Searn led the way out of the Temple courtyard, across the bridge, and toward the castle.

Steigan watched the armor fastened to Searn's horse. Jaxsen had been right about it being the blue and gold armor of a dominus and it was beautiful. He longed to touch it, hoping that when he did a flood of memories would come back to him.

Yet he had no proof that this set of armor was the one he had been found in. It might be some spare armor for Searn, something from his youth.

Steigan noticed an extra sword strapped across Searn's back, a beautiful shiny blade with a golden hilt and scrolling sword catcher. In a strange fashion, the hilt resembled the symbol of the Goddess, even incorporating the circle and three representational lines meaning to protect, serve, and trust the Goddess. Whoever had made that sword had been a devout believer. The breastplate matched the sword, he noticed now.

Searn waved to the guards at the castle gates and they passed the gatehouse into the inner city. Hooves clacked on the cobblestone street. Steigan felt he should pull equal with Searn to ask why they were going to the castle, but he only wanted to hang back and watch the armor sparkle in the sunlight. It made his heart ache, made him crazy with thoughts of the maker. Like his blue, black, and gold doublet, someone had put a lot of work into the armor and sword. A little sorrowful sound escaped his lips before he could stop it.

Danis looked back at Steigan then said to Searn, "I'm going to go on ahead."

Searn also looked back at Steigan. "Aye. Good idea."

As Danis hurried on, Searn turned his horse and came

up alongside Steigan.

Steigan couldn't believe how tight his throat had become, but he had to know, so he forced the question out. "Is that the armor I was found in?" Part of him hoped Searn would say "nay" so he could regain composure and move on.

"Aye," Searn said though he looked like he wasn't sure how to answer Steigan's question. "Do you have any memory of it?"

Steigan glanced back at where it was tied to Searn's horse. "It's mine, Searn. I don't know how I know, but I know it. You have to believe me." He was a dominus. He knew it through and through, but how to make Searn understand it too? Suddenly he couldn't bring himself to breathe.

Searn's eyes were sad. "We need to get to the castle. We're awaited."

Steigan nodded, though his throat felt solid from the lump stuck in his throat. "Who's waiting for us? Please tell me someone's found something out."

"Oh, someone's found something. But 'tis not likely the information you want."

A sudden thought came to Steigan. He'd always imagined that his innocence would be proven. What if the opposite had been found? What if his armor was put before him not to be given back but to be used as evidence against him?

"Let's be off," Searn said as a gentle reminder.

Steigan tried to stay equal with Searn, finding himself unwilling to look at the sword and armor any longer. Being so close and yet not having the right to wear them was too painful. He tried to keep the bitterness at bay.

"I am told that you handled yourself like a dominus at the Temple, " Searn said.

"I was just being me, or what felt like me," Steigan answered, feeling embarrassed now.

"Steigan, whatever happens here, I want you to remember one thing."

He felt trepidation starting to rise again. "What is that?"

"You are descended from a magical line of maeges and domini. You are directly connected to a great man who fought terrible evil. The gift of the domini is knowing our magical roots."

"You sound like I will be cast away from this heritage. Will I never be the dominus I hope to be?"

Searn shook his head. "I wish I could guard you from what's to come."

"What's coming?"

They had arrived at the castle. A stable boy took their

mounts after Searn removed his pack and the armor from the horse. Searn handed the items to a nearby knight who hurried into the castle with them.

"What's coming?" Steigan repeated, following Searn into the castle. His stomach clenched so tightly with fear. Why didn't Searn answer him? "What's going to happen in here?"

The moment Steigan crossed the threshold into the castle, he felt an old, primeval power hit him and icy chills entered his veins. Dropping to a defensive crouch, Steigan hissed as he turned looking for the source.

A movement behind him made him spin around. Laurient stepped out of the shadows with a tightly woven mesh bag in his hands. Before Steigan could ward off the attack, Laurient threw the cloth over Steigan's head.

"Royka piryeian," Searn spoke and Steigan found himself imprisoned in a cobweb tangle of magic. He felt someone close to him.

"Sorry, mate," Laurient said. "Be still and 'twill be over soon."

Fear clenched through Steigan. He waited for a blade to cut into him and end his life. Instead, he felt Searn and Laurient dragging him.

"Stairs," Searn said to Steigan.

So, it was to be the dungeon for him, Steigan thought.

But as he prepared his feet for downward stairs, he felt himself being lifted up.

"Searn, please," Steigan said into the blackness of the bag over his head, "what's going on?" He'd never felt such fear and chills crawled over him like he'd never have sun on his skin again. Nightmares not his own played through his mind: people being killed by magic and beast, blood everywhere.

Searn whispered, "Soon, I promise."

After the stairs, they walked down a short hallway. Steigan heard a door open and a myriad of muffled voices fell silent as Steigan was lead into a room and unceremoniously made to kneel on the stone floor.

Keteria's voice broke the silence. "Was this really necessary?"

Her worried tone made Steigan feel a little better. Maybe it wasn't as bleak as he imagined. Still, he couldn't break free from the images of sharp teeth tearing through flesh and lightning filling the skies.

"I'm sorry, milady," Laurient said. "He felt it. We had no choice."

After a silence longer than Steigan would've wished, Keteria asked, "Cavalier Steigan, can you hear me?"

Cavalier! It galled him to be formally called by this

lesser title. Glad that he could grimace unseen behind the bag, he tried to swallow all the anger to calmly reply, "Aye, Princess. Though I know not what is going on."

"We have a beast of the oldest kind locked in the castle. It is taking everything I have to keep its essence contained within the castle walls," she explained. "If the people of Lilinar felt it, there would be mass panic. Do you understand?"

Steigan bit back on the scoff he felt rise inside him. "I think I get it."

"You must. I can't have you released until I know you have control over your emotions and your magic."

Fear coiled through Steigan. He didn't have control right now. If only Searn had told him what was going on, then he might have been prepared. But the promise of release also had strong appeal.

"I can promise neither, Princess," Steigan admitted.

A chuckle went up around the room as one person gave a nervous, sympathetic laugh then others joined in.

"Honesty, Cavalier Steigan," Keteria said, "is a most uncommon trait. I think we all feel ourselves dangling from that same precipice. Release him."

"Piryeian," Searn said and the tight webbing constraining Steigan disappeared.

The hood came off and Steigan blinked at the sudden harsh light of the room. He noticed Keteria sitting on a throne on a raised dais. He'd never seen her with her tiara on, but her beauty would rival the Goddess. He found himself kneeling between two rows of tables set lengthwise to create an aisle toward the throne. To his right, Sacred Knight Danis sat with several other maeges, knights, and domini he recognized. To the left, he saw Laurient now taking a seat among several people, including the man with the black and gold robes and his maege in white. Steigan wondered if any of the others were also centaurs in human form.

"Cavalier Steigan, I do believe you know most of the people at the north table, but let me introduce those at the south table," Keteria said.

Steigan rose to face the table which Keteria indicated.

"At the far end is Lord Krielic Wevoriton of Montikovert and his Sacred Knight, Hurnric," Keteria began. "Then we have the leader of the centaurs, Chief Rajed. I've been told you already know Laurient de Santz."

Laurient bowed his head toward Steigan and gave a little salute with two fingers at his temples.

Keteria continued, "Then we have Holy Sapere Kelan, High Maege Leloran, and Lord Ithanes Selmik, all from Dubinshire."

Lord Ithanes, the man in the black and gold robes, folded his arms together on the table and leaned forward. He tilted his head, making the blue teardrop shaped gem sway slightly, and his gaze left Steigan for Keteria. He gave her a sly smile, looked as though he was about to say something, then turned his blue eyes back to Steigan and put a finger to his lips instead.

Keteria now addressed the group at large. "Cavalier Steigan is the young man found on the road near Dominus Searn's fief."

"To hear that someone had been bitten by a gargax and lived seemed unbelievable," Kelan, the Holy Sapere of Dubinshire, said. "Not unless you'd fallen through time or something."

High Maege Leloran asked, "Is it not true that he was found in the armor of a dominus? Do you deny him the title now?"

"You know it," Steigan muttered under his breath.

Keteria looked sharply at Steigan. "Until his heritage is cleared up, we decided to not assume anything."

Lord Ithanes leaned over to Leloran and whispered something to her which made her smile. Steigan hated the way Ithanes' icy gaze assessed him.

Keteria clapped her hands to regain everyone's

attention. "Cavalier Steigan, we have brought you to council today for a special purpose," she said. "The centaurs have captured a gaxlor."

"A gaxlor?"

Keteria nodded. "A very ancient beast, older and more dangerous than the gargaxes. Another demon not seen since the time of Sapere Rivic and Lady Alityka."

"Now, to be sitting practically in the shadow of the demon, it seems truly unreal," Leloran said. "Nightmare-ish."

"To have a gaxlor captured live is an incredible feat, even more than the gargax we caught two nights ago," Keteria said. "We have the centaurs to thank and blessings to their tribesmen lost in the undertaking."

Rajed nodded his head in thanks.

"Which brings us to the task we have for you, Cavalier," Keteria said.

Steigan bowed even though the fear in his stomach told him he should run. "I am at your service, Princess."

Keteria motioned for Searn to come forward. "We wish for you to don the armor you had on the day you were found and to meet the beast face to face."

Two things struck Steigan at once. First, she hadn't claimed the armor was his, but only that he'd been found in it. Second, she hadn't said the gaxlor would still be caged. Did they intend on letting the gaxlor finish what the gargax had started? Was this an easy end to their quest for answers?

"What purpose do you hope that serves?" Steigan asked.

"We're hoping that it will either recognize you or that you will recognize it. Either way, we are hoping to have clues," Keteria said.

Lord Krielic of Montikovert spoke up, "If there is one gaxlor about, chances are more are coming or soon will be."

"'Tis imperative that we prepare our kingdoms for what is to come," Ithanes added.

Steigan turned back to Keteria. "What do you believe is coming?"

She glanced to Ithanes as if they shared a secret between them. When Steigan looked at Ithanes' reaction, Ithanes shook his head ever so slightly. Did Keteria not understand that Steigan would do anything for her?

"I rescind my question," Steigan said. "It doesn't matter. I will do as you ask without explanation."

Laurient raised his goblet. "Here, here, mate!"

Searn began strapping the armor plating onto Steigan and fastening the buckles. Steigan looked down at it, the perfectly fitting breastplate and arm plates. Unlike Searn's armor which had been slightly too big for him, this armor fit him perfectly. Lastly, Searn removed the sword on his back and handed it flat to Steigan.

Keteria stood up. "We will escort you to where the gaxlor is being held."

Before Keteria could step from the dais, Steigan moved to block her path. He looked up at her. "Ask me."

"Ask you what?" she asked blankly.

"Ask me what you asked the domini on the night of the tri-lunar ceremony. Don't you believe I at least deserve a blessing first?"

Keteria looked around the room, both taken back by Steigan's request and seeming to ask the permission of those around the room. "Cavalier Ste—"

"Ask me as a dominus," Steigan said firmly. I wear the armor. I have the heart. I need you to ask me as a dominus."

Keteria blinked and looked down at him as though considering his request for a moment. Then she nodded. "Dominus Steigan, coom ra wialca to?"

Steigan stepped back as he griped the hilt of the sword Searn had handed him. He whipped the blade around in a salute which ended with the weapon in his left hand and his right hand over his heart. "Coom ra wialca do, Princess Keteria."

He formed another salute and kneeled before her, his

sword upright at her feet as if being offered to her. "You have my sword and my life. The streets of Gohaldinest are paved with gold, but I seek a richer treasure. Mind, body, soul dedicated to Her service."

"Ha nee," Holy Sapere Kelan responded.

Everyone else in the room except for Keteria and the centaurs responded with, "Porta quinest acay doomasha."

"The Goddess shines Her light on the path," Steigan said as he rose before Keteria.

"Flama'tada lutarien." Keteria put her finger to Steigan's forehead as though marking him.

In that instant, Steigan knew something wasn't right. He bowed, trying to figure out what was different. "Ha nee," he said, holding out his hand to help Keteria down from the dais. "Take me to the gaxlor."

Keteria took his offered hand, stepped down, then released him and started walking for the door. Steigan fell into step behind her, knowing now what had changed: Keteria didn't have any magic. The others in the room stood up.

Laurient slapped the table as he rose. "Leave it to a dominus to turn anything and everything into a ceremony." The centaur in human form hurried around the table to catch up with Steigan as they left. "Way to impress the lady," he added. "She'll not likely forget that soon."

Chapter Eighteen

Princess Keteria led the way through the tangle of hallways until the group came to a doorway where Prince Tanold stood in blue and gold armor, his sword drawn. A look of sheer disgust crossed Tanold's face when he saw Steigan in the dominus armor.

Tanold looked back at Keteria. "The gaxlor has been quiet. Perhaps it has starved to death."

"Not likely," Keteria replied under her breath. She turned to Steigan, her gaze going over him in his armor. "Beyond this door is another. The gaxlor is behind that one."

Steigan wondered what Keteria had been thinking as

she looked him over but realized it was an inappropriate time to ask. "Let's get to it."

Keteria raised her hand to stop him. "You need to be aware of the wall, the one beyond this one. 'Tis a special glass, magic made. We will be able to see into the room where you will be with the gaxlor, but from in there you won't be able to see us. The wall will appear as reflective."

Steigan nodded his understanding. He reached to open the first door and went inside. Just as Keteria had said, there was a small room behind the door and another door straight across from the one they were now entering. The wall beside the door was strange indeed. It looked like dark smoky glass with scrolling wrought iron working its way up through it. He could see beyond into the next room where a cage sat with a large rock contained within.

A rock? Was this some sort of joke?

Most of the group stayed toward the back of the room, but Laurient walked over to the strange glass wall and put a hand on it while pointing with the other hand into the room. "Oh look. The beast is pouting. Give it a good tap with your sword and he should pop right out of that form," Laurient said to Steigan.

Searn stepped up to Steigan. "This is an old and clever demon. Whatever it says to you, no matter what it promises,

Steigan, don't let it out of the cage."

"He's right," Rajed said. "The words of a gaxlor are not to be trusted."

Steigan opened the inner door and stepped inside the room with the cage and the rock. He turned and true enough the wall reflected his form right back at him. He wondered if they were laughing at him yet or if it was just snickering right now. He couldn't hear anything and wondered if they'd be able to hear what he said to the gaxlor.

Feeling like an idiot, Steigan walked up to the cage. "Oh, gaxlor, wake up." He looked back once more at the wall and found only his own reflection looking back at him wondering the same thing he was: was this real or a joke?

He stood there facing the rock. He had to make a decision to take this seriously or to leave. Either way, he couldn't help if this was an elaborate scheme at his expense, but why would they go to this extreme?

Maybe they were testing him to see if he really had the heart of a dominus. At this moment, he didn't feel like one. He felt like some poor sap stuck in a room with a caged rock and a dozen people watching to see what he'd do.

Goddess, he hated this.

With a deep breath, Steigan pulled his sword and approached the cage. "Let me just make Laurient laugh harder," he said half disgusted with himself.

He tapped the top of the rock then gave it a good poke. He even tried to slide his sword beneath it to see if it had a soft underbelly.

It was a damn rock.

He walked around the cage in the center of the room, staring at the rock and never once looking at the reflective wall. Don't go near the cage, every cell in his body seemed to scream. Don't go near the cage.

Worse, he could almost hear the group mocking him, "Oh, don't get too close. The rock might bite." More raucous laughter would follow.

Angry at his thoughts, Steigan stuck his arm through the cage. "Here, want to chew on it like your gargax buddy did?"

The rock did nothing.

Steigan pulled his sword part way out of the scabbard. "Blood maybe? Is that what you need?" He sliced into his arm then flicked some of the fresh blood on the rock.

He hoped they were all finding this hilarious.

The door opened and Keteria came running into the room. "Steigan, what are you doing?"

Steigan leaned against the cage and let his blood drip directly onto the rock. "'Tis a rock. What kind of joke are you trying to pull?"

Keteria stopped, frozen in horror as her hands came to her mouth and she screamed. Tanold and Ithanes rushed into the room, their eyes wide in alarm.

Steigan felt the air beside him shift and magic rippled outward like an untamed force. Instinctively, he pulled his arm out so fast he slammed his elbow into the metal bar.

Tanold and Ithanes dragged Keteria backwards into the protective room and slammed the door.

A large gray arm reached through the cage for Steigan. He tucked and rolled away, coming up to draw his sword. With a defensive stance, he looked at the beast in the cage. It was three times the size it had been in rock form. Large hands with thick fingers tried to pry apart the bars of the cell. It didn't have wings like a gargax, but figured the larger body size prevented flight anyway. Where the gargax was thin and gangly, the gaxlor was large, solid, and obviously destructive.

When it saw Steigan assessing it, the gaxlor turned and licked Steigan's blood from its arm with a tongue similar, only larger, to the gargax. The teeth of the gaxlor weren't nearly as sharp and pointy as a gargax's either though Steigan still didn't doubt it could rip the flesh from its victims.

The gaxlor seemed to enjoy the blood. "Ahhh, the bloodwavez of a descendant of Rivic." It clicked its tongue as it tasted more off the wing. "Steigan, she called you. You haz very tasty magicz, Steigan. I accept your sacrifice and shallz devour you. Come."

Steigan tried to resist stepping near the cage, but his foot slipped along the floor as though under a will of its own.

"Your offering pleasez me. Comez," the gaxlor said. It stretched out its arms, reaching toward him. Long, slightly curled talons glistened on the ends of its fingers and beckoned him.

Steigan couldn't stop his feet from betraying him as he felt the gaxlor's thrall overtake him. He neared deathly close to the cage, feeling his heart beating fast, a heart in its own cage, not seeing what the brain was seeing, but fearing for itself nevertheless.

"I know whatz you did. You slaughtered my brethrenz. But I'z accept your bloodz for theirz," the gaxlor said.

Somewhere through the terror hazing his thoughts, self-preservation must have kicked in and Steigan felt himself almost numbly draw his sword. His heartbeat thundered through him, pulsing in his fingers gripping his hilt.

Steigan's shoulders pressed against the cage bars. He breathed deeply, watching the gaxlor in panic like an animal trapped by a predator.

The gaxlor rushed forward.

Steigan brought the sword up.

The gaxlor screamed as it fell upon the blade.

Spell broken, Steigan shoved the blade deeper into the gaxlor, then pulled it out. The gaxlor stumbled backwards clutching at its chest while golden blood ran between its fingers.

It growled and dashed toward Steigan, stretching its long arms through the bars for Steigan. Raising the sword defensively, Steigan slashed at the arm coming toward him and the blade went clean through the bone. The arm fell away, but landed in as a rock on the floor.

The gaxlor retreated to the far end of the cage. The rock changed to a liquid puddle and seeped toward the gaxlor. Once the two met, the gaxlor went into rock form.

Steigan remembered hearing that the gargaxes could reform, but he still watched in disbelief as the gaxlor retook its demon form fully restored. Steigan kept his sword drawn as he stood against a wall wondering what to do now.

The gaxlor glared at him as it began to pace.

Steigan leveled his sword at the gaxlor. "What are you doing here? Why have you returned now?"

The gaxlor crouched and took a hopping step toward him. "Her magic weakenz on me. I am absorbingz it. I am notz what youz think I am."

There was a shift in the air. Even Steigan had to admit that he felt it.

"So what are you?"

"I am—" Suddenly the gaxlor started shaking, his eyes rolling back so that Steigan could only see black. It looked like the demon was in extreme ~~pain~~.

"What are you?" Steigan repeated.

After another shift, the gaxlor regained itself. "I am olderz than the planet itself. I am a demanding godz."

This felt so wrong to Steigan. He thought of a puppet on strings. "And so what do you want?"

The gaxlor blinked its dark red eyes slowly as though humored. It looked at the reflective wall as though seeing the people behind it. "You are their sacrifice to mez," it said. "Do youz not realize itz? Come, givez your magicz to me."

"I think if I was their sacrifice, I wouldn't have been sent in here with sword and armor."

"I grow bored of thiz sparing with youz."

"How do you think I feel?"

The gaxlor rushed the cage and grabbed the bars. "How dare youz speak to your godz thiz way?"

"My god?" Steigan paused as if thinking about this for a moment. "I would never worship a coarse demon like you, pathetic and trapped."

"But you willz. I havez forever to regain my strength and magic. Where willz you be in a thousand yearz?"

"Where ever I need to be to destroy you."

The gaxlor pressed his head against the bars. "I have thousandz of brethren. You will never destroyz the gargaxes."

"The gargaxes?" Steigan scoffed. "I personally eliminated a whole cave of them a few nights ago. Besides, I don't think you'll be seeing many more days, especially since I've proven you can be hurt. You and your brethren? Not much to fear there."

The gaxlor sank into a low crouch and leaned back his head. Steigan felt the energy of terror come off the demon. He had a hard time remaining still without shaking. If this beast didn't even have ample power yet and could make that much terrible supremacy emanate from it, imagine it at full strength.

The gaxlor stood up and paced the cage again. "After the witch'z spell is broken, we willz fill the sky once more."

Steigan put his sword away as if bored. "And I will be there to hunt all of you down."

"We haz the offering of your bloodwave. Youz should fear us comingz for you."

"Come then, and meet your death by the blade of Dominus Steigan."

The gaxlor's eyes flashed. While Steigan had felt so

good saying the words, he now wished he hadn't spoken so boastfully.

The gaxlor ran for the cage bars again, but this time it didn't stop at the edge. The gaxlor jumped, twisting sideways. Before Steigan could register what was going on, a freed boulder rolled toward him.

Chapter Nineteen

The gaxlor had made it out of its cage.

Steigan sidestepped the boulder coming toward him and watched in horror as it hit the wall and changed back into a gaxlor, its full-height rising well above Steigan. He knew now how this beast could be worshipped as a god.

Arms surrounded him and a woman's terror-filled voice shouted in his ear. "Talcor dun!"

Steigan felt the pull of himself being magically moved and when his eyes refocused he was standing in the protective room behind the glass with Leloran beside him. The gaxlor rushed toward the special reflective wall.

"Is it going to hold?" Tanold shouted.

As if in answer, the gaxlor slammed into the wall and it shook but held.

"I don't know if it can take much of that," Ithanes said.

"We should move," Lord Krielic said.

Laurient pointed toward the gaxlor. "You can't just… oh—"

The gaxlor slammed into the wall again. The noise made Steigan jump. For just a second as he looked at the gaxlor, he swore it had wings.

"You know," Laurient said to Steigan, "Lord Krielic is right. Let's move away from here."

Steigan felt Laurient tugging on his arm and blindly followed. His whole body shook from adrenaline. He looked around and saw Keteria supported by Tanold as if leaning heavily on him. Ithanes stood by her too, whispering to them. Steigan looked once more at the angry gaxlor still pounding on the window and let Laurient move him from the room.

Back in the hallway, Laurient turned to Krielic and asked, "Ancient oaks, wasn't that great? The way he put himself against the bars then stabbed the beast!"

Laurient smiled at Steigan. "You have got some major moves." He made some jabbing and poofing sounds while punching into the air. Then, with an exuberant yip, he turned and continued down the hall to talk with Rajed who also walked along in human form.

Searn pulled Steigan aside. "Are you all right?"

"I'm fine. I'm really getting tired of nothing being in its true form," Steigan answered while watching Laurient walk away. He briefly noticed Lord Ithanes walk swiftly past him,

Searn started to unbuckle the armor. Steigan put his hand on Searn's. "Do I have to take it off now? Can't we wait a bit longer? It feels so right."

"Like your true form?" Searn asked.

Steigan looked toward the small group receding down the hallway. He wondered where the other half was, what they were doing with the gaxlor.

"You have the heart of a true dominus," Searn said. "I know it."

To Steigan, that wasn't good enough. He scoffed.

"Keteria knows it," Searn continued.

He looked back at the door to the room before he could stop himself.

"I would prove it to the world for you if I could," Searn said.

Steigan let go of Searn's hand. "But for now I have to have a form that isn't my own."

"I'm sorry."

Steigan helped Searn remove the armor. He thought the faster he got it off, the sooner his heartbreak would end. It didn't help though. He hung back, watching Searn carry the armor away from him, the sword once again on Searn's back. Goddess, how he hated this.

Temptation to leave now and return to the Temple nearly overwhelmed him. They had made use of him. How could he be needed any further? But Searn turned and motioned to him, so he followed.

As they entered the room where they had first gathered, Ithanes spoke to Lord Krielic. "…'tisn't good. Where there is one, more will follow. Along with them, the Shant'olin will come too."

"Shant'olin?" Steigan asked, vaguely remembering hearing the word at some point.

Laurient was just in the process of sitting down after filling two goblets of water from a nearby canter. He set one before his chief. "Aye, the Shant'olin! You know, the ghosts of old stories, come in the night, steal away your soul…"

"Sorry, still don't get it." He wanted to add that he didn't remember anyone telling him stories, let alone stories of old legends. They all had family memories to give context to this situation, but he didn't. He only had nuggets of information. "Besides," he added, "aren't the Shant'olin a precursor to the gargaxes, they go through a metamorphosis to become gargaxes?"

Ithanes glared at Steigan then let it slowly turn into a patronizing smile as if telling Steigan to back off. "Aye, the Shant'olin and the gargaxes seem to come together, but they are always led by a gaxlor. When you start seeing one, the others are never far behind."

"The gaxlor leads the gargaxes?" Steigan said, trying to remember what the demon had said. "So why would the gaxlor call the gargaxes his brethren? Why wouldn't he call them his followers?"

Ithanes looked annoyed, as if Steigan had asked a question he shouldn't have. "We've never had a gaxlor in captivity. Perhaps our understanding of their relationship is different than what we believe."

Steigan shook his head. "Nay, there was something wrong about that situation. Besides, why don't I still feel the fear that I first felt upon entering the castle?"

"What are you trying to say?" Searn asked.

Steigan turned to Searn. "I'm saying this is a ruse. There's no way that was a gaxlor in there." He looked across to Ithanes, who was watching him with a furrowed, worried brow.

Keteria entered through the open doors. She looked

angry and tired. "Cavalier Steigan, you will sit with Dominus Searn and attend him for the duration of the council meeting. Your conjecture is no longer needed."

Steigan nodded. "Very well." He took his seat quickly.

Keteria stepped up on the dais and sat down. She took a drink from a goblet placed on a little table beside her. "You have now witnessed the threat against us. 'Tis time to decide what needs to be done."

Ithanes turned in his chair to speak down the table to the others sitting with him. "We have to accept that the time of Lady Alityka's prophecy is upon us. I know we all dared to hope that we wouldn't have to deal with such an event during our lifetimes, yet we should be glad it falls on our shoulders and not our children's or our grandchildren's." He looked back to Keteria. "Dubinshire will stand with Lilinar against this evil threat."

"Lord Ithanes is correct," Rajed said. "The centaurs stand ready to assist."

"Thank you, Lord Ithanes and Lord Rajed," Keteria said. "Lord Ithanes, I will need your research on the prophecy."

He smiled in such a way that spoke of more than hubris. "A copy of the translations and my notes has already been prepared."

"I should have guessed."

Chuckles went up around the room, but Steigan didn't see the humor. They all seemed to know something about Ithanes that he didn't.

"Lord Krielic?" Keteria asked as if she'd been hoping the Lord of Montikovert would speak first but she could take his silence no longer.

Krielic sat back in his chair and tucked his fingers behind his head. "Cavalier Steigan has brought forth a good point. Something is not right here." He gave a smug and dramatic pause. "Your two kingdoms have been built on a prophecy that the gargaxes would one day return. Why are you not prepared for this?"

"'Tis been nearly a thousand years. Do you not see that after several generations without signs of the gargaxes, our families would decide that this legend might just have been a story rather than truth?"

Krielic smiled as if anticipating her answer like a rabbit hopping into a trap. "So you are daring to say that your religion is but a paltry false story you continue to follow?"

Keteria looked to the floor as if she could hide her emotions and her speechlessness away from everyone in the room. Ithanes came to her rescue.

"Our young princess only means that we have become

lax in our preparations," he said. "We realize this and admit this. Our people will all pay the price unless we come together to solve this as Rivic told us we'd need to."

"Maybe 'tis time for the mighty powers of Lilinar and Dubinshire to fall."

"Our cities won't be the only ones that fall under attack," Ithanes said. "Once they take Lilinar and Dubinshire, Montikovert will be next. Followed by Hallon and every other city, town, village, and fief. Do you not understand that nothing will be left?"

Steigan found himself enthralled by Ithanes' speech. The Lord of Dubinshire's voice rang out forcefully, yet softened in such a lilting way that it commanded the attention of everyone in the room. Only now, as Ithanes let the unspoken implications hang on his words did Steigan realize the severity of the situation.

"Then what do you propose to do about it?" Krielic asked.

Keteria looked up with a light of hope in her eyes. "We have to find out how the gaxlors and gargaxes were originally driven out. The record has to be there in the histories of our cities. We have to search. In the meanwhile, we've got to bring our armies together to try to keep the number of gargaxes small. We can't keep them from coming, but we can keep them from overwhelming us."

Steigan felt proud as he watched her rising to be the ruler she would be. With the looming threat so near, she knew exactly what to do.

"I thought that was what the enchantment placed on Rivic's lineage was meant to do." Krielic stood up and shook his head. "Princess Keteria, Lord Ithanes, for a thousand years you have been negligent. You trusted none of the prophecies would ever come true, at least not in your lifetime. Leave it to someone else! Here we are now, at the end of your rope, and you wish to hang all of us with the inch you have left."

"Rulers of Montikovert have always been weak," Ithanes said in a chained calm. "Danger comes and you chose to remain neutral until you can no longer. Then you hide in the shadows of Dubinshire like a kid with the blankets over his head."

Krielic slammed his hand on the table. "How dare you?"

"Now is not the time for petty disagreements." Keteria removed her circlet, placed it on her knee, and rubbed her forehead. "'Tis time to quit being rulers of our countries and be leaders for our people."

Rajed clapped. "Well spoken, Princess Keteria."

She still looked tired. "I want you all to pull your

histories together and share with me your findings. I need your oldest spells, no matter how arcane. If it dates back to the time of Gohaldinest, I require it."

Steigan felt a shock at hearing the name Gohaldinest, having always thought it an imaginary realm where temptation reigned. But now it seemed the place might be based in history. Nearly everyone made the sign of a circle on their forehead then over their heart while whispering to themselves, "Goddess protect." Only Keteria, Steigan, Krielic, and the centaurs didn't.

Keteria scoffed as she rolled her eyes and looked up the ceiling. With an exasperated sigh, she said, "Now is not the time for superstition either. The only way we will work out what Alityka and Rivic originally did is to work together to find the truth."

Krielic touched his Sacred Knight's arm and Hurnric stood by his lord. "This does not involve Montikovert," Krielic decreed. "We will not lend any resources to this venture which only seeks to remind the populace of the iron hold of the lands of Alityka and Rivic. We will not subjugate ourselves to your power again, not after finally becoming a free people."

Keteria sank back in her chair as Krielic and Hurnric left.

"You tried," Ithanes said to Keteria.

She gave him a sour look as if he'd said something she really didn't like, as if more meaning lay behind his two words. "We should adjourn for lunch. Afterward, I do believe some research into the extent of the situation is required." She paused. "Chief Rajed, if you and Laurient will contact the other tribes to see if there have been anymore sightings, it would be appreciated. Your alliances will go much faster than any I have. I am sorry we have failed here today."

Rajed nodded.

Ithanes leaned forward over his folded arms and spoke softly to Keteria. "You realized there is nothing more you can do."

"Holy Sapere Kelan and my domini, if you will begin researching at the Temple while Ithanes updates me on his notes, I think we'll cover the most ground," Keteria said, clearly ignoring Ithanes. "Dominus Searn, if you and Cavalier Steigan will attend me this afternoon and assist with High Maege Leloran, we can cover my library."

Steigan's heart leapt as he looked at Searn to see his response. Not only would he be staying in the castle, but he'd actually be serving Keteria.

She stepped down from the dais. Everyone stood to watch her go. After she left the room, Searn motioned for

Steigan to go. "Come on," he said. "You've got to be hungry."

Steigan glanced back over his shoulder to see Ithanes speaking to the centaurs. Laurient waved and Steigan shyly raised his hand in reply. As he and Searn went down the hall, Steigan asked, "Who is this Lord Ithanes? And why does Dubinshire have a Holy Sapere? I thought there could only be one."

"Dubinshire is a kingdom in the east that sits up on a high cliff. Amazing view," Searn said as if enjoying a long distant memory. Montikovert is a port town below Dubinshire and until recently it was part of Dubinshire's domain much like my fief is part of the kingdom of Lilinar."

That explained the animosity between Ithanes and Krielic and why the centaurs had been sitting between them.

"Lord Ithanes is High Lord of Dubinshire," Searn explained, "which means he's equal to King Cirello. Dubinshire has never liked all the titles so they try to keep it simple. Dubinshire, being its own kingdom, does have its own Holy Sapere."

Searn stopped and looked both ways down the hall. He waited for Danis to go around them. Searn continued, "What's important to understand about Dubinshire is that their ruling family is directly tied to the Goddess. Lady Alityka fell in the last major battle with the leader of the gargaxes. There wasn't even a body to return. Sapere Rivic set Alityka's family up to rule in Dubinshire. She had prophesized that the gargaxes would return and that we needed to be ready for them. That is what Rivic really sought to pass on to future generations. They hold all the original magical texts, have the written history of what happened back then, and have all the first ceremonial tomes. Rivic walked away from all that. There are some historians that have speculated that he was really banished."

"But he obviously came this way and settled down here, and set up another Temple," Steigan said.

"Correct," Searn said with a nod, "but there are subtle differences. Dubinshire is more superstitious and Lilinar holds tradition to the letter."

"Why is that so important, especially now? I don't see that it should matter."

"When Alityka's family only wanted to glorify what she'd done, Rivic knew he had to prepare people for what was to come. People needed knowledge and training. When he settled Lilinar, he built upon that premise."

Steigan was starting to see that Krielic was correct when he said that Lilinar had been following a false story as the basis for their religion. Could worship of a once living person even be right? "But he was recreating everything

Dubinshire had?" he asked. "If they hold all the original texts, why aren't we going there to research?"

"You're right. We cannot know how accurate our knowledge is. Now we've been very blessed. The friendship Alityka and Rivic had forged a bond that has held Dubinshire and Lilinar together since their time, even with the slight disagreement Rivic had with her family." Searn went to a window and leaned against the sill while he looked out.

Steigan sensed something was wrong. "What?"

"I personally worry…" He turned away from the window. "Nay, I shouldn't be getting into it."

"Cousin, tell me."

Searn looked at Steigan with sad blue eyes. "I heard a prophecy once from Ithanes' father that one day Lilinar would be no more and Dubinshire would stand alone, that black-sailed ships would bring invaders to attack Dubinshire, and the harbor of Montikovert would run red with the blood of men and centaurs."

"Why would this happen? What would cause it?"

"I asked that very question." A quiet calm came over Searn's face as he seemed to war within himself if he could repeat the answer or not. His gaze darted away from Steigan as he once against looked back down the hall, then came solidly back to Steigan. "Because the Destroyer of Civilization will take his revenge on a son of Rivic."

"Destroyer of Civilization?" Steigan asked, trying not to laugh. "A bit melodramatic, don't you think? Who's to say that this isn't just a story?"

Ithanes came around the corner toward them, his knowing smile on his calm face. "Because some sights that a seer has are variable and can be changed if someone modifies their actions. But those written in The Revelations always come to pass. They are unchangeable." He put his hand on Searn's shoulder. "Now, Dominus, you do seem to have a one-sided view of Dubinshire."

"Is that what you see?" Searn asked.

The smile grew slightly. "Well played, Dominus. I didn't come to trade clever words with you though. I was wondering if I might have a moment alone with Cavalier Steigan."

"The boy is hungry. I took him away from his morning meal and he's had quite the day so far. Too much information on an empty stomach isn't good for a growing lad."

Ithanes seemed to become stone still. He blinked slowly and the smile seemed to fade ever so slightly. "Three cycles I will take and when he returns to you, you will know my prophecy is true."

"What does that mean?" Searn asked sharply.

"Nothing to you now, but when the time comes you will know what must be done for Lilinar."

The air seemed to snap around Ithanes, like little fire flashes hanging in the air for an instant before vanishing. Searn pulled Steigan away, even while he watched the phenomena.

"Come, Steigan. We must get there while there's still food for you," Searn said.

They left Ithanes standing in the hallway. Once they'd gone downstairs and turned a couple corners, Steigan stopped Searn.

"What did he mean?" Steigan asked, trying desperately to understand. "What did he do?"

"He was relaying a vision he had of you," Searn answered with anger like a razor on his voice.

"Was that what he was doing back there? 'Twas like the air was crackling around him."

Searn looked at him like he didn't understand what Steigan was saying. "I don't know. I'm sure Ithanes is up to something."

"I don't like him very much."

The started down the hallway again.

"He's powerful," Searn said, "and his magic is very dedicated. It makes me uneasy. 'Tis hard to not wonder what he sees in your future when he looks at you."

Steigan felt there was more and was about to ask when Searn continued, "He's also made his feelings for Princess Keteria very plain. He would seek a union between Dubinshire and Lilinar by marriage."

Even though they kept walking, Searn looked out a window as they walked by.

"But a child, descendant of Alityka's and Rivic's own lineages," Searn continued, sounding like he was already a million miles off in thought, "that could be the very one which destroys Lilinar and brings Dubinshire to ruin."

Chapter Twenty

Steigan sat with Searn at a long table, a plate piled with bread, cheese, and fruit before him. He looked at the rest of the feast before him thinking that supper at the Temple never looked so good.

But with so much before him, he felt like he ate like a pauper because of what was going on at the end of the table. He put his hand up and leaned his head into the palm so it acted like a blinder to keep him from seeing.

Still, he knew. He could feel the energy of the conversation from where he sat. He wondered what had Keteria and Ithanes engaged in such adamant talk.

He picked at his food. He wouldn't look. He'd focus on what he was doing here and now.

It wasn't working.

Steigan caught Ithanes glancing down the table at him. Ithanes turned back to Keteria with a smile, leaning in close, and sending Steigan another sidelong glance.

If it hadn't been for Keteria's reaction, he might have put his hand back up. Her mouth agape, she shook her head and started arguing with Ithanes. They exchanged sharp words which Steigan couldn't make out. Then Keteria reached up into the air, flicked her fingers sideways like she was sliding open a cabinet door and reached inside.

For an instant, her fingers disappeared before reappearing with a book in her hands.

"What?" Steigan whispered. He nudged Searn. "Did you see that? What did she just do?"

Searn looked up from his meal. "What did she do?"

"She pulled a book out of nowhere as though she had it stored on an invisible bookshelf."

"Dimensional magic." Searn shrugged. "Where Ithanes can see the future, Keteria can work some impressive dimensional magic. Her father even sent her to Dubinshire for several months of dedicated study when she was younger."

So she and Ithanes had a long history between them,

Steigan thought enviously. Steigan tried not to focus on that. "So she's moved the book out of another dimension into ours? Isn't she afraid she'll lose them?"

"Sorry, you're talking to a generalist here. I don't understand the deeper workings of the specialized magic."

"Could anything be put out there like that?" Steigan asked, still curious.

"Finish your meal, Steigan. We'll soon have to be off to work."

Steigan ate mechanically while he watched Keteria flip through the pages of the tome and pointed something out to Ithanes, who laughed in response.

Goddess, how Steigan hated Ithanes. He couldn't just sit here and do nothing while Ithanes tickled Keteria's fancy down at the other end of the table. He nudged Searn again. "Lord Ithanes wanted to see me earlier. Do you think it would be all right if I went to see him now?"

Searn raised an eyebrow. "I really don't see why you'd want to find out what he has to say to you."

Steigan looked back down at Keteria. He just didn't know of another way to separate the two. "I think he'll keep asking until I do and I also think you're very right about your theory. Bad magic wrapped up in that package."

"A little jealous, are we?"

"What possible reason could *you* have to be jealous?" Steigan joked as he started to get up from the table. "But I do have enough for the both of us."

"Steigan, be careful."

Steigan skirted the side of the table and came up behind Keteria so he could look directly at Ithanes. Bowing, he said, "You had requested my presence earlier. I am available now if you wish."

Ithanes looked at Keteria and gave her that knowing smile Steigan hated. To his relief, she seemed not to notice Ithanes at all, but had turned in her chair to stare up at Steigan.

"I did," Ithanes said. "Actually Princess Keteria had a brilliant idea if you were game for such."

Steigan looked at Keteria and he felt the muscles in his face soften and his heartbeat quicken. "A brilliant idea from Princess Keteria? That's not a hard one to imagine."

Color flooded into her cheeks.

Now Ithanes looked irritated. "She told me of your unfortunate circumstances and that 'tis believed you are a cousin to the dominus you currently serve."

Steigan didn't know whether he should be appalled that Ithanes knew all about him or glad because Keteria had been talking about him. What he did like was seeing the look of jealousy now signaled in Ithanes' eyes.

Ithanes continued, "There is a ritual, one rarely performed and extremely complicated in magic, but it looks at the bloodwave and pinpoints your location within it. It might unlock your heritage."

Steigan felt his heart beat faster. He now stood on a precipice of a question he wanted the answer to, yet he feared. Ithanes had just offered Steigan the one thing that could tempt him more than getting his memories back: to prove his lineage. It would mean that no one could keep him from being a dominus. But if he was related to Searn, he'd also find himself related to Keteria. Could he start denying the emotions he felt for her, emotions which weren't becoming in a family? Could he stop his own magic from calling out to hers?

"What do I need to do?" Steigan asked.

Ithanes clapped his hands together and kept them clasped. "I never expected so easy of an agreement. Perfect," Ithanes said. "'Tis really quite simple. I would need only for you to sit through the ritual and give me but a drop or two of your blood."

"When can we do it?"

"Eager even, isn't he?" Ithanes reached out to Keteria and put his hands over hers as though excited that they had succeeded at whatever they had plotted up together without Steigan's knowledge. "So, Princess, when can we perform the ceremony?"

Keteria looked up at Steigan. She sounded breathless as she spoke. "This very night in the library. After evening prayers and meal?"

"Wonderful. I look forward to discovering what we will. It should be exciting," Ithanes said as he rose from the table. "Now, if you will excuse me, I need to rest for a few moments before we reconvene to research."

Steigan noticed the fallen look on Keteria's face. Had she sensed the same thing in Ithanes' words that he had? A sense that Ithanes already knew what they would find? Steigan followed Ithanes out of the great hall.

"A moment please, Lord Ithanes," Steigan requested.

Ithanes kept walking. "Time is preciously short, Cavalier. Ask me on the way."

Steigan caught up to Ithanes. "Have you already seen the outcome of this spell?"

"If I knew the answer, don't you think I'd just say it? I have no need to use my power for expanded parlor tricks."

"Then why did you say it should be exciting? 'Twas like you already knew something."

"As I said, the bloodvision spell isn't performed very

often. When it needs to be performed, 'tis always because the circumstances are unusual. Those are always exciting. All of us will just have to wait to see what happens."

Steigan stopped and bowed. "Thank you for explaining, Lord Ithanes. Rest well."

Ithanes gave a dismissive wave of his hand and carried on down the hall. Steigan watched him for a moment, but before he turned, Ithanes stopped and pivoted around. "There will be a surprise for Keteria though. That I do foresee," Ithanes said.

Ithanes continued down the hall, leaving Steigan with a feeling of cold fear injected into his veins. It wasn't Ithanes usual pompous knowing way, but rather a warning. He couldn't let Keteria go into that unknowing.

Steigan ran back to the great hall in time to see Keteria ascending a stairway. He raced through the room and took the stairs two at a time, nearly knocking over a couple of servants in his pursuit. "Princess Keteria, please wait," he called out.

Keteria turned, her eyes looking tired again. "I was just on my way to see my father. Can this wait?"

"Nay, I'm sorry, it can't. But it won't take long."

Keteria nodded to the knights surrounding her and they stepped off so that Keteria could move off privately with Steigan.

"Milady," he said, "I am most grateful that you have asked Lord Ithanes to perform a bloodvision spell in order to discover my lineage, but I must ask what your true motive is."

A quick play of emotions danced across her face. "My motive is for the truth. We've played this game for long enough. 'Tis time to discover who you really are."

"Is there no other way?"

Keteria looked down. "Tanold has sent messengers in every direction. All have returned with no information."

"So you would just stop with only that action?"

"I've consulted every oracle I know. I even asked Ithanes to…" The admission became too much for her and she looked away.

Steigan waited, hoping she'd find the words and the strength she needed to tell him.

Finally she looked up at him. "I asked Ithanes to do a look-back."

Steigan shrugged, trying to see what was so bad about that, why it had been so hard for her to say it. "What's that?"

"'Tis future-sight in reverse. It goes back over a person's timeline to see where they've been. 'Tis very useful in finding the perpetrator of a crime."

"I take it that since you want to do a bloodvision spell, the look-back failed."

She rolled her eyes as she shook her head, clearly frustrated. "The spell went back to the moment you were found on the road, but all your memories of your life before that incident are locked away, even from magical means."

Steigan thought on this for a moment. "Do you think it could've been done on purpose, maybe because we're not supposed to find out who I am? Could magic be locking away my memories?"

"Don't say things like that," she said, avoiding looking at him. "The person capable of that would be dangerous. You'd be a liability."

"So 'tis possible then?"

She brought her tear-filled gaze up quickly. "Should I lock you away in the dungeons to rot your life away? Is that what you want?"

"Nay, but –"

"That's what you're asking for if you keep going with this line of thought."

"But there must be another way. I just have a feeling that this bloodvision spell is a bad idea."

She raised her chin and claimed her full height. No longer were tears glazing her eyes. "Let me put this very simply. I am your princess and I want this matter put to rest. I am ordering you to go through with the bloodvision spell."

Irritated at her having pulled rank on him, he shoved his emotions down as far as he could and stomped on them. Bowing, he said, "Very well, my princess. As you wish it."

Keteria stepped around him and went down the hall with her knights. He still had a bad feeling about this but now it was her command. Whatever came now was her own doing.

CHAPTER TWENTY-ONE

Steigan waited in the library, his hands on the window sill as he looked out toward the Temple and the lake. The stone of the Temple cast an orange light in the setting sun and the water looked dark beneath it. With his presence now being ordered, Steigan wanted evening to hurry so he could have this done.

He turned away from the window and looked at the rows of books around the room. This afternoon, it had been a bustle of activity in here with them digging through the texts for old spells or any reference to the gargaxes.

It hadn't amounted to much. What they had found had

been so minor and vague.

Two knights entered and looked around the room before taking up positions on each side of the door. After a moment, Keteria entered.

"Ithanes hasn't arrived yet?" she asked.

Steigan shook his head, "'Tis just you and me here."

Keteria sat down at a table, the same chair she'd been at earlier, and began tapping her fingers on the polished wood.

Since she said nothing further to him, he returned to the window and looked out. The orange cast on the Temple was fading. One moon sat on the horizon and a second moon currently rising had a faint glow behind the mountains. Fires were being lit on the edges of the inner city where the shadow of the wall had left them in darkness. The flames looked like sparkling gems.

"'Tis a beautiful night out." Steigan said.

"What's keeping him?" Keteria responded.

"Maybe he had to rest some more," Steigan said, almost needling. "I take it that this whole experience has been tiring for him."

Keteria looked up angrily. "Don't let him fool you. He doesn't have a weak constitution, regardless of what he'd rather have you believe. I promise, you haven't seen the man he truly is."

"You know him well?" Steigan asked, approaching the table. He wondered how Keteria felt about Ithanes. "Searn said that your father sent you to train in Dubinshire for a while."

"Aye, I was thirteen cycles and Ithanes fifteen when we met. I stayed at the castle in Dubinshire for almost a whole cycle. Talk about homesick. I was so glad to get back."

"Tanold wasn't with you then?"

Keteria looked up with shock. "Nay, he wasn't. Ithanes became my surrogate brother while I was there, but it wasn't the same. Ithanes knew what I was going to do before I did it, but he didn't know my thoughts. Not the way Tanold does."

"Was it strange having Ithanes know everything before you did it?"

"You want to know if Ithanes' future sight creeps me out?" She let a crack of a smile show. "Nay, it doesn't. I can't imagine him without the ability. I've always accepted it as part of him just as Tanold is part of me."

Steigan slipped into a chair and leaned forward toward her. "The time away didn't dull your connection with Tanold?"

"Not at all. 'Twas like we'd never parted. Even more, we seemed to know what each other had been doing that whole time." She gave another a little smile.

Her tone made Steigan wonder if he'd had any brothers or sisters and if he had as deep a connection with any of them. If so, why hadn't they sought him out? Did no one wonder where he was, what he was doing? Did no one care?

He shook the thought from him, wishing it had never come. It didn't matter. Even after he'd found his place on the bloodwave, it wouldn't matter. As far as he knew, Searn was the only relation that had shown him any courtesy and was the only one due Steigan's loyalty.

The door opened and Ithanes entered in a sweep of black robes and gold ornamentation which clinked as he walked. Swirling black marks adorned his cheeks, temples, and forehead.

Steigan's head swam from the flood of magic that washed over him as Ithanes approached the table. The air crackled so intensely that Steigan wanted to draw back.

"Good evening. Are we ready to begin?" Even before anyone answered, Ithanes closed his eyes and let his shoulders relax. "Keteria, if you please…"

With a wave of her hand, Keteria dismissed her guard.

Ithanes tipped back his head, exhaling a deep breath through his mouth, and then took in another concentrated inhalation.

"Is there something I need to do?" Steigan asked.

"Quiet please," Ithanes snapped.

The table disappeared from in front of Steigan and Ithanes stepped directly before him.

"Steigan, your origins unknown, your family hidden, memories sealed away in time," Ithanes said. "We seek to unlock some of these mysteries. Do you submit your will to my sight?"

Steigan looked at Keteria, who nodded.

"I do," Steigan answered.

"I am told you believe you are part of the family of Rivic. What proof do have you?"

Steigan turned his right palm upwards. "The birthmark said to appear on all males of Rivic's lineage."

"But you have no idea where you fall on his line?"

"Nay."

"Then having been granted your permission, I take your blood." Ithanes put one hand below and one above Steigan's offered hand.

At first Steigan felt coldness on his skin, then a pinch in his palm. He fought to keep from flinching away, especially as the ~~pain grew~~ and flared. Steigan drew a sharp breath while locking his shoulder to keep from yanking his hand away.

Ithanes withdrew and held before Steigan the source of the coldness he'd felt: a translucent purple gem which had a white swirl curling around like smoke inside. On Ithanes' other hand Steigan saw a band with a small blade attached to it.

Steigan looked down at his palm. A tiny slit ran like a red line splitting the torch-shaped birthmark in two and blood swelled from the line.

"Vapidious," Ithanes said.

Magic swept over Steigan's skin. The cut instantly healed and the blood disappeared. Inside the gem, the white swirl turned red.

"Blocadious tor'na vakan primidious tooka." Ithanes closed his eyes, but not completely, leaving mere slits where Steigan could see Ithanes' blue eyes flickering behind the lids. Ithanes' mouth opened slowly and his body trembled like he was having some sort of seizure. Slower, louder, and more pronounced, Ithanes repeated, "Blocadious tor'na vakan primidious tooka."

Steigan looked to Keteria who watched Ithanes intently while biting down on the side of her index finger.

Ithanes stopped shaking and opened his eyes to look down. Upon seeing Ithanes' gaze completely red, Steigan jumped as memories of the gargaxes flashed through him.

"I see the bloodwave," Ithanes spoke, "and I see your position upon it. Who comes forth to test his position?"

Keteria's fingers were quivering. "I do."

Ithanes turned to her. "Your heritage is known?"

"Aye. I am daughter of King Cirello of Lilinar."

"Very well. Submit."

Keteria held out her hand and Ithanes took it like he had Steigan's. She winced and closed her eyes, teeth clenched. A tear slipped between her lashes.

Steigan started to reach out to her and wanted to tell Ithanes to stop, but Ithanes was already pulling away, leaving similar mark on her hand.

"Vapidious," Ithanes said. The cut was healed and the blood gone, disappeared into the gem. "Blocadious vakan sectido lachar."

Ithanes tipped his head back as he looked up. His eyes moved back and forth as if reading a book suspended above his head.

Steigan realized that Ithanes searched desperately for something.

Softly, Ithanes spoke while still looking up, "Keteria, I need you to go for Searn."

Only now did Steigan also realize that Ithanes' voice hadn't been his own the whole time he'd been in the room with them. He'd been under the influence of magic from the moment he entered.

"Hurry," Ithanes said with a restrained softness. Steigan felt Ithanes trying to hold onto the intense spell while being separated from it. For one moment, it felt as if Ithanes had split himself in two.

Keteria got up. "Talcor dun." She took a step forward and disappeared. A moment later she reappeared with Searn at her side. Searn wore his evening clothes of soft leggings and a long tunic.

Searn assessed the situation quickly. "What's going on here? Keteria said 'twas urgent."

"I need a third heritage marker," Ithanes said, his voice still quietly level as he fought to keep himself detached from the spell.

"Then there is not a match?" Keteria said.

Ithanes started to tremble again as he merged back into the spell. "Who comes forth to test Steigan's position on the bloodwave?" His voice had returned to the commanding magical presence.

Searn looked angrily down at Steigan but stepped forward offering his hand toward Ithanes. "I guess I do."

Ithanes turned stiffly toward Searn. "Your heritage is known?"

"'Tis. I am son of Tanisha, a daughter of Rivic's lineage."

"You bear the mark of Rivic?"

"I do." Searn turned his angry glare to Keteria. "I can't believe you didn't tell me you were going to search the bloodwave for him." Searn's words were broken with a small pause as ~~the again~~ hit him.

"Vapidious," Ithanes said and Steigan noticed he sounded weak. "Blocadious vakan trido lachar."

Again, he went back to reading the unseen above him then his eyes locked on something invisible to Steigan. He looked back down at Steigan with those scary red eyes. "To the family of Rivic you do belong," Ithanes said, "and cousin to Searn. Your markers are close."

Ithanes pointed a finger at Keteria. "Your marker on the bloodwave does not exist. You are a child without." His voice sounded full of damning condemnation. "You are a banished one."

Keteria drew a sharp breath, her hands going to her chest as if covering her heart from evil words. "Look again. I am a cousin to Searn. My marker should be there."

"You are a banished one," Ithanes repeated before suddenly going limp.

Searn kicked out a foot and used it to grab a chair to slide under Ithanes as he collapsed. The chair rocked and nearly tipped over, but Searn caught it and set Ithanes upright. The bands on Ithanes' hands slid off and dropped to the rug on the stone floor.

"That can't be right. I'm Cirello's daughter." She took Ithanes' hand. "Come on, Ithanes, this isn't a joke."

Searn growled, "Keteria, back off. Lord Ithanes is not in any condition to handle your rebuttals."

Ithanes leaned forward and put his head in his hands, supporting himself with his elbows on his knees. He breathed heavily.

Steigan looked between Searn and Keteria. "What does it mean?"

Searn's eyes were still full of rage. "It means you are my cousin, just as I knew you were. Keteria, however –"

Ithanes raised his head and said boldly, "Stop! Speak not another word. If you say it 'twill be treason."

Searn took two steps away then whirled back to them. "She is the one who pushed the issue!"

"I had to know, Searn," Keteria said as she came out of her chair and grabbed his arm. "Not knowing was killing me."

Searn looked at her and seemed to calm some. He glanced back and forth between Keteria and Steigan several times. "Then explain your motives to him so he will know why he must keep up the pretense that this never happened."

"By 'him' I presume you mean me," Steigan asked. "I

wish you'd quit speaking about me like I was still mute."

Searn appeared about to yell at Steigan, then scowled at Keteria and sneered with more fury than Steigan had ever seen before. He took a step in close to her, then waved his hand like he might hit her and backed off. "I'm done here, aren't I, Ithanes? You got your set marker, right?"

Ithanes, with his head once again in his hands, nodded and said breathlessly, "You're done."

Searn waved his arms again like he was casting them all away. "Explain it to him, Keteria. Explain it, and then speak of this night no more." At the door, he paused but didn't look back as he said, "And explain why he still can't carry his rightful title as dominus."

Keteria looked on the verge of tears as Searn slammed the door behind him.

"Is this the surprise you spoke of?" Steigan asked Ithanes.

Ithanes sat back in the chair and nodded. His whole body sagged with weariness from the spell.

"Steigan..." Keteria said. She started to reach for him, then pulled back and covered her face as she sobbed.

Steigan stood up. "I think I'll follow Searn's example. This evening didn't happen." He walked out the door and didn't look back.

Chapter Twenty-Two

Standing on the castle battlements, Steigan watched the stars. Tonight's two moons were close together leaving plenty of sky remaining. He looked toward the mountains, their silhouettes dark against the night. He could make out a small dot of light, a campfire perhaps, on the mountainside and he wondered what it would be like to live out there, far away from the madness of these people.

A shooting star blazed across his vision. He felt he should make a wish, but had none to offer. His dreams might as well be as far away and elusive as the moons; he could see them, reach for them even, but he could never touch them or make them his. There had to be some way to get his memories back. As for his lineage, he knew he was Searn's cousin. That, however, had never been in much doubt, not considering how much they looked alike and the fact they both bore the torch-shaped birthmark. Of course, without proof of his identity, he'd never be allowed his title of dominus.

The rest of what had happened tonight with the bloodvision was nonsense.

He made a wish quickly, hoping it wasn't too late. He prayed that if he had any more memories to lose, he'd forget this evening so it would be like it never happened.

"I had a feeling you'd go out for some air," Searn said behind him.

Steigan shrugged. "Seemed like the best way to get away without actually leaving the castle."

Searn leaned with his back against the merlon and crossed his arms. "I hope she explained everything well enough."

"She explained nothing. I told her I didn't want to know. I thought it would be best if it had never happened."

"You are a better man than I, Steigan."

"Can I go back to the Temple in the morning?"

Searn gave him a shocked look.

"The gaxlor, 'tis a ruse," Steigan explained.

"Aye, 'twas a ruse," Searn admitted. "Because of the vision from Ithanes' father written in The Revelations, Keteria believes we need Montikovert to stand with us. She feels Lord Krielic's support is vital. They had hoped bringing you in would rally Krielic to their side."

"Instead, I undid their plan. Have I ruined it all? Is there nothing that can be done to stop the gargaxes from returning?"

"If there is a way, Keteria will find it. That's why we've got to research."

Steigan turned away. "I don't know what we're looking for in the library. I understand none of it. 'Tis like the context has been removed from my whole life. So I'd do better resuming my studies at the Temple."

"That's actually why I was coming to see you."

Steigan felt relief at being allowed to return to the Temple and knowing that Searn had had the same idea.

Searn sighed deeply. "After learning that you weren't getting the magical training I requested, I had someone look further into the issue for me. Danis came to see me shortly after I returned to my room tonight."

Steigan started to tell Searn about Danis and how the Sacred Knight had refused to teach him magic, but Searn raised a hand and stopped him. "He told me everything. He told me about Tanold's orders. He told me more. 'Twould seem that magical studies aren't only missing from your training but from nearly everyone's."

"What does that mean?"

"At this point I can only speculate, but I suspect a plot against the domini. As soon as the matter with the gargaxes is settled, I'll be doing something about it. Centhya and I should be able to cut to the chase in short order."

"I will be glad to act as your eyes and ears to gather what information I can while I'm there," Steigan offered.

Searn's lips tightened with decision. "You won't be going back. I've already decided that Centhya and I will train you. 'Tis what we should've been doing all along."

The revelation felt like bricks hitting him.

"But my friends…"

"Will still be your friends," Searn said. "You can see them practically any time you want."

"It won't be the same. I enjoy training with them."

"But they can't give you the knowledge you need either. Being at the Temple right now is a complete waste of your time."

"Why?" Steigan asked angrily. "Why do I need to have this knowledge? Why is training me up so important? Why isn't everyone else's training just as important?"

"Because their bloodline isn't so close to the royal family as yours is."

"But you said yourself that I still can't claim to be a dominus. Without that title, Searn, I'm nobody."

"There is another way, if you are willing to be patient," Searn said, raising his gaze to the sky. "We can prove you are a close cousin to me. I've felt ever since I saw you that you had to be my aunt Seleaha's son. Which brings us to our issue. Since Cirello banished his sister, only he can allow her kinsmen back into Lilinar."

Steigan didn't want to say anything or get his hopes up only to have them crushed again, but he also could put two and two together. He scoffed as he looked off toward that distant fire on the mountain. "What you're saying is that if Cirello realizes that I'm here and I'm Seleaha's son, then I'm guilty of breaking her banishment."

"One step at a time. Patience," Searn said. "Aye, we do need to wait until the king has a day when he's feeling like his old self, but then 'tis merely a mention of if her family would be allowed back to Lilinar."

A mention? *If*. His fate would rest on a question? "And if he says nay?" Steigan asked.

"Do you always look for the worst case scenario?"

"I know where the odds are placed. So, if Cirello does have a good day which gives me a good day, does Ithanes just have to come forward to prove I'm part of the same bloodwave?"

"We can't use Ithanes again, but there are plenty of other maeges who can do the spell," Searn said.

"Why can't Ithanes just say he saw it?"

"'Tis a spell that doesn't get performed very often because it's irrefutable and it can only be performed once on a person by a maege. For this reason, it's usually performed in front of the whole court."

"So Ithanes is unable to perform it on me again to prove I am your cousin?"

Searn nodded. "Also, if Ithanes confessed to what he saw for you, he'd have to say who the marker was. If someone didn't believe him, a look-back might be performed."

"Keteria."

"Aye. I don't think she knew what he would find."

"Why? Why would she do it, and do it in private?"

"She's lucky she did." Searn looked around to see where the guards were at in their rounds. He kept his voice low as he continued, "I can't say for certain, but I have my theory. You have to understand, there are few people who can match her magically. Ithanes, Leloran, and a mere handful of other people I can think of immediately. Even Centhya doesn't quite match Keteria's power, though Centhya can hold her own quite well." He finished his sentence with a smile evoked from a memory and for a moment Searn looked lost in recalling the incident. Then he continued, "You, however, surpass what Keteria has. More than that, your magic 'tis wild, unchained and unbroken. 'Tis like dancing with fire. It calls to her."

"You make it sound so dangerous."

"'Tis, for her. But you also have to understand that 'tis more than just physical. Magic is a whole other level. How can I best explain it?" Searn looked around before pointing at the lake. "Ah, there. Water always takes the path of least resistance. It flows to where it can gather. As it gathers, it takes the shape of whatever holds it, whether 'tis a lake or a cup or a rut in the road. When there is too much water to fill the space, it overflows and continues until it finds another spot to fill.

"You are overflowing with magic. It comes off you in waves. Most people already have as much magic as they can handle and they feel the ripple of your magic but it doesn't disturb their puddle too much. Keteria is in constant flow. She works her magic like 'tis part of her. She knows she can take your overflow and work it into hers. 'Tis easy and addictive.

She doesn't have to wait to regain her power with you at her side. 'Twould be there for her, all the time," Searn said.

Steigan hated thinking that Keteria would just use his power, that the magic was the only reason she wanted him around. He smacked his hand against the stone barbican. "Stop!"

"You can't let this go on, for her sake."

"Goddess, do you think..." Steigan rubbed his hands over his face as he tried to find the right words. What would Searn's reaction to the truth be? Steigan continued, "You said it. This magic is wild. I don't know how to use it. I barely know how to control it. And Keteria tells me that half of it is stolen magic. Why would she even want to –"

"Stolen magic?"

Steigan realized Searn had never been told and began to speak quickly as if to explain himself before Searn could pass judgment. "I don't know how or when, Searn. I can't even release it. Keteria tells me that whoever I took it from is probably dead. Does that make me a murderer and a thief?" He wrapped his arms around himself and rocked back and forth against the stone wall. "Searn, I want to go home. I don't belong here. I don't fit in. Why am I here?"

Searn put his hand on Steigan's shoulder. "I'll summon a carriage. You can stay at the Temple tonight if you wish.

Then tomorrow I'll send you on with a letter for Centhya."

Steigan felt like his insides were about to split apart. "That's not home."

"So where's home?"

He ran his hands over his arms. "I don't know. Not here. This place..."

Deep laughter filtered through an open window somewhere in the castle below them followed by Keteria's shout, "Ithanes has never been wrong!"

Searn gave a sigh. "Let's go inside."

Steigan nodded and followed Searn. As they headed back toward Steigan's quarters, there was the sound of doors slamming and footsteps echoing through the castle. They came upon Keteria and Tanold in the great hall.

"I have the mark," Tanold argued. "Maybe I am a child of Cirello and you are not."

"We're twins! How would that even be possible?" Keteria yelled back at him.

"Maybe we were just told we were twins."

Keteria stepped up to Tanold with her hands curled into fists between them. "Then why would I be eldest? Why would Cirello put a child on the throne that wasn't part of Rivic's line?"

Searn hurried down the steps, but motioned for Steigan

to remain where he was. "You two need to keep it down."

"What does it matter?" Keteria asked. "Soon everyone will know the truth anyway."

"Keteria—"

Keteria interrupted, gesturing wildly and shouting as she did so. "I went to see my father. He told me! He admitted that I'm not his daughter, that Tanold and I were given to him by some arrangement. He also said 'twould be all right because the man who had taken his son and brought us to him had returned."

"You really need to calm down."

"Who's the man? Who's the stranger in our midst?" She circled around Searn and pointed up at Steigan. "Him!"

She headed for the base of the stairs like she was going to run up them. "How did you do it? Why? What were you, like negative three cycles old? You hadn't even been conceived when I was born!"

Searn grabbed her arm and pulled her back. "This is all some ridiculous dream you've had," he said calmly. "Now 'tis time to settle down before people start thinking you've gotten a touch of what your father has."

"He's not my father."

"Speak for yourself," Tanold said. "I lay no claim there."

"We're banished, Tanold. Don't you understand what that means?" At first, she sagged as if pleading for Tanold to understand, and then she threw herself back in Steigan's direction. "He's supposed to be banished! Seleaha's son. He belongs to the banished family. Not us. He's banished, not us. He's banished, not us." Her last words were bare mutters among her sobs as she buried her face in her hands.

Steigan wanted to go to her, to hold her, to shield her from these overwhelming emotions. "I'm sorry I bring you so much pain," he said, knowing it was the only thing he could do.

Searn stepped in front of Keteria and with a finger beneath her chin, made her look up at him. He made a circular gesture in front of her face. "Mezzipalor."

Keteria went limp into his arms. Searn gathered her up and carried her to Tanold.

"I'm betting she hasn't slept much lately," Searn said as he passed Keteria off to him. "Take her to her room. When she wakes she'll feel fully rested and I'm certain that her perspective will be much better."

"Thank you," Tanold said. "What was she going on about?"

"A bad dream of an imagined wrong is all. Stress is weakening her magical constitution. 'Tis easy to start seeing demons where there are none."

As Tanold took her upstairs and away down the hall, Searn returned to Steigan.

"I don't think I've ever seen you use magic before except for unlocking the tower door when we took Centhya to the Cauldron," Steigan said.

Searn smiled and gave a small chuckle. "You can thank the new baby for that spell. I've become quite practiced at it."

Steigan looked at the floor as they headed down the hallway. "I feel like this is all my fault."

"You can't take on her blame. Don't wear that mantle. This is all her doing."

"Aye, but she did it because of the attraction of our magic," Steigan said as they reached his quarters. He opened the door. "Were I not here, none of this would've happened. I don't want to cause more trouble tonight. I'll stay here. You can send me back to your fief tomorrow. Blessed evening, Searn."

He stepped inside and closed the door before Searn could respond. Leaning against it, he listened as Searn's footsteps faded down the hall. Steigan stood there, head back against the wood while he decided what to do next.

Chapter Twenty-Three

Steigan woke the next morning while the castle was still quiet. He kicked the blankets off him and sat up, looking around. Daylight tinted the window. He listened, but he wasn't sure for what noise.

He sensed something very wrong.

His skin felt like he was plunged in icy water, not to mention the tight feeling in his chest like he needed to fight or run.

Dressing, he looked around for something to use as a weapon. Unable to find anything, he transformed a chair into a sword with scabbard and silently thanked Jaxsen for this little trick. If something fouled the magic, he'd rather wind up with a chair in his hand rather than a candle.

Opening the door, he looked out into the hallway, surprised to see absolutely no one. This feeling...

Shaking, he closed the door behind him and started navigating the maze of stone hallways on instinct with no destination in mind. A couple knights roamed the corridors and he ducked out of view before they saw him, but Steigan felt the guard wasn't normal but rather reduced from what it should be for the protection of the royal family.

At last, Steigan found himself in a space he recognized: the room where the gaxlor was being held. Making sure no one had spotted him, he went inside.

From behind the protective glass, Steigan watched the demon move around in the cage. Not only was it smaller, but it now had wings. He wasn't sure he could trust what he saw. Was it really a gargax, or had the gaxlor metamorphed?

Slowly, he opened the door and went into the inner room with the demon.

The beast stopped pacing in its cage and closed its eyes. "I iz having my revengez. My revengez." In a crouched position, it undulated as though in deep mythical prayer. It opened its mouth and exhaled sharp breaths, sounding almost as if it were panting.

Steigan came forward, unsure of how close to get, yet fascinated. "You are a gargax, not a gaxlor?"

The gargax whirled and spread its wings. With a hiss, it rushed the walls of the cage. It seemed genuinely surprised and frightened.

"What are you doing?" Steigan asked, knowing that this feeling of wrongness came directly from the gargax.

The gargax folded its wings and hunkered down, looking very small. "The witchz... both of themz. Revengez I had for what they did."

"Who? What did they do?"

"The witchz, both of themz, they used mez." The gargax's voice grew frustrated. "Puppet on a stringz I waz to themz."

Steigan wanted to understand. "So 'twas you in here with me, not a gaxlor?"

"It waz."

"They changed you," Steigan said, touching the sword at his side, "to look like a gaxlor." He had known it was a ruse, even had that confirmed by Searn, but he hadn't imagined that Keteria would used magic to transform the gargax into a gaxlor.

The gargax backed off. "Why I tellz you this? Get outz!" It rushed the cage again.

Steigan drew his sword, afraid that the gargax would shift and come through the bars again, but it didn't. As he backed away from the angry, hissing beast, he wondered why it would remain in the cage if it could get through the bars. Had that been another illusion?

Once again in the room behind the reflective glass, Steigan watched the gargax a bit longer. It paced inside the cage, then sat back and started its chant again. Steigan wished he understood the gargaxes a bit better. This one seemed irritated, nay, *violated* at having been used. Was it possible that they had emotions? If so, wouldn't it also mean that magic had emotion since the gargaxes were magic-based life forms? Why else would magic want to create life?

He raised his right hand and flexed his fingers. The gargax was definitely doing something. On a level so deep, he felt it. He couldn't define it, but he sensed it like an abstract notion. All the way to the blood running through his veins, he knew a gargax's revenge wouldn't be good.

His skin began to crawl and he wrapped his arms around himself. Why did he seem to be the only one feeling this?

Steigan left the room and hurried toward Searn's quarters. If he'd stayed any longer, he'd go back in and kill the gargax. Whatever plans it had, they weren't good.

Searn would know what to do. He'd put forth his case to Searn and find out why they were keeping the gargax alive.

Hearing footsteps coming up behind him, Steigan looked for a place to hide. Before he found one, Sacred Knight Danis came running around the corner toward him.

Danis slowed to a stop. "Where's Searn? Is he still sleeping?"

"Aye," Steigan replied.

"Please fetch him while I get Princess Keteria."

"What's going on?"

"There's an incident at the Temple. Go quick." Danis continued running.

Steigan ran to Searn's quarters and pounded on the door until Searn opened it.

"What's going on?" Searn asked sleepily.

Steigan shook his head as if trying to indicate that he didn't have a whole lot of answers. "There's something going on at the Temple. Danis went to get Keteria."

"One moment."

The door closed in Steigan's face. He waited impatiently for it to reopen. When it did, Searn was dressed and trying to strap on his armor. Steigan stepped inside to help him buckle it.

"Have you seen them yet?" Searn asked.

Steigan assumed he meant Danis and Keteria. "Nay. 'Tis been quiet."

"Not a good sign."

That reminded Steigan of the initial reason he had been heading to Searn's. "I think the gargax is doing something."

Now prepared, Searn headed out of the room. "Impossible. 'Tis locked away."

The tone told Steigan to shut his mouth and follow Searn without arguing. On the way to Keteria's chambers, they met with Danis returning down the hall. Searn pivoted as Danis approached and matched the Sacred Knight's pace.

"What's going on?" Searn asked.

"I think Mierk is burning the books," Danis replied.

"Burning the books?"

Steigan quit lagging behind hoping that Keteria would catch up to them and hurried to join the other two men. "The originals or the translations?" he asked.

Danis shrugged. "I don't know. If I had to guess, I'd say the originals."

"Translations?" Searn asked. "Steigan, what do you know?"

Steigan ignored Searn. "Why would he do that? He promised Keteria he'd keep them safe."

"He never said any such thing," Danis said, glancing at

Steigan. "Only that they would be kept separately. Now he means to destroy them."

"Again, I ask why?"

"Because he doesn't want us to defeat the gargaxes. He wants to bring them back."

"I don't believe it," Searn said. "Mierk wouldn't do that."

"The gargax is up to something I tell you. Can't you feel it?" Steigan knew they both were wrong but didn't know how to get that across to them. Even as they continued on, it seemed like they hadn't heard him.

Keteria appeared right in front of them with her back to them. She turned and pointed at Steigan, though she spoke to Searn, "He'll need his armor."

"Aye, milady," Searn responded.

Then, to Danis she said, "Get Tanold. Bring him to the Temple."

"Milady, I should stay with you."

Keteria's gaze jumped to Steigan. "'Tis Steigan…" She looked like the words were hard for her to admit, but she pressed on. "Dominus Steigan who must help me now."

Danis didn't look happy, but he nodded. "Aye, milady."

Both men started in separate directions, but watched as

Keteria stepped up to Steigan. She reached out a hand and touched his arm. "Talcor dun."

In the space of a blurred heartbeat, they were outside the castle. She repeated the spell and they appeared in the Temple courtyard.

What they found there was chaos.

A huge bonfire sat in the middle of the courtyard. Maeges sobbed, some too distressed by this scene collapsed in their white robes onto the grass. Knights and domini gaped horrified at the fire. Everyone seemed to be in a state of stunned disbelief, no one quite sure of what to do. Even for Steigan, the sight of it made him pause.

"By the Goddess," he heard Keteria whisper.

Why wasn't anyone doing anything?

Suddenly, books appeared out of thin air above the fire.

Keteria raised her hand toward the books. "Radin'loo malleit trapesa rhosh'a," she spoke quickly. A spark of blue lit in the space beneath the falling books but blinked out of existence.

With a crackling snap, the books dropped into the waiting flames with a crash and sent sparks flying into the air. Steigan realized that the bonfire was made from the furniture in the library, tables, chairs, bookshelves, but the main bulk of it was books. Paper blackened in smoldering leather bindings.

Dominus Colwyn came running over to Keteria. "There's a shield around the fire. We can't get through. We also can't get into the Temple. Mierk is in the library sending the books out here."

Keteria approached the invisible shield with her hand stretched out. "'Tis strong." She turned to Colwyn. "Who's helping Mierk?"

"We don't know," Colwyn said as though surprised that she would suggest that someone was helping the Holy Sapere destroy the Temple's library. "There was a diversion which pulled all of the knights, maeges, and domini outside. The pages and cavaliers are still inside."

"He's got the children?"

Colwyn couldn't look at her any longer. He licked his mouth and gave an aggravated shake of his head like he didn't want to take the blame for this situation. "And we can't get back through," he admitted harshly.

Keteria watched another load of books drop onto the bonfire. "Nalorium breticham," she tried.

Nothing happened.

"The maeges have tried everything they can think of. If Centhya was here… This magic is strong."

"Mierk's not capable of this. His magic isn't that powerful and he's sworn to be a guardian of the knowledge,"

Keteria said, more voicing her thoughts aloud than speaking to be heard. "Why?"

Before Colwyn could answer, a maege screamed. Steigan followed the maege's pointing gesture to see a child dangling in the air above the flames. The boy squirmed as if trying to get away from the invisible hands that held him then froze as he realized his position above the flames. He screamed too.

Gasps filled the air as smoke surrounded the boy, misting him from view.

"I have an idea," Keteria said to Steigan. "'Tis crazy."

Steigan looked down at her. "Whatever you need done."

Keteria grabbed Steigan's hand. "Radin'loo malleit trapesa rhosh'a. Talcor dun."

As the strange blur faded from his eyes, Steigan found himself very close to the bonfire with Keteria beside him. She'd gotten them not only through the shield but actually through the bonfire to the other side closest to the Temple. The air here was thick with heat and smoke.

When he looked back to where Keteria had been standing, he found her gone.

"Get ready to catch him," she called through the smoke.

Catch? He could hardly breathe, let alone think about catching someone. Suddenly the boy fell toward the flames. His scream turned into a horrified shriek.

"Shi'baten to'a helcord," Keteria shouted.

The boy changed direction and instead of falling into the bonfire, he shot sideways and slammed into the side of the shield. Steigan held out his arms, fighting the tears rising in his eyes from the stinging smoke. The boy dropped into his arms and the weight knocked Steigan over. As the boy landed on his chest, the remaining air was knocked from Steigan's lungs.

"Steigan!" the boy yelled as he rolled off and to his feet.

Steigan tried to follow the boy's lead and get up. The blond child helped. As Steigan blinked to clear his burning vision, he saw the boy was Urlane, Merkor's son.

Sweat broke out on Steigan's face and dripping down the back of his neck.

"What do we do now?" Urlane coughed.

Steigan pulled his tunic over his nose and mouth, hoping it would help him breathe better and used his arm to shield his eyes from the light of the fire. "Keteria, where are you?"

There was no answer.

Grabbing onto Urlane, Steigan tried to make his way

around the bonfire to find Keteria. "Who's in the Temple doing this?" Steigan asked Urlane. Not only were his words meant to gain any information, but also to distract himself from his own worry. Precious little air remained and they needed to get out. The heat, the fire, they wouldn't last long against it.

Searn ran up to the shield and shouted something Steigan couldn't hear. It was like everyone in the courtyard no longer existed. Searn banged against the shield, yelling in what looked like slow motion as if trying to get Steigan to understand. Steigan shrugged. Couldn't Searn see he was a little busy?

Steigan kept trying to walk around the bonfire. A shadow appeared and he looked up to see another load of books come crashing down onto the fire. Sparks showered them. Steigan turned and covered Urlane with his own body, feeling the sparks nip through his tunic. He stepped back into the shield to smother the flames.

He continued on, pausing only to pick up Urlane when the boy dropped to his knees in a fit of coughing. Where was Keteria?

More books appeared and Steigan turned, preparing for another spray of embers. It never came. Daring to look up, Steigan saw a thin blue line floating over the fire.

Where ever Keteria was, she still worked magic. "Keteria?" he called, the attempted scream coming out as more of a gag.

Urlane pointed. "Look."

Steigan glanced toward the bonfire, following Urlane's gesture. The hot fire seemed to shimmer and a moment later Keteria walked right out of the flames completely unharmed. She passed a hand in front of her and Steigan felt a rush of cool air, though it was short lived as it got sucked into the vortex of the fire, making more sparks fly and the flames deepen.

Keteria stepped up to Steigan and Urlane. "Miex'calidori. Badimazulien."

Steigan realized that the previous rush of air had been Keteria releasing the bubble she had been in so that she could create another around all of them. Breathing again, Steigan set Urlane down.

Keteria watched the bonfire and the blue line above it as more books appeared, dropped, and vanished as they crossed the threshold of the line. "As long as whoever is in there doesn't drop another child, that'll keep the books from being burned."

Steigan bent down to Urlane's level. "Who is in there doing this?"

"I don't know," Urlane answered.

"Why were you thrown out like that?" Keteria asked.

"I don't know." Urlane shook his head and shrugged. "I was in the room with the others, and then I was hanging in midair. Everyone's so scared."

"Someone must have been trying to do something and Urlane was used as an example to the others," Steigan said.

Urlane gave a slow nod. "Jaxson. He was trying to pick the lock on the door to get us out.

Steigan turned to Keteria. "'Tis getting hot in this bubble too."

Keteria watched a pile of books on the fire as they slacked a little when books lower in the pile crumbled to ash. "I can't stop it," she said helplessly. "Even if I could, I couldn't save the books."

Steigan wanted to tell her that what was done was done. They couldn't go back now. They had to move forward. "Then let's figure out how to get into the Temple and stop him."

Chapter Twenty-Four

Several people standing outside in the Temple courtyard tried to get Steigan's and Keteria's attention. When they noticed, Searn once again pounded on the shield and made wild gestures. Keteria watched closely and started to nod.

"What's he saying?" Steigan asked.

"He's trying to push something to us," she said. "I don't know if I can open up another portal while I've got one open. We've got to save the books."

"I'll do it," Steigan said, nodding trying to seem more confident than he truly felt. "What do I need to do?"

"'Tis highly advanced magic. I'm not even sure Searn is capable of it."

"'Tis our only choice."

Keteria exhaled a deep breath. "Imagine a doorway that slides open. Imagine it in front of you. Slide your hand as though you are opening it, and say, 'Ra'loo malleit jakca rhymastadi.'"

Muttering the words to himself to remember them, Steigan braced his stance and took a deep breath. He pictured the door as she had said and made the motion while firmly speaking, "Ra'loo malleit jakca rhymastadi."

Nothing happened.

He tried a second time. Nothing. "What am I doing wrong?"

"There's no way you can control that amount of magic, especially with no real training," Keteria said.

"Then what do we do?"

Searn banged on the shield again. He did the gesture and pulled out Steigan's breastplate and held it so Steigan could have a good long look at it. Searn raised an eyebrow as his lips pursed. Then he slid it back beyond the unseen boundary and the breastplate was once again invisible.

"He's trying to send you your armor," Keteria said as though Steigan needed her explanation.

Glimpsing the armor and knowing that Searn had done the magic filled Steigan with warm strength. He could do this. He rubbed his hands together. "I'm feeling strangely motivated now," he said, with a smile to Urlane as he distributed his weight over his stance again. "Ra'loo malleit jakca rhymastadi."

A memory of vegetable soup, fresh and warm with just a hint of spice, came to him strangely out of nowhere. It didn't quite seem to fit, this thought of a gentle, nourishing brown broth on the spoon, but the comfort it brought him like none he could recall.

Like a shot of lightning, Steigan felt the magic course up his spine and over his arm. He reached into the air before him and made a flicking motion with his hand. As though it had leapt for him, the breastplate appeared in his hand. From the clattering sounds, he knew there was more and he reached further into the invisible hole and tried to not be concerned that he could no longer see his hand or most of his lower arm. Inside, he also found greaves, arm plates, and his sword. He handed the pieces to Urlane as fast as he could pull it out.

"Is this your armor?" Urlane asked. "Are you really a dominus?"

"He is," Keteria said, bouncing on the balls of her feet with her hands clasped against her chest. "He really is."

Steigan strapped on his armor as though it was second nature to him. It felt so comfortable having it on. Now he could take on the world. He turned to Keteria. "How do we get into the Temple?"

Her excitement fell away. "We can't take my cousin," she said, putting a hand on Urlane's blond head. "'Twill be too dangerous."

"And 'tis getting hot in this bubble. So let's get him out there with Searn."

"That's our issue. We can't just pop him back there. If this maege in the Temple is any good, which I have reason to believe he or she is, he felt the moment we passed through," she explained. "I had the one shot backed with a lot of magic. It won't work a second time."

"Searn slid my armor through to me. Can't we do the same with Urlane?"

"Again, that was probably a one shot deal."

"So he stays here and we hurry," Steigan said. "With only him, the bubble will stay full of air for a while."

"If I leave, the bubble will collapse. Urlane could maintain his own for a while, but I'm also not sure about my dimensional spell."

More books dropped from above the fire and disappeared through the portal.

"What do you think will happen when the library is empty?" Steigan asked.

"Depends on who is doing this and why."

"I need options, Keteria."

She closed her eyes and bit down on her lips before she spoke. "The only one I see involves you going in there alone."

Steigan nodded. "I'd rather keep the princess of Lilinar out of harm's way. Speak your magic."

Keteria nudged Urlane to stand behind her. "Close your eyes and spin around," she said as she started making a twirling motion in the air with her upwards pointing finger. "I'll do the rest."

Steigan felt a little awkward. He made one turn, taking a peek as he came around to see what Keteria was doing. She stood with her feet shoulder-width apart and her arms duplicating the triangular stance of her legs. Her eyes were closed. A breeze blew her hair back from her face, little curls dancing in the air.

"Keep turning," Keteria said. "Faster."

Steigan spun around and around, feeling a bit like a kid trying to make himself dizzy enough to fall down.

Keteria's voice rang out loud and strong, "Kachy lore'icantica bascemium ra'to acia. Kna'cripitium roosha fortunic."

A thousand knives flicked sharp blades over Steigan's skin. With a cry of alarm, he opened his eyes and dropped to a crouch expecting to see an attack. Instead, he fell over dazed onto the stone floor. He shook his head trying to recover. As the spinning world settled, he realized he lay on the Temple floor.

Standing, he found several cuts on his tunic and leggings where the armor offered no protection. His jaw tightened, willing himself not to feel the ~~pain of the~~ nicks on his skin, some of them starting to bleed.

The halls were quiet but an acrid heaviness hung in the air. The after effects, Steigan realized, of strong magic being worked.

Steigan drew his sword. Would this maege sense him coming? If ever there was time when Steigan wished his magic wasn't so abundant, so stolen, it was now. He hurried along, trying to walk on the balls of his feet so his footfalls wouldn't echo on the stone.

He approached the ajar door of the Holy Sapere's office. Peeking in, Steigan saw the office in disarray and Mierk slumped over at his desk. Steigan slipped inside and went over to Mierk. The Holy Sapere was alive, but unconscious. Steigan didn't know if that fact filled him with relief or dread. If not the Holy Sapere, then who was behind this?

Turning to leave the office, Steigan noticed a box which had fallen on the floor. The lid had opened in the tumble and remained slightly open on the floor with a couple deep red stones lying nearby.

Absorption stones, Keteria had called them. They hadn't completely taken away his magic, due to the stolen power he possessed, but it had diminished it. A maege possessing only his own energy would be rendered defenseless around these stones. Steigan scooped up the box and the stones and with the lid closed, he felt his full strength return. The box, it seemed, blocked the stones' ability.

Steigan continued on and went up the stairs to the library on the third floor. As he got closer, he could smell smoke. But if it was all contained within the bubble outside, where was the smoke coming from?

Reaching the second landing, he remembered the cavaliers and pages still trapped in the Temple. Did he continue on or did he help them now? If he hurried, he might be able to stop the maege and end this quickly. If the maege overpowered him, who then would be able to help the others?

Steigan paused at the door to the first dormitory. Would it be magically locked or would he be able to kick it in? Once he did, would the maege know and punish the children Steigan hadn't released first. How could he choose?

He couldn't. He had to choose one dormitory and trust that they could think of something to help the others. Decision made, Steigan broke down the door to the girls' dormitory. As they ran out, Steigan grabbed one of the young maeges running from the room and said, "You've got to stay and help the others. I don't know if I can get to them before he finds out."

Several more girls paused and indicated their willingness to help.

"Get these doors open and then get out," Steigan said before continuing on his way with a hope that they really did understand him through the panic they were feeling.

Steigan slowed on the stairs right before the outer door to the library. He crept up and put his back against the wall. Expecting to encounter a barrier spell, he reached out and opened the door.

Heat and smoke came out to greet him. Then a raspy voice followed, "I've felt you coming, demon! You won't make it in here."

A flash of fire soared out of the room, reaching hungrily for the wooden roof above then retreating quickly back. Inside, the area was filled with white and gray smoke. Steigan thought he could make out the dark brown shadows of bookshelves beyond, but he couldn't be sure.

Steigan yelled, "I'm no demon. Come on out."

"Come dance in the flames!"

Steigan stepped inside. All the furniture that remained in the room was on fire. Wooden shelves burned lighting the room with a brilliant yellow-orange glow. In the center of the room, a dark figure danced.

Steigan opened the lid on the box he carried and slid it across the floor as far as he could.

"Cazidor palikiem!" the figure shouted.

The magic struck the box and the blow knocked it into the air where the carved wooden box erupted into flames. The stones tumbled back to the floor amid ash and metal.

Steigan rushed in, running straight for the figure who shrieked at the oncoming attack.

"Shi'baten to'a helcord," the silhouetted magic cried out.

The magic left the maege's hands and the stones sucked the power into them. Steigan approached, sword raised. The figure stumbled backwards and as he tripped, the round metal circle of a crown hit the floor. The figure tried to pull his own sword from his belt, only to find it also caught up in the cloth of his heavy cloak.

"Back demon," the figure said tugging at the material covering the hilt. When he realized he'd be unable to draw his sword, he dove for the crown.

Steigan stared in disbelief as the man tried to shove the metal back on his head. "King Cirello?" he asked.

"Do not foul my name by speaking it! You hold no power over me."

Steigan lowered himself to one knee and reached out a hand. "Milord, why have you done this? Please, take down your barriers so others can come in and put out these fires."

Cirello adjusted the crown, tapping it for good measure as if to keep it there. "They mustn't get our knowledge. This is the only way to keep it safe."

"You're destroying everything your family has built up. Please, let the barriers down."

Cirello leaned forward and squinted. "I know you. How is it that you still look young now and I am decades older?"

"I don't know what you're talking about."

"You took my only son. Are you bringing him back? My son?"

A bookshelf collapsed behind them, knocking over another bookshelf with a thunderous crash. Cirello jumped and put his hands over his ears.

"Everything is going to be all right, milord," Steigan said, sliding his sword away in the scabbard and crawling a little closer to Cirello. "Come this way with me."

"Nay, 'tis not all right. You would let them have everything. They can't have it. My son, he's the only one who can stop them."

Steigan tried not to let the heat get to him. He inched closer, trying to keep his hand out toward Cirello at all times. "Stop who, milord?" he asked. If he could just keep Cirello talking for a little longer…

Cirello's eyes widened. "The beasts who take to the sky. The guardians of the dead and the old ones. Shh, they might hear you." He looked around. "I must find my son. You took him."

"How do you know I'm the one who took your son?"

"The armor. 'Tis wrong. I remember." Cirello's brow furrowed as he pointed at Steigan's chest. "You were wearing my nephew's armor before."

"Searn's armor?" Steigan wondered if the pieces of the puzzle were coming together. "Did Searn take your son?"

Cirello started to snicker. "He was just a toddler at the time. You think I don't remember. You think I'm crazy. 'Twas you, but you were wearing Searn's armor when you took my son. Where did you hide him?"

Steigan reached forward and grabbed onto Cirello's arm. "Come milord."

"You'll take me to him?"

Willing to say anything to get Cirello out of the burning library, Steigan tried to say that he would yet the words wouldn't come. He couldn't even nod. "Let's go," he finally managed, hoping Cirello would take that as acceptance.

Another bookshelf crashed. Sparks came down and lit Cirello's cloak on fire. Steigan tried to stomp out the flames, but Cirello saw what was going on and screamed.

Steigan grabbed the cloak off Cirello as the king turned in a panicked circle. Now the king's long nightshirt had caught on fire. Steigan whipped the cloak around, trying to get it around the squirming king, but Cirello broke free in a mad dash of curses and ran out of the room and down the stairs. Dropping the burned cloak, Steigan ran after Cirello. On the second floor, Steigan looked around for Cirello. The king hadn't gone toward the dormitories.

Centering himself quickly, Steigan let his magic reach out for Cirello and found that the king had gone into a massive chamber which Steigan figured could only belong to the Holy Sapere.

He heard a scream, deep, yet short. Then more screams.

Steigan ran through the room to where the balcony doors stood open and curtains blew in the breeze. Steigan stepped out desperately hoping to see Cirello on the balcony.

In the courtyard, people were clustering toward the building. Steigan looked over the wrought iron rail, knowing what he'd see even before he looked.

King Cirello lay dead on the stone entryway beneath him.

Chapter Twenty-Five

Steigan's world fell into slow motion.

Maeges tried to revive the king. Searn restrained a sobbing Keteria. People were running up the stairs to the third floor to put out the fire. Steigan felt the magic being used all around him.

Amid the chaos, Steigan walked against the crowd. It seemed like everyone was trying to get to the Temple. He went against the flow, shaking and numb.

The gargax had had its revenge.

Steigan wandered across the bridge, then through the town. He contemplated getting a room at an inn, but realized he had no money. He thought about making camp in the forest, but what if the gargaxes sensed him there like a campfire on the mountainside? He waited in the forest for the sun to set. Somehow, that felt like the right thing to do.

He wished he could remove himself from existence.

When everything seemed to settle down, Steigan went into the Temple stables, made a bed of straw in one of the stalls, and fell into a deep sleep.

Bells for morning service woke him the next day. He wasn't sure he wanted to head across the bridge, wasn't sure what would await him at the Temple, but he did so anyway. Washing in a bucket of water he pulled from the Temple well, he went inside and took a spot on the pews. He wondered why people were staring at him until he realized he was still wearing the dominus armor. Goddess, he'd completely forgotten about it. He'd slept in it like it was a second skin. How could this not be part of him?

He rose to go up to the dormitory to take off the armor, but a knight stopped him and handed him a sealed letter and package. As he slid his finger beneath the seal and unfolded the letter, he wasn't sure if he had thanked the knight or just grunted.

Of course, it was from Keteria. How could it not be? Reading her light script, he realized that she was asking him to attend her for her father's funeral later in the morning.

Feeling more drained, Steigan returned to the pew and sank down.

How many times during morning prayers did he tell himself that he needed to snap out of this fugue? How many times did he merely open his mouth to pretend to speak the words back to the sapere leading the service?

Worse still, Steigan realized he really couldn't attend Keteria with armor that he wasn't entitled to. Knowing that he now *had* to take it off brought up a strange resistance in him. He picked up the package he'd ignored until now and opened it. Inside was his black, blue, and gold doublet.

He found renewed strength to walk upstairs. It still smelled like smoke and the walls were marred with soot. In the dormitory, he changed and stored the armor in the wardrobe where he'd first found Jaxsen. That incident felt like a lifetime ago. He wondered if he were to look in a mirror now would he find old eyes looking back at him.

Goddess, what could he have done differently?

That was the question that plagued him. It surfaced now from the corner of his mind where it had stayed hidden, crouched and scared.

Keteria arrived. He felt her enter the courtyard before he looked out the dormitory window to confirm it. She paused as she climbed out of the carriage to look up at him. Dressed in a layered purple gown and robes, adorned with all the proper symbols, and with the royal circlet on her head, he hardly recognized her by sight.

Steigan went downstairs. She never looked at him as he came out of the Temple. Was she even aware of his presence? He fell in behind her and stayed there while a small procession gathered in the courtyard. A funeral carriage lead by two white horses brought in the body of Keteria's father. Banners of blue and gold streamed off long poles in each corner. Cirello had been wrapped in white cloth bound with ribbons of black, blue, and gold. In a disheartening way, the look of it reminded Steigan of the doublet he currently wore.

The carriage rounded the well and pulled up in front of the castle. Lord Ithanes and the other representatives from Dubinshire walked behind the carriage. Six domini marched out of the Temple to pull the body off the carriage and carried it back inside.

The halls of the Temple were lined with maeges, domini, and saperes singing soft lilting tones. The sounds of sorrow made a knot rise in Steigan's chest and into his throat.

Keteria swept along into a lower room filled with tapestries and podiums, shelves and objects containing magic that Steigan could feel as he passed. This was a room where the scribes worked, but none were at their books now.

A carpet of white, blue, and gold lined the way to a door in the far back wall. Keteria stepped away from the crowd to come around them and stand in front of the door.

"Hallow rist'a kah'tay misha stalay," she said.

Gold patterns began to glow within the wood grain of the door. It swung open on its own. Keteria stepped aside and resumed her position at the back with only Steigan right behind her.

Torches on the wall were already lit. The carpet ended shortly beyond the door, leaving only the bare dirt floor. Several slots in the walls housed decomposing bodies. Skeletons with graying flesh and no eyes stared at Steigan, who kept moving ahead trying not to look at the macabre scene.

What about the sight of death bothered him? He was a dominus. He knew his fate.

Wait! An elusive thought remained just out of reach. He wished he could take a moment to stop and think, to try to regain that emotional memory that had flashed by.

The domini ahead of them were beginning to sing, carrying on the low drones they'd left behind in the hallway. The tunnel grew darker even though there were just as many torches on the wall here as there had been at the beginning.

The floor sloped slightly, enough to let Steigan know they were going further underground. The smell of decay gave way to musty earth.

Keteria reached her hand back toward him and Steigan could scarcely believe it as her fingers wiggled trying to draw his attention. She didn't look directly at him. He tentatively reached for her, not really sure if she wanted him to take her hand, but as they brushed together, she grabbed onto him and pushed her fingers between his.

He hoped this signaled that she'd be able to find forgiveness within her grief. The last thing he wanted was her anger. Please, Goddess…

He yielded to his secret prayer and closed his eyes for but a moment. When he opened his eyes again, he found they had come to a stop before a door with battle scene frescoes carved into stone. Mierk and Tanold stood on each side of the door.

"Who comes to the Hall of Kings?" Mierk asked.

"My father, King Cirello Taburath of Lilinar," Keteria replied. "Who stands ready to receive him?"

"I, son of Cirello and Heir Prince of Lilinar, stand ready to receive my father," Tanold said.

"What legacy does he leave behind?" Holy Sapere Mierk asked.

"Born on the twenty-fifth day of Salaoh, sixty-two cycles ago, to Kardian of Lilinar, he left us on the sixth day of Pinth. He leaves behind two children by Queen Lanadela of Lilinar," Keteria answered.

Tanold continued, "He leaves behind a brother, Merkor. The life status of his sister, Saleaha, is unknown. He is greeted into the Goddess's realm by his eldest sister, Tanisha, as well as by his uncle Tonashad, his father Kardian, and his mother Marru."

"He reigned for twenty-seven years as King of Lilinar."

"During his reign, he has fought in numerous battles where he declared victory in all of them due to his powerful magic. He personally fended off an assassination attempt on his life the very night his twin children were born," Tanold said.

Steigan noticed a scribe off to the side making notes of everything they said.

Keteria said, "He changed the banner colors of Lilinar from red and gold to blue and gold. He remained a steadfast dominus and continued his duties as a domini as long as he was physically able."

"He held charge over the city of Lilinar as well as ruling council of its twenty fiefs. He oversaw the construction of the Temple on the lake. He always saw to the best care of his people," Tanold finished.

Steigan wondered how his own life would pan out, what they would say about his legacy. He'd never given pause to think about what he might be leaving behind. It hadn't seemed important. Besides, he had nothing to his name. Hadn't his night in the stables proven that? What right did he have to even think he might provide a legacy of any value to anyone?

There was Keteria.

He looked at her and saw tears rolling down her cheeks. His life and everything he did in this life belonged to her. His legacy would be to make her the grandest queen ever. Never did he want to see her cry again. She was the only thing that held value in his life and he would spend every day making sure she knew that.

"The giver and the receiver of the body have spoken," Holy Sapere Mierk said. "Do any others wish to add to the record?"

Searn spoke up from his position as one of the domini holding the body. "I, Searn Bytherhourn, wish to add my thanks to him for saving my life during a skirmish with the Plenelians. I would not be here today if not for him."

"Here, here!" the domini cheered.

"The record is noted. Any further?" Mierk asked.

Steigan hadn't even realized that Searn as one of the domini carrying the body. Looking closer, he realized that Merkor was another.

When no one else said anything, Mierk turned, raised his hands, and the door before him opened. "Enter now, King Cirello of Lilinar into the Hall of Kings."

Once the doors opened, Steigan realized there was woman already in the room; Centhya dressed in her maege robes.

"Enter now to the realm of the Goddess," Centhya said. She tilted her head back slightly. "Coom ra wialca to."

Holy Sapere Mierk glared at her as if she'd misspoken. Centhya matched his flashing look with challenge of her own. Steigan wondered what had happened that he had missed.

Keteria squeezed Steigan's hand before releasing it. She wiped the tears from her cheeks as she went up to Centhya and whispered something to her. Centhya nodded and went to the head of the room. Tanold looked questioningly at Keteria and made his way over to her.

Before Tanold could say anything, Keteria whispered to Tanold, "I can't do it."

"You've never let yourself be unable to perform your duty," Tanold said.

"This is a little different."

"But the kingdom needs you to be strong."

"Centhya is High Maege," Keteria said. "'Tis her rightful position. I can't do it now. But when the time comes, the kingdom will have their strong queen."

Tanold backed down as Centhya began the chants. "Coom ra wialca to," Centhya said.

Mierk stepped up beside Centhya and said sharply, "For the Goddess in Her love I serve."

Keteria gave an exasperated sigh. "The old rites, Mierk, please. That is the way my father was raised and lived. 'Tis the way he wanted it."

Mierk glared at her, but did bow. "As you wish it, my princess."

Steigan wanted to rip Mierk's snide tone right from his throat. Besides, what did it mean, 'the old rites'? What were the new rites?

At length, they slid Cirello's body into a vault and sealed the area with a rock that took four knights to lift. The domini resumed their chant of low tones as they left the chamber.

Once upstairs where the air didn't smell like musty earth, Steigan fell back from the group. He wasn't sure what would happen next. The family exchanged hugs and talked about a dinner later that night. Steigan realized in an unsettled fashion that he hadn't even had breakfast.

"Princess Keteria, will you be heading back to the castle now?" Mierk asked. "I don't know if you want to get back to matters of state right now or not."

Keteria nodded to Mierk. "Actually, I thought the coronation should happen today. I can't keep the delegation from Dubinshire waiting while we mourn."

Mierk looked displeased but forced a smile. "Very well, milady."

Keteria walked off down the hall. Steigan stood against the wall wishing he could evaporate into the stone.

"Steigan, you look lost," Mierk said.

"I am not use to idleness or mourning," Steigan replied, trying not to let Mierk grate him.

"I hope you realize how much we appreciate what you did yesterday, even if it did have such a tragic end. We might have lost everything."

"A good portion of it is still gone. None of that can be brought back," Steigan said.

"We have our lives and those of the children. Besides, history may look back on this as a necessary purging."

"Necessary purging?" Even speaking the words had a distasteful sound in his mouth.

"Aye," replied Mierk, "to make way for the new. The

scribes still have all the translations and new ceremonies you provided for us down in their workshop as they are busy copying them."

Old rites versus new rites. Steigan understood now. He'd almost forgotten about the exchange he'd made with Mierk: translated texts for a new generation, to make it related better, in exchange for Mierk's prayers of health to Jaxsen.

"What you did will be instrumental in our rebuilding," Mierk added. "The Goddess knew what she was doing when she sent you to us before this tragedy."

"I'm sure," Steigan said, feeling suddenly sick to his stomach. "Now if you will please excuse me, I should see where I can lend a hand."

"Don't run too far away today. Your presence will be needed at the coronation today."

Steigan couldn't imagine why he would be needed, why his presence would be important. He nodded, though he felt like the strength had drained right out of him. All he really wanted to do was saddle horse and take a long ride. So long a ride that maybe he'd find a quiet place to start a new life. Maybe Telimas would come for him.

As he started down the hall, he wondered why he had a feeling he'd be regretting his actions for a long time to come.

Keteria stepped out of a crossing hallway ahead.

Steigan wished he could change course, but it seemed like she'd been waiting for him. He stopped while she approached.

"Steigan, I wish for you to walk with me," she said.

He fought every nerve which told him to run. After all, hadn't he just pledged himself to making her a grand queen? Would he run from that personal oath so soon? "Very well, milady." Then he followed her out of the Temple.

CHAPTER TWENTY-SIX

Two knights stepped up beside Keteria as she and Steigan left the Temple. Her carriage waited a short distance from the steps. She nodded to the driver, but continued walking around the carriage. The knights had to catch up.

"We're taking a walk," Keteria said over her shoulder to the knights, who remained close.

A few more steps deeper into the courtyard, Keteria turned to the knights and made a motion with her hands as if telling them to scurry away. "I'm with Dominus Steigan," she said. "Can you give us some room?"

The knights looked displeased, but hung back.

"Dominus?" Steigan asked as they continued toward the gatehouse.

"I'll explain momentarily."

They crossed the bridge in silence and started around the lake. It reminded Steigan of the trek he'd made for several mornings when he'd go to sit in the soothing, cooling mud on the east side of the lake. This memory combined with her silence made him feel uncomfortable.

"Why did you sleep in the stables last night?" she asked, her words barely more than a whisper so that Steigan felt they were more awkward than the silence.

"How did you know?" he asked. "No one else does."

Now Keteria looked a little distressed. He wondered if she'd been afraid that he'd ask how she knew, like the answer might be too hard for her to reveal.

"I woke last night and just had a feeling you weren't around," she said. "I went to your quarters and found them empty. I woke Searn who told me he thought you'd stayed at the Temple." She was staring at her feet as she walked. "So I sent a knight to fetch you. He returned saying that you were gone. I feared you'd left for good."

Keteria stopped and looked out over the sparkling lake. "Then I did something I've never done. I cried for fear of losing you." She paused, biting down on the inside of her lip, then continued. "To make it worse, I did something I never thought I'd do."

"What was that?"

Her gaze flickered toward him for just a second then returned to the lake as if it were easier for her to look at the water than at him. "I cast a heart search spell."

"What's that?"

"I thought 'twas an old wives' tale." She glanced around Steigan for a moment as if checking on the location of the knights following them. "'Tis said that one can find a person they love by tracking the light. Of course, I couldn't just leave the castle in the middle of the night and certainly not alone, so I used remote viewing to follow the light and found you sleeping in the stables."

"We don't have to speak of this."

"We must. I don't want you to have to rely on the Temple or myself for anything, but I realize that you've been given nothing to help you in that direction."

Steigan felt his rising discomfort. "I don't need anything. I just wanted to be alone."

"I don't want it happening again. My Numen should not be in the stables."

Irritated over her seeming possessiveness as well as not knowing what she was talking about, he snapped, "Fine. I won't. No one saw me. Your image is intact."

"My image?" She almost laughted. "You think I'm worried about how you sleeping in the stables affects me? That's not what this is all about." She shook her head.

"Then what is it about?"

"I want to restore your title and give you land of your own. There's a road, little maintained mind you, going south west from Lilinar. 'Tis mostly forest country, but quite a few travelers from the south come in that way. I think there's great potential for a village. I want you to gather people and start a fiefdom there."

Steigan couldn't believe what he was hearing. "Really? A fief for me?"

Keteria smiled. "You are a dominus descended from Rivic. 'Tis your due right." She nudged a rock with her slipper. "There is another matter of a more tricky nature, but I believe we can manage."

Still reeling from the shock of being offered his title and land, Steigan tried to focus on listening to her. "What would that be?"

"I want you to officially be my Numen."

There was that word again. "I don't know what that means."

"Well, this is where it gets tricky. Please don't refuse

until you've heard me out."

"Very well."

Keteria breathed heavily as though extremely nervous and trying to fight it back. "The noble maeges have always tried to stay together. It helps to keep the magic in the bloodwave straight. Whole complicated thing I'm not sure I fully understand. Of course, Rivic's bloodline is the most important as 'tis the line of prophecy."

Seeing that this was so hard for her, Steigan turned toward Keteria and took her hands in his wishing to give her strength.

Keteria continued, "Centhya is from a very powerful family. Her mother was once High Maege, as was her mother's mother. When Searn came of age, he chose Centhya to be his Numen."

"So this is a position made in matrimony?"

"Nay, maeges enter into a Numen bond to share and balance the magic. Without this Numen bond to balance magic, especially the higher level magic, it can be bad." Keteria's eyes filled with tears. "I think King Cirello went crazy because he never made another Numen bond after his wife died."

"I'm sorry."

"I'm afraid that the same thing will happen to me, but

no one's been strong enough to wield the level of magic that I do until you came along." She paused, biting down on her lip once more. "But I'm even more afraid for what a Numen bonding would do to us and what it could mean."

"Again with the non-understanding."

Keteria released his hands and turned away. "Most, not all, but most Numena result in marriage between the paired maeges."

A light of understanding began to dawn. "Which would be an issue of for us because..." He wasn't sure how to phrase it.

"Because we're both supposedly of Rivic's lineage and yet we both know the truth."

"So that's why you want me to have my own fief too? So it looks like there's nothing which could be considered improper going on between us. After all, we're cousins." Steigan stepped up behind her and put his hands on her upper arms.

She turned her head and leaned back against him. "Aye."

"But won't you need me nearby to be your Numen?"

"After I train you, you'll be able to flash to me in an instant. I'm betting your dimensional magic is stronger than mine."

"Thank you," he said, referring to everything she had just said. The words felt so small and insignificant compared to what she offered, but what else could he say. His whole life had just changed. "I know it'll have to be all proper between us, but we can do it."

Keteria turned back toward him, tears renewed in her eyes. "I'm glad you think so. I wish I had that faith in my own feelings."

"What else could we do?" he asked. "I would burn this mark from my hand in an instant if it would help."

"Don't," she whispered, leaning her forehead against his chest. "I know in truth I have no real claim to the throne of Lilinar, except that my heart does belong to a son of Rivic. It has to be enough."

Steigan wanted to embrace her but knew the knights were watching not too far away. Everything from here on out had to be proper between them. No missteps.

Keteria looked up and smiled. "Just promise me a small cottage on your fief where I can go to get away."

"A small cottage to start," Steigan said with a nod. "Then a small castle where you can hide away whenever you like."

"Sounds nice."

For a moment, silence dropped between them while

they listened to the longings in their imaginations. Then reality came back.

"I need to return to the Temple now," she said.

Steigan nodded and fell into step a little behind her. The return trip seemed too quick for his liking. He much rather enjoyed being with Keteria while looking to the southwest and thinking about what he could do with his land. It felt so strange to even be thinking about it.

At the Temple, Keteria dismissed the guards and headed upstairs. Steigan watched her go until she disappeared from his sight, yet she seemed to know when she was at that edge and looked back to send him one last smile.

It would be hard to keep things proper.

Chapter Twenty-Seven

The main worship hall of the Temple had filled with people. Domini stood at the perimeter of the room while knights stood up on the balconies around the room. Steigan waited to the right of the raised dais against the wall while Mierk's secretary issued final orders to people around the room.

Sacred Knight Danis and Dominus Colwyn entered the room. "Domini, knights, stand tall."

A chill went through Steigan. It had already happened. The new rites he'd been a part of creating were being institutionalized. Ithanes' words came back to him: *Lilinar will be destroyed*. Had that started with him, the changes he'd suggested and Mierk had adopted?

Merkor entered first. He came and took a position on the dais to the right of the Goddess' statue. Searn came in second and went to the left of the statue. Both wore their domini armor.

Third to arrive was Tanold who wore a blue and gold cape in addition to his domini armor. He stopped at the edge of the dais and did a quarter turn to face toward the wall to the right.

Holy Sapere Mierk entered next wearing white robes with thick gold braids and scrolls on it and a sunburst collar which rose up above his head. He came to stand at the edge of the dais, also turning a quarter of the way so that he looked toward Tanold.

The audience rose and turned to face the door where Keteria now stood. She swept into the room in a gown of blue and gold. White pearls and gold beads adorned her hair which had been pulled up. She looked every inch the queen.

Keteria walked down the aisle and took Mierk's offered hand. "Why Keteria," he said, "you look fantastic."

Keteria ignored him and reached out to take Tanold's hand. Tanold smiled at his sister. Together, Tanold and Mierk put their hands beneath Keteria's elbows and ushered her up on the dais. She turned to face the audience.

"Tanold, son of Cirello," Mierk said, "you are the second born and do hereby become heir apparent to the throne should your eldest sister falter in her duty to Lilinar and the Goddess. Do you understand?"

Tanold nodded. "I do, Holy Sapere."

"Do you believe Princess Keteria capable of her duties?"

Tanold briefly looked at Keteria. "I do, Holy Sapere."

"Support of one's family is honorable in the eyes of the Goddess. Thank you, Prince Tanold."

Centhya came down the aisle now carrying a crown on a little blue pillow. She handed the pillow and crown to Tanold.

"Please kneel, Princess Keteria," Mierk said.

Keteria went down on bended knee, her skirt tucking in beneath her leg. Mierk took the crown from Tanold and turned toward Keteria.

"Keteria, princess of Lilinar, do you swear before your people to uphold the laws of the land?" Mierk asked, holding the crown over her head.

"I do, Holy Sapere," she replied.

"Do you promise to be decisive and just, bringing trust from all those who serve you?"

"I do, Holy Sapere."

"Do you promise to honor the Goddess with your actions and remain noble of heart even in times when it might be hard to do so?"

"I do, Holy Sapere."

Mierk set the crown upon her head. "Then by the will of the Goddess, I now pronounce you Queen Keteria of Lilinar. Rise and stand tall for your people."

Keteria stood and smiled.

"I now give you Queen Keteria," Mierk said to the audience, who started to clap and cheer.

Keteria curtsied to the crowd, then after a moment she turned to Mierk and said, "Thank you, Holy Sapere. Now there is another matter to attend."

"As you wish it, my queen." Mierk stepped back, but as he did so, he looked at Steigan with a smirk on his lips.

Keteria went to the edge of the dais and held out her hand toward Steigan. He felt his heart jump into his throat as he moved forward.

Keteria held out her hand as if to help him up on the dais. "We have done a great disservice to this gentleman."

Steigan turned to face the audience as Keteria continued, "I'm afraid the wrong-doing started with me. He was brought to me when I filled in for Centhya as High

Maege. He was sick, alone, and unknown. He wore the armor of the court of Lilinar, but we could not prove his identity. I ordered his armor removed and his title not spoken. This has been a grave injustice as he does bear the mark proving his lineage. I rescind my prior decision and restore his dominus title to him."

Mierk approached. "Steigan, kneel."

An excited tingle went through Steigan as he bent one knee down onto the wood dais and looked up at the Holy Sapere. Dominus Searn stepped forward and offered a sword to Mierk.

"I stand before you with the Goddess' sword of truth," Mierk said, pointing the blade toward Steigan. "If you be false, you would rush up on it?"

Steigan loosened the ties of the doublet and pushed it aside. He leaned toward the sword so the tip pressed against his skin. "If I be false, may it pierce my heart and send me directly to the Goddess for Her will."

"Upon the Goddess' sword of truth, what is it you seek?"

Steigan tilted back his head. "Goddess, You have my life and my sword. The streets of Gohaldinest are paved with gold, but I seek a richer treasure. I serve for Your wisdom."

"Upon the Goddess' sword of truth, what is in your

heart?"

Now, looking back to Mierk, Steigan replied, "Truth, loyalty, honor, courage, strength, compassion. 'Tis all in the heart of a dominus. My heart as a dominus."

Mierk took the sword away from Steigan's chest and a spot of blood quickly blossomed where Steigan had let the tip pierce him. He wiped away the blood and spread it down the flat of the blade while Mierk held the sword steady for him. Then, saluting with his hand over his heart, he applied pressure to the small wound with the heel of his hand.

Mierk placed the sword upright before Steigan and said, "By your blood oath and by the trust placed in me by the Goddess, I now bestow upon you the title of dominus, including all the rights and privileges thereof. Rise, Dominus Steigan."

Thrill burst through Steigan and he grinned as he stood. It took him a moment to realize that people were shouting and clapping. When he looked out at the audience, he found Jaxsen and all his newfound friends from the Temple standing up on the chairs clapping and cheering. He waved to them.

Holy Sapere Mierk held out his hands to settle the audience. "I have to admit that this is a most fortuitous time," Mierk said. "First we have a coronation, then a titling, but I have further announcement."

Keteria stepped up beside Steigan as she stared at the Holy Sapere. Steigan felt the nervous tension rise within her magic. This hadn't been planned. "What's going on?" she whispered.

Steigan shook his head as he watched Mierk step to the edge of the dais.

Mierk continued, "Queen Keteria is correct. This young man standing before us tonight is quiet accomplished." He turned and started applauding in Steigan's direction. "I have to hand it to you, son. I don't know how you've done it all."

Mierk turned back to the audience. "By now, I'm certain you all have heard of his climbing down the well to save his friend. After that, he took some time to help us rework the religious texts that have now been handed out to the people of Lilinar and several of your fiefs."

Steigan hated the way Mierk boldly announced how far his reach was now extending.

"You wrote the books?" Keteria accused in a whisper.

Steigan's anger hit with a quick shot back, "You took my title?"

"Yesterday," Mierk continued, "he risked his life to save many old texts as well as the life of the inductee, Urlane, along with all the other children. Without his efforts, the

Temple would lie in complete ruin."

Goddess, he wondered if that's really how the people in the room saw him. He wondered if anyone else could feel the anger coming off Keteria in waves.

"As tragic as yesterday's events were, I hope we come to look upon this as a purging of the old." Mierk stepped forward swing his arms wide. "Now we must till the land and bring forth new life."

Keteria choked.

"In honor of his accomplishments and the new age he brings to the Temple with making the rites and rituals more accessible to the common man, I hereby deem Dominus Steigan as a saint."

"I can't believe this. How could you?" Keteria's mouth dropped open as she gave a little scoff and she turned to walk away as if unable to face Steigan. She staggered past Tanold and went to stand at the side of the dais. Tanold went to her.

"Hail, hail, Saint Steigan," Mierk said.

The crowd returned the cheer, "Hail, hail, Saint Steigan."

Steigan looked back over his shoulder to Searn who looked stunned.

Mierk crossed the dais and grabbed Keteria. He returned with her to the center and put Keteria's and Steigan's hands together as he raised them high. "I now give you Saint Steigan and Queen Keteria!"

The audience shouted, "Hail, hail, Saint Steigan. Hail, hail, Queen Keteria."

Keteria pushed away from Mierk then fled down the aisle toward the doors. Steigan tried to catch up, but she shook him off.

"Keteria, wait," he pleaded.

"Not now, *Saint*." She spat the bitter word from her mouth.

"'Tis important. I've got to speak to you."

She held her hand up to defend herself magically if necessary. "Then I suggest a better time when I haven't been completely blindsided and my temper has cooled."

Keteria hurried out of the room. Steigan shifted from foot to foot wondering whether or not to chase her. He looked back at Searn, who returned a shrug with his palms up, then pointed toward the door.

Steigan needed no further urging to unstick his feet and run after Keteria. He didn't see her in the hallway, but figured she'd probably go upstairs. He took the stone steps two at a time, pausing on the second floor to listen.

Nothing.

He went on up to the third floor. The door to the library

had been boarded over. Keteria sat on the floor before the door sobbing.

She heard him coming and turned her tear stained face toward him. "Go away," she begged.

Steigan sat down on the last stair and leaned toward her. "I can't do that and I think you know it."

"Goddess, how stupid am I? I didn't even see it coming."

"What?"

"The devastation you cause through my life, like a storm that flattens all the crops."

Steigan sat quietly to let her have a moment.

After a long pause, she said, "You disrupt my work, you come to me with magical mysteries I can't help but want to solve, you give me feelings that I can't stop and only threaten to grow." She looked down, her eyes growing wide as if in shock from her own admission. She shook her head and sniffed. "You were attacked by gargaxes and yet you survive, even before I knew the gargaxes were returning. I find out the truth on the bloodwave that you are and I'm not. You've been undermining everything I've ever believed in and ever done. You are the one making the rites more accessible when I'm trying to take magic education to all the people. Another cycle and people would've understood the ceremonies the way Rivic wrote them."

"I'm sorry."

"Sorry. Why?" Tears refilled her eyes as she looked at him. "Are you sorry that you brought the gargaxes back? Or that our capture of one pushed my father into a magical panic that made him destroy, nay, *purge* the very knowledge from the Temple which may have helped us defeat the gargaxes? Or are you sorry that I watched my father jump to his death with you coming out behind him? Were you trying to catch him or were you convincing him to leap?"

Steigan felt the numbness he'd felt after that event returning to him. Was that really how she'd seen yesterday's events or was that how she saw them now with Mierk's dark shading?

"Are you sorry that I didn't put the pieces together before I granted your title back to you?" she asked, her voice starting to rise. "Are you sorry that your actions have made you a saint? I doubt you are sorry for any of this. Rather you are glad. Aye, Saint Steigan, killer and destroyer." She looked away. "You have ruined everything for me. Everything."

Steigan felt small. He didn't know what to say. He ached so badly and yet couldn't say anything, couldn't move, couldn't slink way like a beaten animal. He had to stay and face the daggers created from her words.

"Do you feel any remorse about making me love you and then shattering my heart?" she asked.

Steigan shifted so that he knelt on the stair. He put his forehead down on the stone before her. "You have my life and my sword."

"Don't," Keteria sobbed.

"I only have my life to give you in penance if you think me capable of wronging you so. I cannot heal any of your ~~pain~~ or make you believe I never meant you any injury. After all, that is why our heart is caged in our chest away from the reality our eyes see. If your heart has shattered because of what your eyes tell it that they see, there is little I can do to correct it." Steigan raised his head and pushed up just far enough to reach out to take Keteria's hand. "I cannot help what I have been made into, but if you say the gargaxes and the new thoughts coming from the Temple are your enemies, then they are mine as well because I can only live to serve that which my heart tells me is right. I serve my queen."

He kissed the back of her hand before he stood up, his fingers lingering with hers for a moment longer. Drawing away from her, he took a lasting look at her tear-stained face not wanting to forget that sight for a long time. Steigan turned and started down the stairs.

"Steigan," she called after him.

He kept going, running downstairs to find his armor still tucked away in the wardrobe of the dormitory.

Until he could restore the Temple to what it once had been, he wouldn't be returning. Charged with his new mission, he packed his belongings and walked out of the Temple, never looking back.

A figure waited at the end of the bridge and while Steigan couldn't say it shocked him to see Lord Ithanes standing there, it did surprise him. But Ithanes had probably known all along what would happen.

"I serve Queen Keteria and Lilinar," Steigan said to Ithanes.

"Then you know the only way to save her and to get the answers you need is by coming to Dubinshire," Ithanes returned.

Steigan nodded. The original texts and ceremonies were there. The origins of truth to defeating the gargaxes were there as well. Rivic had started his journey in Dubinshire, so it only seemed right that Steigan should begin his quest there as well. "Then to Dubinshire I shall go."

Ithanes clapped his hands and High Maege Leloran and Holy Sapere Kelan came out of the stables with Telimas all decked out in black and gold tack.

"In Dubinshire," Ithanes said with a smile, "you will

realize your full power."

Steigan took Telimas' reins as he admitted to himself that he liked Ithanes' words: his full power.

Kelan nodded to Leloran.

The High Maege of Dubinshire raised her hands. "Talcor dun proximitious."

With a single step, Steigan welcomed a different life and a new quest.

Dawn Blair grew up on a farm in a rural town. The space and old buildings provided inspiration for her imagination and she thrived on stories of unicorns, princesses, heroic knights, and hidden rooms waiting to be discovered.

Today, she writes, paints, and illustrates with her love for Steigan's story being a driving passion in her life.

She currently lives in Idaho with her teenage children, two cats, and two dogs.

sacredknightblog.blogspot.com

SACRED KNIGHT on Facebook
http://on.fb.me/nHAySu

SACRED KNIGHT Art & Extras
http://bit.ly/ylRx1P

MORNING SKY STUDIOS
www.morningskystudios.com

Made in the USA
Charleston, SC
20 January 2013